THE
SCORNED

ALSO BY DAVID PUTNAM

The Bruno Johnson Novels

The Disposables

The Replacements

The Squandered

The Vanquished

The Innocents

The Reckless

The Heartless

The Ruthless

The Sinister

THE
SCORNED

A BRUNO JOHNSON NOVEL

DAVID PUTNAM

OCEANVIEW (PUBLISHING

SARASOTA, FLORIDA

ISBN 978-1-60809-494-3

Published in the United States of America by Oceanview Publishing

Sarasota, Florida

www.oceanviewpub.com

10 9 8 7 6 5 4 3 2 1

PRINTED IN THE UNITED STATES OF AMERICA

*Dedicated to Mike Fasari,
a bold and fearless partner while working the streets*

A great friend

He passed away during the writing of this novel

Rest in Peace

THE
SCORNED

CHAPTER ONE

I TURNED TO check behind me for the hundredth time since my bartending shift started—something fugitives do out of instinct. Chacho, my partner for the afternoon, came down the walk from the hotel at the Punta Bandera Beach Club and Spa, heading toward the Lido cabana bar. On his shoulder he carried a large round tray filled with drink garnish—wedges of pineapple, oranges, limes, lemons, papaya, and mango. He always had a huge smile, displaying perfect white teeth bright enough to blind. The smile wasn't faked for the tourists. He was one of those rare folks who loved life with all its blivits and blemishes. And why not? He was born and raised in paradise and had not experienced the real world.

The sky was cerulean blue and the hot Costa Rican sun bore down on the sunbathers, baking the brown-skinned tourists, skin glistening with cocoa butter in bikinis made of strings and postage-stamp-sized material. The humidity so thick words hung suspended a moment longer before dissipating. The deep blue ocean, calm, slick as glass, with the gentle lap of nonexistent surf. Children frolicked on the fringes, laughing, enjoying a life that had not yet kicked into full throttle, one filled with responsibilities and choices. Millions of choices.

I opened the pass-through for Chacho. He stopped and leaned back to read the nameplate pinned to the bright floral Hawaiian shirt the hotel now supplied so we all looked alike in a world of individuality. Something Darla Figueroa, the Food and Beverage Manager, had instituted. I had to admit, the new style gave the hotel a bit more *je ne sais quoi*.

Darla, a slinky feline sexpot—this according to my wife—was a master manipulator with a hand in every detail of the hotel. Marie had met her only once and shook her hand. Marie could size up a person in one meeting—from one touch, one look into the eyes.

I used the occasion to reassure Marie that I loved her more than life itself, that she was the very breath in my lungs, and I meant it.

Dad, my true friend and life counselor, had told me something when I was very young that I still remember decades later as if it were yesterday: "Son, don't be a man with a wandering eye; don't go out for a tasty cheeseburger when you have steak and lobster at home." Marie was my lobster. Darla, well, she definitely fit in the tasty cheeseburger category.

"Hey . . . ah, Ted." Chacho's eyes caught mine as he winked.

"Ted" was the new name for the next two-week period. I changed my name on a regular basis, mostly out of paranoia. Nobody much cared or noticed. Bartenders could be innocuous if they worked at it. And I worked hard at it. Traveling patrons who frequented the bar, drank to get drunk, the alcohol clouded their memories, unfortunate events or folks in their lives they'd rather forget.

Chacho patted my shoulder. "Good to see you, my friend."

I could only smile, nod, my hands on the blender making a drink, the noise a loud rattle.

A fat man in a light-blue seersucker suit with wet sweat stains under his arms walked up with a woman of questionable background. They took stools at the bar on the shaded side of the cabana. The sun, making its daily run for the western horizon to hide from the night.

He wore a straw boater on an all but bald pate, his face layered in fat, too flushed and puffy to be out in this heat drinking alcohol. The woman wore a hat with flowers and a floral dress that didn't match the black goth tattoos that peeked out. She was thin and pale and at least twenty years the fat man's junior.

I didn't trust him. My old deputy sheriff radar alerted anytime he came to the cabana bar. The man had been staying at the hotel off and on for several months. His name was Otis Brasher and all he ever drank were grasshoppers.

Otis slapped the bar. "Two of those green blended drinks and keep them comin'." He lowered his voice, turned to face the woman, and spoke purposely loud enough for me and Chacho to hear. "Look, honeybunch, I didn't know Negroes were this far south. We came here to get away from all that mess up north."

He was referring to me. He was putting on; he knew me well enough. Chacho lost his perpetual smile and opened his mouth to chastise the intolerant customer. I put my hand on his shoulder and shook my head. "He's not worth it."

No way did I believe Otis had left the hotel on one of his extended visits away and returned with a wife. I didn't want to be critical, but she could easily be a high-paid lady of the evening—only in this case, the afternoon.

I'd seen him coming, knew what Otis would order, and poured his drinks—fresh grasshoppers from the blender.

The day slogged on like they all had for the last couple of weeks. I wanted to be home and felt empty inside when I wasn't. Marie was about to give birth any day to our son.

Even though the hotel was only two miles from our house, my current anxiety level made it seem more like a hundred.

Three hours in when the sun had just crossed over the top of the cabana, Darla Figueroa appeared in her body-hugging Hawaiian dress, teetering in stiletto heels that made her three to four inches taller. She wore red lipstick that matched her nails and stopped at the edge to the concrete. She reached down, pulled off her shoes, stepped in the hot sand, and pretended it didn't burn her feet. She traversed to the shade of the cabana bar in five steps.

She made every employee nervous, including me. She had no compunction at all about firing workers. She'd created her own system for tracking minor hotel infractions, three violations, you were out, no excuses. Hard-core. We called her the Ice Princess.

She raised her hand to get my attention. "Ah, Gaylord." For some reason I could not fathom, she'd taken to calling me *Gaylord* even though that handle had never been one I'd used as a cover. And since she used it, most of the other workers did as well.

I came over. "Yes, ma'am?"

"I'm going to be in a fluff piece for NewsSix. They're coming here right now to shoot it. I would like you to stay out of the shot. Chacho? Chacho, come here."

Chacho did as she asked with his smile a bit tarnished. He, like everyone else, stepped lightly around her.

"Chacho, you stand right here while we're shooting. I want you as background, local color."

"Yes, ma'am." He kept his smile and spoke in a forced whisper through clenched teeth, "What? Now I'm a store window mannequin?"

"Better you than me, pal." And I meant it. I wanted nothing to do with a video that ended up on the net. I was wanted in California for robbery, murder, and kidnap.

CHAPTER TWO

Twenty minutes later, Darla, the Ice Princess, set her Manhattan down, pasted on a fake smile that was more predatory, turned, and welcomed Rebecca Sanchez, the newscaster from NewsSix, the darling of Costa Rica news.

The men at the bar started talking about Rebecca as she made her way down past the hotel pool.

When she arrived at the cabana bar, she and Darla shook hands, both phonies wanting something from each other—Rebecca a fluff piece for the news and Darla free publicity for the hotel. She was the food and beverage manager, for crying out loud. She must be going for Herb Templeton's job, the hotel manager.

Darla turned, caught my eye, and nodded to the side, reinforcing that she did not want me in the shot. I waved and smiled.

With the niceties over, Rebecca tried to set up the shot that now included Otis Brasher, the fat pig in the sweat-stained seersucker suit. Darla didn't want Otis in the shot so she moved down the bar leaving Rebecca standing there with her cameraman. They had to move if they wanted the story. I smiled at the two women playing tug-of-war power games.

The phone rang. I picked it up. "Punta Bandera Beach Club and Spa, Cabana Bar."

A mouthful, but the Ice Princesses did spot check phone calls on employees. She'd be listening now with a cocked ear.

"Bruno?"

I recognized the voice—it was Dad. He never called me at the bar. "Dad, what's wrong?"

"Son, I need to talk with you."

My stomach knotted. His tone said it was something serious. He'd just finished chemo and radiation for his stomach cancer and had been declared officially in remission. Yay.

But phone calls out of the blue made for some rough moments.

"Dad, I'm working right now, my boss is . . ."

He wouldn't be asking if it wasn't important. He knew the value of a good job. This had to be serious.

"Okay," I said. "I'm on my way home now." I started to take off my apron. My eyes, all on their own, scanned the surroundings out of panic for what my dad had said. Had law enforcement caught up to us? Were the U.S. marshals closing in as we spoke?

Then my eyes fell upon Dad.

He wasn't calling from home. He stood on the concrete walk between the sand and the cabana bar. His eyes caught mine and we stared, the dead air on his cell phone in my ear.

Now I heard the ambient noise from the frolicking in the hotel pool behind him coming through his cell.

Dear Lord. He'd come to the hotel to talk to me. He knew the rules—no guests or family allowed. Him even standing there was one strike—that is, if Darla figured out he was my dad.

Dad knew the rules, the risk.

Yikes.

"Dad, meet me in the Beachcomber Bar inside the hotel. I'll be there in five minutes."

I hung up and looked over at Chacho, Punta Bandera's newest mannequin. He had a beautiful wife named Gloria whom he adored and an extended family to support. He'd jump through any hoop the Ice Princess held up. When he smiled big, his eyes went to slits. I didn't know how he could see.

I said, "I'll be right back. I have to go get more garnish."

He turned to look at me. He knew we didn't need garnish. He lost his smile, his eyes urgent as he nodded toward the Ice Princess who stood next to Rebecca, an ice cream cone mic in her hand as they both talked to the camera about the inane and the mundane.

I stood outside the camera shot, held up my hand with five fingers, and mouthed the words, "Five minutes."

He shrugged, as if saying, "Go ahead; it's your ass."

He knew I needed the job. I had ten kids at home to feed and another on the way.

During the day, the Beachcomber bar supported vacationers who required alcohol throughout their stay, not just at the nightly parties. Alcohol that ruled their lives. The shadowy dark allowed them concealment from the lie they lived. No one noticed when I walked into the quiet murmur. I nodded to Jaime, an ex-MS13 gang member who worked mainly as a sous chef but took shifts as fill-in bartender. I rarely frequented the Beachcomber, if at all when not working. Wearing the hotel Hawaiian shirt made me stand out. But the Ice Princess was busy out at the cabana bar. I'd make this fast. Five minutes tops.

Dad knew the risks involved and took the far corner booth, the darkest part of the bar. I slid in, my entire body humming with nervous tension. His need to talk had to be his cancer, the evil disease had returned, and this was the way he'd tell me, away from the family, in a public place to limit my keening wail.

We stared at one another as the second hand swept around and around the dial. Finally, he reached over and put his warm, overly wrinkled hand on top of mine. His eyes now naturally watery and occluded with a light white film. He looked so old, too damn old. My heart ached at the thought of losing him. He'd been my anchor throughout my life, someone I could always depend on, ready with the right answer any time day or night, to say the comforting words when I needed them the most.

I leaned forward, closer. "Dad?"

He stared some more.

"Dad?"

"Son, I'm going to ask something of you that is very difficult." His voice came out soft and creaking in places.

I swallowed hard. "Okay." My body clenched waiting for the ugly black word: cancer. He wanted to tell me and me alone. That's why all the clandestine, 007 moves.

"What? Dad?"

He looked down at his hands. He never did that. No matter what the topic he always looked me in the eyes. Oh, God, this was going to be bad.

Real bad.

He spoke to his hands. "I want you to forgive your mother."

I sat back in the blood-red vinyl booth. "Forgive my . . . what?"

He looked up at me, his jaw set firm. "You heard me. I want you to forgive your mother. Treat her nice, treat her like a mother."

Oh, I wanted to treat her like a *mother*, all right.

She'd committed a robbery when I was still an infant. I wasn't old enough to roll over yet when she and two cronies robbed a telephone man of his dimes, bags and bags of dimes from phone booths. Mother had wanted a life more glamorous than Dad could offer, a life of the rich and famous and thought the quickest route to her goal was knocking out a workingman and stealing.

While counting the booty in a shabby motel room on Long Beach Boulevard, greed overwhelmed her two cronies and both died at each other's hand. Mother fell squarely into the felony murder rule: If someone dies during the commission of a felony, it's considered murder.

Covered in blood and not knowing what to do or where to go, Mother ran home to Dad. She begged him to help her.

Dad never told me the story until four decades later. I was far better off believing dear old mom had just run away, unable to handle the constant crying of a newborn—that and the huge responsibility that came with keeping a child safe in the ghetto.

Mother did her time in the joint, got out, and never looked back even though we still lived in the same house. She didn't come over to see how her child was doing, never called, never so much as sent a postcard.

Once out, she'd picked up where she left off in her criminal life, frequenting the prison with its revolving door.

What made it impossible for me to forgive her—every time I thought about it, I ground my teeth and wanted to punch something—was that night she came home blood soaked and asked my dad to take part in her crime by harboring—or serving as an accessory after the fact. She put him in an untenable situation.

Asked him to make a horrible choice.

Dad loved her more than anything in the world. I knew my dad, the decision to forsake the law over his wife would have torn him apart. He was a moral and upright man. To him, right and wrong was as simple as black and white. If anything could, love had the ability to shift anyone's beliefs.

That blood-soaked night Dad made the most difficult choice in his life and called the sheriff on his wife.

That's why I couldn't forgive Mother.

She came back into our lives two months ago with criminals on her tail, the state about to violate her parole, once again sending her back inside. She appeared at our hotel suite door in a wheelchair asking for help. That was the first time I'd ever met my mother, when I was forty-nine years old.

Forgive her? I didn't think so, not ever.

Dad squeezed my hand. I was being torn in half by his request. In that moment I realized how difficult his decision had been to pick up the phone that night and call the cops.

CHAPTER THREE

TWO YEARS AND six months ago—ancient history now—I shot and killed my son-in-law for crimes he'd perpetrated on my family. Dad, for the love of his son, set aside his strong moral beliefs and helped Marie and me. We'd kidnapped Alonzo, my three-year-old grandson, from his biological father's family—the parents of the monster who had killed his twin brother and my beautiful daughter, Olivia. I absconded from my parole and fled to Costa Rica with Marie and Dad and seven other mistreated children living in toxic homes in South Central Los Angeles: Toby and Ricky Bixler, Randy Lugo, Sonny Taylor, Marvin Kelso, and Tommy Bascome. We'd taken another child with us, Wally Kim, but later found his natural father in Korea and returned Wally to him. Had we not taken the children, they would've died horrible, abusive deaths. And then there's Little Bosco, the child of my son, Bosco, whose violent death is still too raw to comprehend.

Dad had made his choice to go with us, had chosen to break the law.

When he had not for his wife, my mother.

Now sitting next to him in the Beachcomber bar, he'd asked me to forgive my mother. There wasn't any way I could refuse him.

Mother was a con artist right down to the bone—it was built into her DNA. She sat in a wheelchair even though she could walk as well as the next person. She sat in the wheelchair because it gave her an edge over anyone who'd underestimate her. She always kept a gun handy by the side of her leg. She too had a violent past, one that tended to rise up and bite her in the ass when she least expected it.

I'd not only have to forgive her but also deal with her constant scandalous behavior.

I put my other hand on top of Dad's and looked him in the eye. "Sure, I can forgive her, Dad. I've been a horse's ass the way I've been treating her. I'm sorry, I promise to do better."

He smiled. It warmed up my life. I'd do anything for him.

Anything.

"I have to get back to work."

"Wait."

"What?"

"That wasn't the reason I came down here."

Ah, shit, here it comes.

That ugly word *cancer* again raised its malicious head. Dad wanted to get his affairs in order and me burying the hatchet with Mother was high on his list.

I held my breath.

He reached into his front pants pocket. He struggled to pull out a thick packet. He slid it over to me, a yellow envelope folded over.

I opened it and found hundred-dollar bills, a fat sheaf of them. "What's this, Dad? There must be seventeen, eighteen thousand dollars here."

"Twenty thousand."

"Okay, what's this for?"

"That's the reason I came to the hotel today. To ask you a huge favor, one I have no right to ask."

My forehead broke out in beaded sweat. Dad had withdrawn his entire savings account and he was giving it to me for a reason, one I didn't want to contemplate.

The bad Bruno who periodically appeared on my shoulder now kicked me in the side of the head and whispered in my ear, "He's paying you to bump off your mom."

No way, no how. Go away.

"Dad, what's this for?"

He reached and tried to take it back. "I have no right. No right at all to ask this of you."

"Dad, what's going on? You're scaring the hell outta me." I held onto the packet and wouldn't let him take it back.

He shook his head from side to side. "It's too dangerous. The risk is too great."

"What? Tell me!" Sweat now rolled down the sides of my face and into my eyes. The tension tightening, pulling my shoulders together in my back, my heart doing a rapid rat-a-tat-tat. "What's too dangerous?"

He said, "Marie will kill me for asking you."

"Tell me!"

I'd raised my voice to my dad.

He hesitated, looking me right in the eyes. He nodded. "I'm going to do it. I'm going to ask you. This thing has been eating me up for days now. It's not healthy. You're smart, you've done this before. You can get away with it."

"Dad!"

"I want you to take this money and escort your mother back to the States." He held up his hand to stop me from objecting. "Just get her on the ground in LA and make sure she gets off okay. That's not asking for a lot, is it, Son?"

"Dad, I'm about to have a baby."

A fat tear welled and rolled down his cheek. He nodded. "I know. I know. That's why I just want you to fly with her, make sure she gets in a rental car. A six-hour flight, a couple of hours on the ground, then a six-hour flight back. You take the red-eye; you'll be back before anyone even knows you're gone."

I didn't say it out loud, but Marie would never allow it. She'd said under no circumstances was I to ever again set foot in that violent world.

"Dad, what's going on? Why is *Mother* going back to the States with your entire life savings?"

He set his jaw. "That's personal between me and her."

That's why Mother came back two months ago—to weasel her way back into Dad's good graces and then take him for everything he had. His deep adoring love masked his good sense.

I knew his tone, the expression that included his jaw muscles grinding away. He would not budge an inch.

I said, "I'll go—"

Before I could finish what I meant to say, he smiled and patted my shoulder. "Thank you, Son, I knew I could depend on you."

"On one condition."

He froze and waited for me to say it.

"I have to know what she needs the twenty thousand for?"

His anger flashed. He grabbed the money packet from my hand and slid out of the booth without another word. His anger hurt the same as if someone stabbed me in the gut with a serrated knife.

"Dad? Dad, wait. Let's talk about this, okay. Let's just talk about it."

He kept going out the entrance to the bar into the hotel area where he took a right to the front door.

I sat there stunned over what just happened, trying to put together any possible motivation for why he'd ask something so desperate and dangerous, and couldn't find one.

He suddenly reappeared at the bar entrance. He raised his voice and shook the money packet as if choking a chicken. "Fine. I'll go myself."

"Ah *shit*."

CHAPTER FOUR

WHAT DAD HAD said—the way he'd said it—weighed on me the rest of my shift. I couldn't think of anything else when I should've been thinking about my new son on the way. A new son flying in any minute, hanging from a diaper in the stork's mouth.

I tossed the apron in the dirty clothes bin on the way out, pulled my bike from the rack in the employee area, and started home. I'd take the long way to think over what was about to happen. This new responsibility—a brand-new son—scared the hell out of me.

And it shouldn't have.

I'd lost a son and daughter—and even a grandson—in the most horrific ways. Parents are not built to outlive their children. A new child, my child—our child—I just couldn't imagine losing another one. The ache from that fear in my chest wouldn't let me enjoy the lush flora, the angel's trumpet, African tulip tree, bullhorn acacia, and the purple foxglove; rainbows of color that sweetly scented the path. The longer way home circled Tamarindo Park, a place we often took the kids, and sparked wonderful memories.

On top of everything else, Dad's desperate conundrum kept horning in.

We lived in an expat's house that was more a compound with tall walls covered in flowery vines and bougainvillea that surrounded the entire two acres. The owner, the expat, had grown tired of paradise and craved the depravity and social unrest the U.S. afforded. He rented us his villa and fled back to the chaos. Two eight-foot-tall wrought iron gates guarded us against the outside world. We didn't keep them closed to protect us from unforeseen evil, we kept them closed for peace of mind, to know that our children were corralled and safe behind the walls and under our careful watch.

Or I wouldn't have been able to sleep at night.

I grew up in South Central Los Angeles, in the Corner Pocket on Nord Street, worked as a deputy sheriff, then went to prison for killing my son-in-law, who had killed my grandson Albert. When I got out, my wife Marie, Dad, and my two-year-old grandson Alonso fled the U.S. and took up residency in Costa Rica. On our way out of the States we scooped up a flock of children who were abused and left unprotected by Child Protective Services. Kids who had fallen through the cracks and would surely die without our intervention—seven wonderful children who we taught to again love life and to live without fear.

At the same time, they taught us things about ourselves, how love has an endless depth, a bottom no one has reached.

Since we first arrived in Costa Rica, the violent world I thought I could leave behind called me back to the States three times. I had to go or risk that same violent world, that evil seeping into our lives like a kiss from the black plague. Once smitten by Mr. Evil, the bastard never lets go. After the last time, Marie had said never again. On those trips back, I'd managed to bring other children who'd been trapped in desperate situations. I also brought back bumps and bruises and gunshot wounds, but worst of all, images of violence that haunted my dreams, images I'd never live down.

* * *

Outside the tall double gates to our property, off to the side, sat paper grocery bags recently left, filled with clothes and food. The heartfelt community we lived in had long ago heard about our extended family and continuously left donations. What we couldn't use, we gave to the church. We appreciated the food the most—growing children eat like ravenous locusts.

The sound of children cheering came from the side of the house. I eased the gate open to keep it from clanging. I didn't want to disrupt their fun. Once inside the estate, I peeked around the side. Dad and his long-estranged wife Bea—recently reunited—now sat in dueling wheelchairs racing each other on the paver-tiled terrace while the children followed along and cheered. The joy in all their expressions gave me a warm feeling I'd always cherish. New memories to tamp down the old.

Tommy Bascome, one of the original kids we'd taken to Costa Rica, looked up and caught my eye. He was growing into a wonderful young man, acclimating so well, and becoming a leader among the children. He paused and nodded to me, then went back to cheering the race, his bright smile was all I needed to live on. How far he'd come from the shattered kid with the spiral shaft humoral fracture who'd been traded by his mother to a drug dealer for a bag of meth.

Dad didn't need a wheelchair, but when Bea—my mother—showed up in one, he feigned the need. I didn't question his wheelchair request. Dad got whatever he wanted. He was a man with stalwart moral convictions, who never wavered when it came to sacrifice for his family. *Mom*, on the other hand, did or said something daily that caused me to grab my hand to keep from slapping her silly.

Dad tried his best to please her, overcompensating for making that phone call nearly fifty years ago, the phone call that sent her to prison.

Mother, I admitted, had changed Dad's life. I wanted to forgive her just for that reason but couldn't—not with her daily egotistical arrogance and sharp-tongued condescension.

Someone punched me in the back.

I turned to find my lovely wife, Marie, the crown jewel of my soul. She looked up. Filtered sunlight on her beautiful countenance created an angelic aura. Our baby was one week overdue, and I had never seen a woman more pregnant. As big as she was, Junior would be able to walk the minute he came out, maybe even play catch.

For the last week she'd been in constant motion, too uncomfortable to sit or even lie down. She had to be exhausted from the lack of rest. The doctor was coming by in twenty minutes to check on her and Dad, a house call. Marie was a certified physician's assistant, and before she'd gotten too pregnant, she worked at the local clinic in Tamarindo, donating her time.

"Thanks for coming home on time, you big lug." She went up on tiptoes for a kiss. I met her halfway and tried to hug her and couldn't. She was now one of those fully extended Jiffy-Pop popcorn pans.

I never questioned her love for me; her eyes always told the story.

"You okay, sweetie?" I asked.

She turned and waddled toward the villa's double-door front entrance she'd left open in order to sneak up on me. She said over her shoulder, "I just wish Alfred E. Neuman would finally make his appearance. *I am so tired of this.*"

I took her hand and walked with her. "I know you are, babe."

"This is all your fault, you know."

"Yes, I know."

"I mean, me being pregnant."

"Yes, dear."

She abruptly halted, looked up at me. "Thank you, Bruno. Sometimes I don't say that enough." She had again caught and wrestled to the ground her overly aggressive hormonal response brought on by the pregnancy.

I might've been overly sensitive regarding her roller-coaster emotions due to my fear of having another child. I was over the moon at the prospect of being a father and at the same time conflicted.

What I needed most was to pull Dad aside and talk to him about the new-father fear I couldn't shake. If I could only work up the nerve. But now I had the other problem to deal with—escorting dear ol' mom back to the States. No way did I want the job but couldn't see any way around it.

The children continued to cheer the racers, cheers that now continued to make laps around the house in an echoing Doppler effect.

I moved behind Marie and hugged her, put my head down on her shoulder. I nodded. "Babe, I had this great idea while I biked home."

She continued her waddle, and closed the big doors behind us, so the kids wouldn't see us. "Enough with the ideas. I'm just going to do it. I'm going to the big library in town, climb up and down the stairs. That'll shake Alfred E. Neuman out of his lair."

She wanted to name our son *Albert* after the grandson we'd lost to my son-in-law's brutality. I didn't nix the generous offer, but I also didn't outright agree. That name would be a constant reminder, one I didn't need. She, of course, sensed my trepidation and tagged our unborn son with Alfred E. Neuman, after the big-headed, jug-eared *Mad* magazine icon. Each time she said it without mirth, it made me smile. Her second choice was *Xander*, after Dad. No way could I dispute that decision, and I tacitly agreed. I'd told her I kind of favored *Zeus* or *Hercules*. It made her smile.

Our poor kid.

She stopped in the huge entry to the great room, the house interior ten degrees cooler than outside. She put a hand on her hip and canted to that side. "What's this great idea? Red peppers? Castor oil?" She raised a finger. "If it's sex you have in mind, no! That's how you got us in this mess." She smiled.

She'd been the one who wanted a child. I'd gone along because Marie got whatever she wanted, and I was more than happy to comply.

I kissed her forehead. "I'll be right back."

I took off.

"Where are you going?"

"To get a hammer, some nails, and pieces of wood."

She yelled after me, "I don't think that'll work. Bring back one of those come-along thingies—you know, a winch. We'll hook it to Alfred E. Neuman's feet and yank this baby out."

CHAPTER FIVE

I LEARNED LONG ago after being shot, spit on, incarcerated, losing a daughter, a son, and grandson—you take happiness as it comes— small doses or in large spans. Doesn't matter, you grab it and hold on dearly. Savor every second. The thought of having a child made me glow inside, a feeling I never wanted to lose.

Marie and I were finally through to the other side. We'd left that violent, abusive world behind. Never again were we to leave Costa Rica. The decision left in me a quiet calm I treasured.

Or at least it had until Dad showed up at the hotel, standing on the sidewalk staring at me while talking on the cell phone. Twelve hours total, there and back, how could I refuse? But I had to.

I rolled around on the great room floor wrestling with five of our kids. This time Bea and Dad watched from their wheelchairs laughing, all the while holding hands. I couldn't help but believe Bea was no more than a poser in love, that she was after something that came with a price too costly to consider, the crushing of Dad's faith and hope.

My previous life gave me a tough-as-leather cynicism that tended to cloud logical thinking. Taking Dad's life savings back to the States was more than a red flag—it reached the level of "reasonable cause" for an arrest, a legal term needed to get a warrant. No way could I tell Dad what I really thought.

He wouldn't care, love had the power to obscure all logic, cloud the road until you drove off a cliff.

The kids who thought they were too old for childish games cheered and laughed from the sidelines.

Five kids, ages five to ten, were a mob that took me through my paces on the floor as they tried to subdue the "monster." I definitely needed to increase my running routine, up from three miles a day to six.

The doorbell rang.

Half the children froze; they were still terrified of boogeymen; still had night terrors—PTSD brought on by evil parents. The fright that filled their faces caused an emotional pain the same as if someone punched me in the gut.

"Whoa, kids, take it easy. It's only the Doc. What's up, Doc? Remember, like Bugs Bunny?"

Their expression instantly transformed back. They jumped up and bounced on their feet echoing, "What's up, Doc? What's up, Doc."

I made my way to the door with two youngsters hanging on, human leggings, cute as the dickens.

I opened the door to Aleck and Alisa Vargas. Aleck a beloved doctor of Tamarindo and his wife, Alisa, a good friend of Marie. Aleck wore an eggshell-colored linen suit with a vermillion dress shirt open at the neck, his jet-black hair combed straight back. He also sported a well-trimmed goatee with gray streaks.

I reached and shook his hand. "Come in, my friend, come in." He stood even, eye to eye with me at six foot one, tall for a Costa Rican. We dwarfed Alisa's five foot four. She had amazing brown eyes, the first thing anyone noticed about her. She wore her glistening black hair straight and down to her waist. The modern Costa Rican style floral dress hugged her curves. She wore red lipstick that stood out against smooth light-brown skin, an Aztec goddess.

She grabbed a hold of my Hawaiian hotel shirt—I hadn't changed from work—pulled me down, and laid a big smooch on my cheek. I blushed as red as her lipstick. She patted my face. "You're too easy, Bruno. You shouldn't let women control you with just a kiss. Where's your lovely bride?"

"She's lying down."

"Lying down? I thought you said she couldn't do that anymore. You kinda made it sound important that we come over and cheer her up." She lowered her voice. "That's not really why we came, though." She lost her smile, then it returned just as quickly. She winked. "You know this is all your fault?"

"Yes, I've been so informed on a number of occasions."

They both stepped deeper into the house. The children mobbed them, yelling, "What's up, Doc? What's up, Doc?"

Aleck laughed and opened his black doctor's bag, the kind carried by Dr. Marcus Welby, MD, on late-night TV. Aleck pulled out two smaller paper bags, one each of Morenitos and Tapitas, two classic Costa Rican candies. Some of the children checked over their shoulders looking for Marie. She rarely let them have candy.

When they didn't see her, they looked to me for approval, hoping I'd once again enter into their conspiracy to break house rules.

"Okay," I said. "Tommy, can you make sure the candy is given out evenly, two apiece for right now."

The children cheered. Tommy nodded and took the bags from Aleck.

"Wait." I held up my hand. Everyone went silent. "What do you say?"

In unison came: "Thank you, Doctor Vargas."

"Hey," Alisa said. "What am I, chopped liver?" A purely American colloquialism. Alisa was an American expat who'd settled in Tamarindo twenty years ago, now more Costa Rican than American.

"Thank you, Alisa." The kids surrounded Tommy in a throng, arms outstretched, hands open as they moved into the great room.

"You'd think the poor children never had sugar." I started to turn away and again caught a fleeting expression on Alisa, one of deep concern I'd never seen before. She recovered quickly and pasted back on the smile I now knew to be phony. Something was up.

Dad wheeled down the long hall with Bea in close pursuit. He shot me a quick scowl over not taking on his crusade to get Mother to the States.

Dad smiled hugely and shook hands with Aleck. He liked Aleck and he was a great judge of character. Aleck had also come by to check on Dad, who refused to go to the clinic for any reason. More so now that Bea had arrived to complicate our family structure. He didn't want anyone fussing over him, as if all of a sudden, his stomach cancer had turned into this huge military secret.

He didn't want Bea to think him weak.

His Afro, cut short to his scalp, was all white, and he'd finally lost the cadaver-like appearance after putting on a few pounds. Mother—Bea—had helped with that by gently cajoling him to eat when he wasn't hungry. I couldn't fault her for that and marked her down with a couple of points in the near-empty "good" column. All of those favorable numbers wiped away now for conning a vulnerable old man.

Dad said, "You two here for dinner?" Before they had a chance to reply, Dad said, "Yes, you are, no arguments. I'll tell Rosie two more for dinner." He spun his wheelchair around like a pro and headed toward the kitchen. He continued to roll away and said, "Bruno, you better hope Marie doesn't find out about that candy, especially this close to supper."

He was right, that was an error in judgment, the part about being so close to supper. His tone hurt. Turning him down was going to be a death by a thousand lashes.

"Dad?"

He stopped wheeling but didn't turn around.

I said, "I'm sorry. You know I'd go if I could."

His back stiffened. He nodded and in a half-whisper said, "I know, Son. I shouldn't have put you in that situation." He continued on. His voice had cracked. I was a heel for denying him any request, even if it meant leaping into a spewing volcano. I owed him.

Aleck snapped his satchel closed. He lowered his voice. "At his age and physical state, I'm worried if he stays in that wheelchair much longer, he's going to lose muscle and won't be able to walk even if he wants to."

"I'll have a talk with Bea and get it sorted out."

Dad had been on his feet at the hotel.

Alisa said, "Where's Marie?"

"Come on, I'll show you." I led the way to the master bedroom at the end of the long hall.

Halfway there, we heard loud snoring. I stepped aside and allowed Aleck and Alisa to enter the bedroom.

As they did, their jaws dropped and they froze.

I said, "She couldn't sleep lying down or sitting propped up so . . ."

Aleck said, "I've never seen anything like it. What a brilliant idea."

Alisa grabbed my shirt, pulled me down, and gave me another big smooch on the cheek. "I've never seen anything so romantic. You built this for her. My friend, you're very close to changing my mind that she's too good for you; maybe it's the other way around."

I blushed.

I had nailed two-by-fours to the wall, picked up the head of the bed, the legs, and nailed them to the two-by-fours. I used Gorilla tape as an extra measure to secure the two bed legs still on the floor to the paver tile. This put the bed at a steep 45-degree angle. Marie wasn't lying down, and she wasn't quite standing up.

Earlier, when I brought Marie into the room, she turned to me with tears in her eyes. She was so tired she didn't have the strength for words. She shuffled over to the bed, kicked off her shoes, mounted the bed, and fell right to sleep. I used the soft decorative rope, the tie-backs for the drapes, as a safety belt to keep her from rolling off.

I said, "I think she'll sleep for hours."

I eased the door closed. Aleck and Alisa stayed close instead of moving ahead down the hallway. I turned and almost bumped into them. "Oh? What's going on?"

Alisa took hold of my hand in both of hers. "Can we talk with you?"

"Of course. How about out on the terrace?"

CHAPTER SIX

I EASED THE two French doors closed behind us and held out my arms as a guide. "Please, have a seat." The sun filtered down through the jungle trees, the birds sang, and the tall estate walls kept everyone safe, the world at bay.

Aleck sat in the cushioned redwood chair, his legs crossed at the knees. He took out an engraved silver cigarette case, extracted a brown cigarette, and lit it. His ingrained Costa Rican manners wouldn't allow him to even ask if he could smoke indoors. Whenever out in the open air, he automatically lit up. A halo of blue-gray smoke over his head, enhanced by the country's constant humidity, created a rainbow prism.

As Aleck sat, Alisa paced, wringing her hands, her shoes clacking on the large paver tiles. She always wore heels to add to her stature.

Their nervousness created an electric static in the air that transferred to me, and I was now fighting the jitters. I wanted to flee as fast as my feet would carry me back to the bedroom to watch Marie sleep. I had to know she was okay.

Something was up. "This isn't about Marie's condition, is it?"

Aleck waved his hand, the lazy cigarette smoke swirling. "No, not at all."

"Dad? Is it something with Dad?"

Alisa bolted over to me and looked up, her eyes fierce. "Would you quit with your egotistical arrogance. The world doesn't revolve around Bruno Johnson, for cripes sake."

I took a step back. I looked over at Aleck, his mouth open in shock. "Alisa, we are guests in this man's home. What is the matter with you? Bruno, I apologize for my wife's rude behavior." He still had not taken his crossed leg down off his knee, his tanned hand rested on his leg.

Alisa took another step toward me. I put my hands on her shoulders. "Take it easy. Let's talk about this, okay? Whatever it is, we can work it out. Why did you ask me out here?"

She knocked my hands off her shoulders, stepped in, and wrapped her arms around me, putting her head against my chest. I felt my heart beat out of control over her erratic behavior. What was this about? These were our two best friends in Costa Rica and for some reason they were hurting.

I held her as she sobbed into my chest, her tears soaking through. I let her have a minute, then I escorted her over to the picnic table bench, eased her down, and sat next to her holding her hand. I took a handkerchief from my pocket, possession of which was something instilled in me by Dad, and daubed at her wet cheeks.

She took it from me. "I'm sorry . . . it's just that . . ."

"What? Tell me." I looked up at Aleck.

He said, "It's our daughter, Layla."

"What's happened to Layla?"

Layla was their only child, and in my opinion, a little too pampered—spoiled actually. She was a student at USC in Los Angeles. Marie, who had gone there for a few classes, said USC really stood for University of Spoiled Children.

I knew Layla was a huge financial drain on my two friends. In her second year, she had already burned through all the money Aleck and Alisa had set aside for her four-year education, a bloated sum that should've been more than enough.

"She's in trouble. But we don't want to make a federal case out of it. We want to keep this . . . ah . . . discreet."

"What kind of trouble? I promise I won't say a thing to anyone."

Aleck was the front-runner for Governor in Costa Rica, the political party's choice going forward. He would need discretion if Layla's problem got too ugly. He'd want someone he could trust to handle it.

Alisa said, "I'm sorry. I shouldn't have snapped at you. I guess I'm just upset—it's the situation—the favor we have to ask you. It isn't fair."

Aleck cut in. "We . . . ah, know your situation, how you have an issue back in the States."

I sat back, the table edge holding me firm. My voice came out a little hoarse. "What's going on with Layla and how can I help?"

What I really wanted to know was how they knew about my background. Marie wouldn't have said anything. The only other people who knew were Dad, Salvador Perez, and Mom. No way would Salvador let the information slip out—that only left dear old Mom.

Aleck had always been there for my family, the kids, and Dad when we needed a doctor. And now he'd been taking extra good care of Marie.

What was that worth?

Was it worth the risk of going back to the States? I had friends in the Los Angeles County Sheriff's Department, and a good friend in the FBI, but if I got caught out on the street by any other agency, those folks wouldn't be able to help. I'd go to prison for the rest of my life. I couldn't do that to Marie and the kids, to my new son about to arrive any day.

But what would happen if I turned down Aleck and Alisa, and Dad . . . and something happened to Mother or Layla. Could I live with myself? Anger flushed my face hot. How could these people, including Dad, ask this of me?

I tried to put myself in their place, and for the first time, it seemed absolutely logical.

Then Alisa's earlier words returned and echoed in my brain. *"Would you quit with your egotistical arrogance. The world doesn't evolve around Bruno Johnson, for cripes sake."*

Aleck took out another brown cigarette from his silver case, tapped the tip against the case, and lit up. "Layla has a stalker. She's scared to death. She wants to come home for a couple of weeks to think things through. To be someplace where she can sleep without worry."

"Has she gone to the police?"

"She has, and they told her that since she doesn't know who this guy is they can't do anything about it. I'm worried, Bruno. We're both worried."

"As you should be. I would be as well."

Next to me, Alisa said, "Scared to death really. I'm sorry I said those horrid things."

I patted her hand as I tried to wrap my brain around the situation. The issue wasn't something exclusive to my skill set. If they wanted, they could hire private security to take her to the airport. But I could see how they'd want a personal friend to handle it. If it were Marie at risk, I wouldn't let anyone near the situation I didn't know. I'd handle it, no questions asked.

Aleck blew out smoke. "It's a turnaround trip—fly there, six-hour flight, pick up Layla, and fly back, fourteen-sixteen hours max." It almost sounded as if he'd been talking to Dad with this "turn-around" bull crap. I fought down my anger. Calling me egotistical and arrogant, the nerve.

I had to weigh Dad and friendship against leaving Marie about to give birth. This was a no-brainer.

"I'm sorry," I said. "I would help if I could. You know I would, but I have to think about Marie. I have to be here when our son is born."

I'd already turned Dad down.

Aleck stood, unlimbering from the chair, came over, and offered his hand. "No hard feelings. We understand."

Alisa stood and shoved Aleck. "No, we don't understand. This is our daughter. Her safety is at stake."

I said, "Am I missing something here? You can hire personal security to escort her to the airport. No big deal, it's done all the time for VIPs."

Alisa took two steps back. "Private security? Layla saw this man with a gun."

"What?" Aleck said, alarmed at this new information. "When did this happen?"

I said, "She saw a gun but doesn't know who it is?"

Alisa looked at me. "Last night. It happened last night outside her building in the parking lot. We're only asking you because we know about you, your background. You're absolutely the best choice to handle this."

Aleck reached into his suit coat pocket and extracted an envelope. "Here's a thousand dollars. I'll get you more if you like. I'll just need some time. Also, in there is your private investigator's license. I pulled some strings."

When I first came to Costa Rica, I thought I'd hang out my PI shingle. I took the written test and passed. Then I showed up for the "administrative paperwork." They wanted my fingerprints. I chickened out and fled. Took the job as bartender, nice, safe, quiet, camouflaged, hiding in plain sight.

Then I realized why he wanted me to take the money and the reason for the PI license. He wasn't just asking for my discretion; he was guaranteeing it.

And we were supposed to be friends.

"I'm sorry," I said, "really I am. But if something happens to Marie during her delivery, I'd never forgive myself if I wasn't here at her side."

Aleck said, "I'm sorry, Bruno, I wasn't told about this gun issue. I'll go myself and hire security like you said. That makes absolute sense."

No, it didn't. His new plan would ruin his chances at governor. The press would find out.

"No! No!" Alisa said. "It doesn't make sense. This is our daughter. If Bruno is the best out there, that's who we want." She broke down crying. Aleck took her in a hug.

I eased into the house through the French doors. Let them work it out. The guilt over not helping them or Dad pressed down on me with a smothering weight.

CHAPTER SEVEN

ONE HOUR LATER the whole family, sans Marie, sat at the long dining room table—the kids, Dad, and Bea, along with Alisa and Aleck, all eating dinner; plenty of fresh fruit, vegetables, handmade tortillas, sopa negra, and olla de carne. For dessert, the kids' favorite, arroz con leche.

I sat at the head of the table trying my best to enjoy the wonderful family atmosphere. Aleck and Alisa sat quietly, her eyes swollen and red from crying. I wouldn't let the guilt tarnish the day. Aleck had found me right after they had come back in the house and apologized for putting me in such an untenable situation.

Everyone abruptly stopped mid-bite, mid-word, and stared my way.

I turned to the right.

Marie stood in the doorway to the hall, one hand on the doorframe, one hand under her huge belly, a pain-filled grimace on her face. "Bruno, my water broke . . . and something . . . something's wrong. I'm not supposed to be having this kind of pain. These kinds of pains." She looked down at her feet. Blood droplets speckled the tile.

I jumped out of the chair and scooped her up.

I'd faced down the most dangerous murderers that ever walked the streets of Southern California, a truly evil crop of killers, and had never experienced fear like I did in that moment. With it came a total sense of vulnerability that begged me to curl up on the cool tile floor and pretend none of this was happening.

With Marie in my arms, I looked around, bewildered. I didn't know what to do.

Aleck jumped up, knocking his chair back. "In here, Bruno. Bring her in here and put her on the couch. Darling, get my bag."

Eddie Crane, a sweet kid we rescued from Montclair and who didn't talk for months after we got him home, had taken to humor as a stress outlet. He leaned over to one of the kids and said, "Should Doctor Vargas be calling Bruno Darling?" He got no response.

I hurried into the great room and gently laid Marie down on the couch. She writhed in pain, trying to fight it, not wanting to upset the children even more. Clutching my arm, she said, "Bruno, get the kids out of here. Take them to the park." She wrenched to the side, her eyes squinched shut. "*Bruno!*"

Rosie burst from the kitchen, running through the dining room, jumping into action as if on a Navy ship and general quarters had sounded. She stuck her arms out wide and herded the children. "*Niños, venga, venga aqui.*" She said something else in Spanish. The kids knew to obey. They all disappeared out the front door with Rosie.

I paced, wringing my hands. "What can I do? Doc, what can I do?"

Aleck said, "Call for an ambulance." He'd just started examining Marie, who had her fists full of couch cushion, her face in a tight grimace, a thick scent of blood in the air, metallic and humid.

Aleck said, "No, never mind. It's too late for that. Put a large pot of water on to boil. Get a plastic sheet if you have one, some clean linen. Hurry."

My first step, I stumbled. I was breathing too fast, not thinking clearly. I yelled as I hurried away. "What's the matter, Doc? Is Marie going to be okay? Tell me. Talk to me!"

He didn't answer; he had his black bag open on the coffee table. I came out of the kitchen after putting on the water. Dad appeared at my side, standing on his own two feet, his arms loaded with fresh bedsheets. He handed them to me and clutched my arm. "Take it easy, Son, it's going to be okay. The doctor's right here."

* * *

Three hours later, or maybe it was only one, Marie's screams had reduced to murmurs and yelps. I stood at the stove waiting for the water to boil to sterilize additional instruments. I wrung my hands. I should be in there. Dad came into the kitchen and put his hand on my shoulder. "Come on, Son, let's go outside and get some air."

"I can't. Aleck told me to watch the water until it boils. I'm to wait for sixty bubbles a minute, then put in the instruments. Then let them boil for twenty minutes. Take them out, let them cool, and bring them to him."

"Bruno?"

I couldn't take my eyes off the bubbles and stared at them trying to count. Would they ever make it to sixty per minute? *Come on. Come on.* I silently counted a string of bubbles.

"Bruno?" Dad's hand came up flat against my cheek and turned my head to face him. He looked so terribly old it scared the hell out of me. I didn't know what I'd do without him.

"Yeah, Dad, I'm right here. I see you."

"No, you don't. He moved my head to look at the bundle of instruments on the tray next to the stove. "Son, you're not thinking straight at all. You're not doing anyone any good."

"What are you talking about?"

He pointed this time to the instruments. "Those are for dental work."

He didn't have to say more. Doctor Aleck assigned me busy work to get me out from underfoot. Even the doc saw the state I was in and outsmarted me with a simple little trick that any other time I would've seen right away.

Dad gently took me by the elbow and guided me outside to sit in the shade of the scented bougainvillea and magnolia trees. He held on to my hand. His had a faint palsy that never went away. He was so damn frail. Cancer had eroded his core and left him a shell.

I needed to get back inside to help Marie. I had to help Marie.

We sat for a minute. I knew he wanted to tell me something and was working up the nerve.

My knees bounced all on their own; the anxiety wanted to bleed out and couldn't find a path.

"Why don't you just go on and say it?" I said. At least I could still read him.

He nodded.

"I'm going to tell you something and I don't want you to interfere. I want you to respect my decision."

"Okay." I girded my insides and waited for the shoe to drop. What could it possibly be after the bombshell he dropped in the Beachcomber bar?

Come on. Come on, please talk faster.

He finally spoke. "I've decided to make the trip back to the States myself. I'll be gone about five days."

I said nothing. My jaw clenched and ground enamel. This was Bea's doing. She'd worked her way into Dad like a tick on a dog. She latched on and started again, sucking at the blood to his soul. She was a woman, but just the same, I wanted to sock her in the chops. I waited, counted to ten. "Dad, I do respect your decision, but you are too weak to make a trip like that, and there are warrants out for your arrest. If you had to move fast, a turtle with two broken legs could catch you. I'll do it. No argument. Like you said, I'll only be gone twelve hours."

"I can't ask this of you. If something happened, I could never forgive myself. Bruno, I don't want to go to war with you over this. You know how stubborn I can get, especially when I know I'm right."

"It's okay, Dad, you don't have to go anymore. I'm going anyway for something else."

He leaned back to get a better look at me. "I taught you better. You've never lied to me."

"I'm not lying."

"Then tell me, why are you going?"

He sat back on the two-person wicker seat we were sitting in. I'd made a promise to the Vargas' not to tell a soul. I broke eye contact. "I promised not to tell anyone."

"Bruno?"

"Dad, it's the truth."

He looked away and over at the bright red bougainvilleas mixed in with banana plants as his mind worked the problem.

He looked back at me. "You're doing something for Aleck and Alisa."

"I can't say. Like I said, I made a promise." I looked him directly in the eyes, so he could see the truth. The man might be old but was still sly as a fox. He'd read the play.

He nodded and again looked away. "This is dangerous, Son."

"Nothing I haven't done before." But for the first time a faint trickle of fear told me not to go.

"You poke the devil too often, he'll turn and bite you."

"It would be a safer trip if I had all the information. What's Mother got going back in the States?"

I felt sorry for trapping him. He, at her behest, promised not to tell anyone. Didn't want the heinous crime to be discovered; financial elder abuse, embezzlement, theft under false pretentions.

"It's a personal issue that you need not bother with." His tone turned icy. He stood on wobbly legs and walked back into the house.

I was a grade-A heel.

But once I had dear old Mother back in the States, she wouldn't be under Dad's protective umbrella. I wouldn't do anything to harm her. I just had to look the other way while she slithered back to the place from whence she came.

Under a big rock.

CHAPTER EIGHT

I PACED THE hall outside the bedroom where Doc Aleck worked with Marie to deliver our baby. The clock on the wall let me know time chose that day to change its rhythm, extending each minute to twice its length. While I'd been outside with Dad, they moved Marie into a bedroom and closed the door. Locked it. With each pass, I stopped and came in close to listen; the wood door darker where I left sweat from my ear and hair.

Marie's yelps had dropped to low mews. I wanted to go in and help, hold her hand, comfort her. Each time I put my hand on the doorknob ready to twist and rush in, to console the jewel of my soul, I knew nothing had changed, it would still be locked.

I could take the door down with one kick, splinter it out of the frame. I'd done it a hundred times chasing murderers. My old boss Robby Wicks called my right foot "The State Key—it can open any door in the state."

Doc Aleck and Alisa were doing everything they could to help Marie. I was a heel for turning them down. If everything came out okay with Marie and the baby, I'd tell them I'd go.

How could I not.

During one pass, my head to the door, someone took my hand. I looked down.

Eddie Crane.

"Come on, Bruno, come watch TV with me." His eyes pleaded. My pain had turned into his pain. It was too easy to forget the kids experienced the same kind of emotional pain over Marie. Eddie was a kid I'd rescued the first time I'd returned to the States adding him to our family. He worried the most about getting pulled back into his old environment and needed reassuring.

"Sure, okay." I let him guide me to the great room where we sat on the couch sans the cushions. Rosie must've taken them outside to clean and let air-dry. I could handle the sight of anyone else's blood and had many times, maybe even in the thousands of times. But blood from a loved one was a game changer. I couldn't do it. Panic set in each and every time I saw it.

All the other children were outside under the shade trees playing board games or reading books. Marie had book clubs going with the different age groups. Eddie sat next to me inches away. He usually wasn't so demonstrative with his affection; he was more like a feral pet who didn't trust any quick moves or raised voices. He'd flinch and move away, fear in his eyes.

Marie said the kids would get better at their own pace and that they would all react differently. We were to go slow and not push them. Eddie had made a large leap, by coming to me asking if he could help, and any other time I would've reveled in his progress.

He had the TV tuned to the local station that played ancient movies to keep their overhead costs down, unable to afford first-run shows from the States.

The Lone Ranger rode his horse, Silver, in pursuit of the bad guys. A make-believe world where a guy with a black mask goes against the social fabric and takes the law into his own hands.

The monotony of the show, its fantastical depiction of what it was like to chase evil, allowed my mind to ease off the problem at hand.

The scene on television reminded me of something. I chuckled at a real-life incident where life imitated fiction.

A short pursuit entered into Lynwood's area, LAPD units chasing a murder suspect who fired a semiautomatic handgun from his car, jeopardizing uninvolved citizens. He couldn't drive and shoot at the same time, lost control, caromed over a curb, and crashed into a tree. He came out of the car firing.

The conga line of cop cars skidded to a stop. The cops got out and unloaded on the crook, returning fire. The score: Good guys one, bad guys zero. I didn't fire, there were too many other cops. One LAPD uniform started to get back on his motorcycle to leave the scene. I said, "Hey, what's your name for the report?" He wore a helmet and sunglasses, so I couldn't identify him even if I had to. He smiled, took a bullet from his belt, and flipped it to me. The Lone Ranger's calling card. He laughed and roared off.

"What's so funny?" Eddie asked.

"Nothing. This show just reminded me of something about work."

"Yeah?"

"No, I'm not going to tell you."

Marie and I decided a long time ago we would shield the children from the world we'd left behind. An all-too-real world.

He nodded. He knew the routine. The rules.

"Hey," he said, "if you work for a living, why do you kill yourself working?" He made me smile. I knew the movie he was quoting. More humor.

"Okay, here's another one," he said. "You know the King Kong movie? If the natives built this big wall to keep Kong out, why did they put in a gate?"

My mind had wandered back to Marie, and I only half-heard him. "You see, it's because—"

Eddie put his hand on my face and turned it to look at him. "Bruno, it's called observational comedy. You're supposed to laugh."

"How old are you?"

"Ten, why?"

"You talk like you're in college."

"I know how to read a book." He smiled. "Can I ask you a question?"

"You know you can."

"Could you . . . I mean can I . . ."

He got my attention. I moved to the side and faced him. "It's okay, you can tell me anything. You know that."

He nodded and looked away as tears filled his eyes and threatened to overflow. My heart sank. Something had happened, and I'd missed it. "What is it, son. You can tell me."

He shook his head. "No, never mind."

"Tell me."

"It's too selfish."

I took in a breath and let it out; at least it wasn't what I'd thought. "You know I will give you anything if it's possible. And within the realm of reality." I tickled him. "Tell me."

"Okay, stop. Stop."

I stopped and waited.

He looked down at his hands. "I . . . I was hoping . . . that maybe you and Marie . . . you'd adopt me. I want to be a Johnson."

A big lump rose up in my throat, choking off my air. This *was* within the realm of possibility. I had it within my power to grant him this wish. "I'll talk to Marie about it."

"You will, really?"

"Yes, of course I will." I'd spoken too soon. With all that was happening, he'd caught me with my emotions laid bare. Once I thought about it, if we adopted Eddie, all the kids would want the same. But what did it matter—ten children weren't too many—well, eleven, if Alfred E. Neuman would finally cooperate and make his grand appearance.

CHAPTER NINE

HOURS LATER, DOC Aleck appeared like a disheveled apparition at the entrance to the great room. His hair no longer perfectly coifed, his sleeves rolled up, face haggard as he wiped his hands on a towel. I jumped to my feet and rushed to him, put my hands on his shoulders, and looked him in the eyes. "Tell me." I wanted to shake it out of him but resisted the urge.

"It was a very difficult delivery. The baby was breech. And, quite frankly, too large for a woman of Marie's stature."

"Doc?"

His solemn expression broke into a smile. "Congratulations, you're the proud father of a healthy baby boy."

Three tons of solid weight lifted off my chest, and I could breathe again.

I tried to move around him. He stepped in my way, blocking my harried advance, searched for my hand, and shook it. "Congratulations, Bruno."

"Yes. Yes. Thank you." I tried to look around him to break away to go see Marie.

He held onto my hand. "Bruno, it was a rough delivery. Marie is worn to a frazzle."

I stopped trying to go around him. "Is she okay?"

"Yes, but exhausted. I had to do an episiotomy so she has stitches."

I had no idea what that was, but *stitches* didn't sound good.

"Okay, okay," I said, not knowing what else to ask.

"I can only give you a couple of minutes with her. She desperately needs rest and absolutely no stress. You understand? None. Not for three to five days at least—a week would be better."

"I understand." This time I physically moved him out of the way just as Alisa appeared holding a swaddled baby.

Tears burned my eyes.

Alfred E. Neuman looked so pink, too pink. And his head . . . maybe a little too cone-shaped. I looked back at Doc Aleck, suddenly scared to death.

"I told you it was a tough delivery, and I have to say that baby has the largest head I have ever delivered. The shape will go back to normal in a few days, don't worry about it." He patted my shoulder as Alisa handed me the little bundle. "Say hello to little Bruno."

I took the warm bundle. It wasn't heavy enough to be a human life.

"No, Xander. His name's Xander."

Alisa smiled more broadly. "Not according to Marie."

I nodded in agreement as something solid inside me, something emotional, snapped. I was holding my child. My son. Suddenly all the horrible things I'd dealt with in my world slammed down on top of me, snatching my breath away. The death and mayhem, how it came so easily to vulnerable and unprotected children.

How would I ever be able to protect him enough? How would I keep him from all the heinous criminals who slinked around the underworld forcing their tyranny on the weak? I thought about how I'd fight off that tyranny and felt hopelessly inadequate, that I could no longer hold my own on the streets and didn't know how I had in the past.

Weakness filled my body, my muscle and bone, but far worse my confidence. My mojo had left my body, with just the touch of my newborn son.

I'd never let him walk out of the house. He'd grow up in the estate behind the high walls where the world couldn't touch him. I'd never leave Costa Rica again. Never.

It occurred to me that this was abnormal, a product of latent PTSD from the violence I'd actively pursued in another life. Sure, that was it.

But I had to leave.

Doc Aleck saved my wife and gave me a son. I had no choice but to help them. Just for twelve hours though, no more. Then I'd be back. Twelve hours, a small price to pay. And I'd be killing both birds.

Alfred E. Neuman took hold of my finger in his little pink hand with the grip of a plumber. The simple action snapped me out of my foolish fugue. Tears rolled down my face. "Hi there, little guy." I wanted to hug him and never let go. I kissed his forehead. He already smelled of baby powder, a delightful scent that brought back so many wonderful memories of Olivia.

All was right with the world.

Doc Aleck: "Remember what I said."

"What?"

Doc Aleck: "If Marie wants to name him Bruno, she gets whatever she wants for the next three to five days. And just be aware, her body is awash in hormones, and if she seems off-kilter in any way, you just nod and tell her, 'Yes, dear.' No stress, Bruno. I'm not kidding. She's one worn-out girl."

"Don't worry about me, she always gets her way." I smiled through blurred tears. "I'm going to the States for you. Twelve hours though, that's all I can give you."

Alisa reached up, put her soft hand on my cheek. "Thank you. You really don't know what this means to us."

She tried to take little Bruno from me. I didn't want to let him go.

She said, "You can have him back after your three minutes with Marie; she's waiting for you. She won't go to sleep until she sees you. Go."

"Yes. You're right." I carefully handed little Bruno over and hurried to the bedroom.

I slowed, stopped at the bedroom door, hand on the knob, and took in a deep breath. I entered with a silent reverence.

Marie lay on the bed propped up with pillows. Dark half-circles under her eyes, against too-pale skin slick with perspiration, confirmed everything Doc Aleck said. I no longer felt confident that everything would be all right; that confidence had somehow leaked out through my feet onto the floor.

She sensed my presence and slowly opened her eyes. A smile filled her face, lighting up the room with a thousand watts that made the skin on my back prickle from unbridled joy.

Her hand twitched. Was she trying to raise it? I hurried over as Doc Aleck's admonishment echoed in my brain. *She's exhausted. Only three minutes, then let her rest.* A clock started clicking in my head. Three minutes were not near enough to tell her how much I loved her.

On my knees at the bed's edge, I held her hand and gently stroked her head. She tried for a half-smile. "You see him? Isn't he beautiful?"

"The most beautiful baby in the world."

I looked down at her hand I held.

"Babe, I can't stay. The doc says you need your rest."

"I'm tired, Bruno, so very tired."

"I know you are, babe, and now you can have all the rest you need."

"We have a big healthy baby boy," she said.

"Yes, we do. You go to sleep. And sleep for a week. You deserve it."

"A week. Yes, a week sounds so luxurious." She closed her eyes for a moment, then opened them. She was fighting sleep to talk with me. She said, "Will you take care of things while I rest? I only need a couple of hours. I'll be right as rain in a couple of hours."

Sleep deprivation and exhaustion made her delirious.

I struggled up from my knees and stood when she again closed her eyes. I turned to go.

"Bruno?"

"Yeah, babe?" I'd stopped halfway to the door and turned around.

"We owe Doc Aleck a lot."

I came back toward the bed. "Yes, we do. We owe him the world. No need to worry about a thing. I'm here. I'll handle everything while you rest."

"Thank you, Bruno. Now I can sleep. Thank you, Bru . . ." The land of nod reached up and tugged her down into a deep slumber. She'd be out for a couple of days. A lot more than twelve hours.

I went back down on one knee and took hold of her hand. "Babe, I have to go back to the States. It's just for twelve hours. I'll be back before you wake." I squeezed her hand.

I was, for sure, a grade-A heel.

But she'd understand in a couple of days when she woke up, once I explained it to her.

She always understands.

CHAPTER TEN

THE NEXT DAY I stood in line at the airport next to Bea's wheelchair, of all people to be stuck with. Next to her stood Alisa. I didn't want to go. I wanted to stay with my wife and newborn son but sometimes responsibility overruled strong emotional responses to a situation.

I had an expertly forged passport in the name of Gaylord Johnson, the moniker Darla Figueroa—the Ice Princess—randomly assigned to me for no reason. How did Aleck get that name? Had he talked with the hotel's Food and Beverage Manager?

I didn't know how Aleck pulled it off, but the PI license was also in Gaylord Johnson's name. The license would add one more level of cover if confronted by law enforcement. It also ensured that I couldn't talk about my mission, an added level of discretion for Aleck. He was a smart political operator; he'd do okay if elected. What was disconcerting was the fact he had the passport and PI license in hand when he asked for the favor.

I wore dark sunglasses, a ball cap pulled down low along with a two-day growth of beard. I looked nothing like the photos law enforcement had back in the States.

Talking about going back to the States was one thing. Standing in line about to be scrutinized was another thing altogether. I would be okay on the Costa Rica end, but coming back through U.S. Customs might be tricky.

Bea—my mother—wouldn't tell me why she needed to go back. The authorities were looking for her as well. The risks remained high for the both of us. I would say to hell with her, but I couldn't walk off and leave her in a bad place. I would never be able to face Dad. In just a few short hours, my idyllic life had shifted, and I'd landed in a high-walled box without an exit. The kind of box I'd made a promise that for the rest of my life I'd avoid at all costs.

But a plane ride to and from wouldn't be that bad. Sure, I could handle that much. If all went well, I'd be back with Marie and baby Bruno in twelve or eighteen hours. Twenty-four on the outside. Marie probably wouldn't even be awake yet.

Mom already had her own forged passport—the one she used to get out of the U.S. Passports weren't the problem. If the government ever perfected and instituted facial recognition, we'd be in a world of trouble.

I tugged the ball cap pulled down lower over my dark sunglasses and put a Band-Aid across the bridge of my nose, an old trick I learned from a bank robber.

I already missed Marie something fierce. And baby Bruno.

As the line moved closer to the departure counter, I reached into my back pocket and took out a white paper bindle and carefully unfolded it. Inside contained a lock of Marie's hair. The sight of her hair gave me solace and elicited a small smile each and every time—I was turning into a doddering old fool. What happened to the fearless warrior who chased the worst of the worst? That life was gone forever. I liked this one much better, a father and bartender at a resort hotel.

"What's you got there?" Bea said, reaching up from her wheelchair seat to pull my hands down.

"Don't get handsy, old woman." I pulled away, refolded the bindle, and put it back in my wallet. To let Mom in on something so intimate defiled the reason for having the lock.

Several times, she'd tried to strike up a conversation with me, only I didn't feel like talking. Not to her, not the way she'd hoodwinked Dad. He'd paid for her ticket and given her money to live on. I still didn't know her purpose for the trip and didn't care. She'd gotten what she'd come to Costa Rica for, and as soon as the plane landed, she'd be in the wind—gone for good.

I finished putting my wallet back and said, "My guess is that you're not ever coming back, right?"

Alisa, who wore a big floppy straw hat and sunglasses that covered most of her face, said, "What'd you just say? Bea won't be coming back? Are you kidding?"

Bea shot me the evil eye. She didn't want me to blow her cover, reveal how she'd been using Dad. She put on that fake smile and used her best saccharine tone. "No, silly, I'll be coming back. Of course, I'll be coming back. Bruno just likes to tease me, that's all. Right, Bruno?"

I grunted.

The short line cleared. Good thing Doctor Aleck insisted on upgrading our coach tickets to first class. This allowed us to stand in the premiere line. I didn't want to push Bea's wheelchair, but I did. She reached back and patted my hand. "Thank you, Son."

I whispered, "Don't call me that."

Alisa looked back over her shoulder at us. I was acting like a spoiled brat.

I couldn't help it.

At the counter, a nice clerk with an airline-branded kepi and long brown hair called for a skycap. He took over and pushed Bea through the airport terminal and deposited her at the gate. Bea took a dollar out of her purse and tipped the man. I said, "Hey?" He stopped and came back. I gave him a five. "Sorry she talked your ear off."

He smiled. "No problem, that's my job."

Bea took a ten out of her purse and tried to hand it to me. "You know, Son, you can be real hurtful. Now run over there to that store and get me three or four of those gossip magazines and a box of Jujubes. We should've stopped at the store on the way like I wanted to; the prices here are outrageous."

"Not gonna happen, old woman. Besides, those chewy candies aren't good for dentures."

"Why, I never. I don't have dentures and you know it."

I smiled.

Alisa stood close enough to hear the exchange. "Bruno! I'm ashamed of you." She took the ten. "I'll get them for you." She walked off to the store across from our gate.

Out of habit and training, I watched Alisa. I'd taken the assignment to keep her safe and that's what I intended to do. She pulled her cell phone from her oversized purse and made a call while she walked. She still wore sunglasses and the big floppy hat, her resplendent long hair up in a bun and out of view.

Bea nudged me. "Hey, you gonna tell me what's going on with this woman and her daughter? I'm kinda involved in this thing too, you know."

"No, you're not. I'll handle it. You won't tell me what you have going on, so why do you expect anything different from me?" I could hear my words. They sounded juvenile and petty.

"What did I ever do to you?" she asked.

As if she didn't know.

"I saved your life not two months ago," she said, "and you treat me like this?"

That let the air out of me.

She was right; she had shot a man when he was about to finish me off. He stood over me with a smoking gun after he'd already shot me once. That was when I found out she really didn't need the wheelchair, that it was just one long con.

"You're right. I do owe you a great debt. But nothing I owe will compensate for you working a con on my father."

"What are you talking about? I love your father, I always have."

"What about that packet of money, the twenty-two thousand dollars, money he withdrew from his savings account. The money you're sitting on? He emptied his savings account for you."

"You went through my things. You ought to be ashamed of yourself. A woman's things are sacred ground." She'd raised her voice on purpose so the other travelers sitting at the gate would hear.

What a wicked old crone.

"Keep your voice down. Your damn straight I did. Anything that concerns my family, I'll do what I have to, to protect them."

"I'm your mother."

"Yeah, I know."

She leaned over and swatted at me.

I moved out of the way.

She sat and fumed. I'd taken my eyes off of Alisa and couldn't see her in the store across the way. I moved a few feet and spotted her at the end of the checkout line. I sat down. I kept my eyes on Alisa and said to Mom, "Don't pretend to be some kind of put-upon martyr. The way I figure it, twenty-two thousand dollars is a small price to pay to be rid of you. I'm just not looking forward to dealing with Dad when I come back without you. You're going to hurt him badly. You're going to crush him. But I guess that's what you do."

She took sunglasses from her purse and put them on to hide her tears. My bitterness over being abandoned by this woman who came into our lives right out of the blue and was now conning Dad somehow turned me into a despicable son. I wanted to take back the harsh words.

She took a hanky from her purse, one with Dad's monogrammed initials, and dabbed at her cheeks below her sunglasses. "You know what, Son? You're an asshole."

"Thank you for that." She'd taken the edge off me being a heel.

Forty minutes later I pushed Mom along the ramp and into the plane. I stopped the chair at her seat. She waited. I leaned over close to her ear and whispered, "Old woman, I am not going to lift you out of that chair when you are perfectly cable of doing it yourself."

An ugly grin crept across her face, showing no teeth. "Can someone please assist me in getting into my seat? My ungrateful son refuses to help his poor old mom."

Heads in the first-class cabin turned to look, all with expressions of disdain. A flight attendant hurried down the aisle behind us. I couldn't afford the attention. We needed to stay low-profile.

I gritted my teeth and whispered, "All right, you old biddy."

I picked her up. It was the first time I had touched her since she came to live with us.

As a kid I had stayed awake many nights, far too many nights, dreaming about the mother I never had, coming home and hugging me. Taking up with Dad and me like nothing ever happened. She'd make my lunch for school and kiss my forehead. With each passing day, each passing year, I dreamt less and less about her and became more and more bitter about the abandonment.

In my arms she was lighter than I thought she would be. I always equated evil with a dense heavy weight, which would make her weigh the same as an aircraft carrier.

I didn't want her to be my mom, I didn't want her to work her malicious ways, weasel in under my skin, and take over my conscience like she'd done with Dad.

She'd liberally doused herself in White Shoulders, an ancient scent that harked back to a childhood—one so far back I had no right to remember. I eased her down in her seat. As I pulled my arms out from under her, she patted my cheek. Then she put a hand on my neck and held me there while she laid a wet smooch on my cheek. "Thank you, doll," she whispered.

That kiss shook me. The wetness remained, a harbinger of an evil I couldn't control.

My *mom* had kissed my cheek. A nostalgic, high-speed dream reel of life ran past, pulling the strength out of my legs. I eased down in the seat next to her. I had to get up and move. I couldn't sit next to her, not next to the Spider Woman. The flight would give her too much time to cast her web.

Before I could get up and move, Alisa came and sat in the aisle seat, trapping me. "Ah, can I please switch with you?" I asked.

She dipped her head and pulled her sunglasses down a tad to look at me. "Don't be a jerk, Bruno, sit there next to your mom and be good." A flight attendant hurried by. Alisa shifted, raised her white-gloved hand. "Ah, waitress? Waitress?"

I said to no one, "Dear Lord, this is going to be a long six hours."

"It'll go by faster than you think," Mom said. "Be a baby doll and order me a Courvoisier."

The request came with a sickening sweet smile she used on Dad. Courvoisier. Who did she think she was, the Queen Mother? I took a breath, eased back in my seat, and hoped I could get through the plane ride with my sanity intact. I closed my eyes and tried to think about home and the kids.

The distraction didn't work. My thoughts flashed back to Dad telling me the story of my mom being present when two of her cronies killed one another with a straight razor and a knife, the blood-filled images clear and crisp as if her story was happening right in front of me.

CHAPTER ELEVEN

"Baby Doll, your momma needs to use the facilities." I woke in my plane seat to find Mom inches from my face, her breath warm and heavily laden with cognac. I wanted to return to the dream world.

I rubbed my eyes trying to wake up. "You have got to be kidding me."

She patted my face. My stomach rolled at the thought of carrying her to "the facilities." Dad had described for me, at a very tender age, the moral fiber of an upstanding young man: "A young man will never shirk his filial duties." Dad's words are what commanded my legs to stand, to pick Mom up and carry her to the restroom. She opened the door. I stood her inside. Once out of view from the passengers, she smiled hugely, squinting her eyes, and fluttered her fingers at me. "Don't go away. I'll only be a minute."

Alisa stood over by the flight attendants in the galley, talking with her hands. All the while I waited by the lavatory door like some kind of jerk giving into Mom's charade. She'd lived in the world of con artists and subscribed to their time-proven precepts: pay attention to the details. But the more important one: never break character.

Who did she think she was conning now? No, she was making a grade-A chump out of *me*.

The lavatory door opened. Mom flashed a smile that looked genuine, and I melted a little more. Her method that worked on Dad now sank its evil claws into the vulnerable part of my emotions. I stood there helpless while one of those flying monkeys from my nightmare carried off my common sense. I couldn't shake her loose no matter how hard I tried. I reached into the small bathroom, picked her up, and carried her back to her seat. I set her down. She patted my cheek. "Thank you, Son, you do love me."

I growled, sat down next to her, and checked my watch. Only two hours had lapsed, four more to go. No matter how hard she tried, she would never crack the emotional barrier created by the twenty-two-thousand-dollar packet of cash in her purse, Dad's life savings, an unforgivable breach of his trust. There wasn't a valid excuse for that kind of con artist theft.

I closed my eyes and tried to sleep and knew that wouldn't happen.

"Bruno, why don't you order yourself a warm cookie. They'll bring you a warm cookie if you ask. They are marvelous. Trust me, I've had three already."

I leaned over and whispered, "Old woman, I'm only human. You keep eating like that and you'll need a tow truck to take you to the can."

She giggled like a little girl and pushed my face away. "See, you do love me."

"How did you derive that from . . . Never mind." I took out my phone and pulled up photos of Marie and our beautiful baby boy. I smiled and my chest turned warm.

* * *

Four hours later, the plane touched down in Burbank. LAX would've been too rife with law enforcement.

We made it through customs without a hitch and stopped as soon as we found a place to push to the side in the hallway out of the flow. In case we somehow got separated, I told them both the hotel where I'd made reservations, a place I'd spent two months recuperating after being shot the last time I'd visited the States. We also had each other's cell phone numbers.

I figured Mom would wait for the first and best opportunity, then take the twenty-two thousand and run. That much money to a con artist was a good haul. We'd never see her again. It'd crush Dad for sure. But there was nothing for it.

I looped our two carry-ons to the wheelchair handle and pushed Mom through the terminal. Alisa stayed close with her own carry-on; she wouldn't let me tote it. The way her head continually turned from side to side, she must've really been afraid of the big bad world. I needed to calm my resentment toward these women dragging me away from my new son and get in tune with their motivations.

In another of life's many lessons, Dad had said that all humans by nature tended to think of themselves first. Not their fault, it was the nature of the beast. Self-preservation. But a good human tried to see past themselves; they tried to put themselves in the shoes of others to see how they viewed the world. Basically, I needed to get over myself, get the job done, and get back home. The way Dad would say it, "Quit with the 'oh, poor me act' and get to it."

Mom in the wheelchair waved as we started to pass the restroom. "Son? Bruno?"

I leaned down and whispered, "I am not carrying you in there."

"Don't be silly, they have handicapped stalls. Just push me up to the entrance. I can take care of myself."

I stopped short of saying "Gladly." Alisa already thought me a monster by the way I treated Mom. I could explain about the 22k but didn't want to air the family's dirty laundry.

I stood with my back to the wall and waited. Alisa stood close by in her big floppy hat and sunglasses, hand on her hip, one leg in a model's forward cant. Men passing by paid homage with uninhibited ogles.

I said to her, "You going to call your daughter and have her meet us at the hotel? We can stay there for six or eight hours until the next flight and be on our way."

"Yes, of course. And thanks again for helping with this. I can't tell you how much we appreciate it." Anxiety made her voice high and a little tight. "I'll call her right now."

She reached into a purse large enough to hold a six-man pup tent, took out her cell phone, and stepped away. With all the people flowing past, I only caught glimpses of her, which raised the nervous hum in my core.

Why had she not gotten on the phone as soon as we landed? Why did she wait to be asked? Why had she stepped away to talk? Too many questions left unanswered spelled trouble with a capital T.

A throng of people comprising several large families passed in a cluttered herd. I again lost sight of her. I looked one last time at the bathroom entrance.

No Mom.

I moved out into the flow of people trying to locate Alisa.

She wasn't there.

My heart rate jumped.

I hurried faster.

And faster.

Bumping shoulders through the crowd that now moved too slow. I jumped up again and again to get higher trying to spot that big floppy hat. "Alisa? Alisa?"

We came to the double exit doors where the crowd funneled shoulder to shoulder to get through. I made it outside to the curb and checked both ways.

Alisa was gone.

Why would she take off? She wouldn't. Had a bad actor grabbed her? What the hell was going on?

CHAPTER TWELVE

I PULLED OUT my cell phone and called up the app. While Mom and Alisa slept on the flight, I'd used the time to clone both of their phones and also added a tracking app. The red dot that indicated her cell phone moved along the street that led out of airport circle. The need to run back in and check on Mom or to follow Alisa tore me in half.

I made the choice, flagged a cab, and jumped in just as the red dot disappeared. Alisa had turned off her phone.

Or someone else had.

I paid the driver a ten, jumped out, and ran back into the terminal, fighting the flow of outgoing people. I broke out of the throng. The hall shifted from full to near vacant. I kept my eyes on the restroom exit as I approached. I yelled into the restroom, "Bea?" Nothing. "Bea, quit messing around and answer me."

I couldn't go in and risk being jammed up by an airport cop for being a perv. What was I going to tell Aleck? What a mess. A simple turnaround trip just shifted into a colossal screwup.

What could I have done differently?

A gold kepi atop a lovely airline employee appeared and headed into the restroom.

"Excuse me."

She stopped, smiled, and came back out. "Yes?"

"My mom went in there a while ago. She's in a wheelchair and I'm worried about her."

The kind woman lost her smile, her expression shifting to concern. "Of course. I'll be right back." She disappeared inside. Less than a minute later she returned. "There's no one in there, but there is a wheelchair. Oh my God, what do you think happened?"

I clutched her hands that wanted to grip my arm. "Thank you very much." I hurried away.

She yelled from behind me. "The police kiosk is the other way. You should notify the police."

I kept walking, increasing my pace without running. Mom had ditched me just like I thought she would.

I caught the tram over to the car rental and rented a crossover. I drove out of the airport while dialing my phone. Karl Drago picked up on the first ring. "Who's this? Speak or I'm hanging up."

"You still have that boulder-sized head sitting on those puny shoulders?"

"Bruno! How the hell are ya, man? Are you in town?"

"Yeah, big guy, and I hate to call only when I need help."

"Not a problem. You wanna meet. Give me a location and buddy, I'm there."

It was so good to hear his voice, his excitement to see me.

"That same place we stayed the last trip. Twenty minutes. In the lobby."

"Got it." He clicked off.

I dialed Alisa's phone; it rang and shifted right to voice mail. I pulled up her text messages. She wrote:

I'm here and I have all the money. What do you want me to do now?

All the money?

My foot involuntarily came off the gas pedal.

The car slowed while I tried to absorb this new information, words indicative of a kidnapping. What the hell was going on? I wanted to call Aleck and ask if he'd heard from Alisa but played that conversation over in my head. He'd reply, "What do you mean? She isn't with you?"

If I asked him if his daughter had been kidnapped and he didn't know about it, I'd have kicked over an entirely different hornet's nest. No, it was better that I developed more information before making any kind of decision.

The kidnapper had not replied in text. He must've called her with the directions.

I drove in traffic. I wouldn't make the twenty-minute meet-time in the hotel lobby. There were just too many people. A good chunk of them uncaring or evil, a sad reminder of why I didn't like the States. Especially Los Angeles. The sprawl, the disconnection from the world. Its frenetic activity was like bending a paper clip and sticking it in a light socket.

Drago had once said Los Angeles was filled with people who were born just to be buried. He believed that since Los Angeles was on the San Andreas Fault, sometime during an earlier earthquake, out slithered the souls of evil: pederasts, rapists, murderers, and exploiters of the weak. He made it his life's work to shove them back down where they came from. And if he made a few dollars in the process, well that was a small token for a lone-wolf crusade.

Forty-five minutes after I hung up with Karl, I pulled into the hotel in Glendale that overlooked the Galleria.

Karl sat in the lobby, huge and foreboding, everyone sneaking glances at him making sure the exits remained clear for a hasty retreat if the beast roared. He was as out of place as a whale amongst sardines.

Marie and I met him way back during the caper when we recovered Eddie Crane. Back then Karl *was* a beast, wild and uncontrollable. I had to shoot him in the leg to get his attention. Marie worked her magic, soothed and tamed him. He became a good friend and an ally I couldn't live without. Always giving and never asking for anything in return. He had a little crush on Marie and made no bones about it.

Okay, maybe a huge crush.

But Karl lived by the sword and one day his account would come due and I didn't want to be there to bear witness.

He wore his usual football jersey to cover his bulk and any weapons he might be carrying. Today's jersey was a Rams white-and-blue with the number 29 that matched his blue and gold Rams ball cap. A thick gold chain hung around his neck with a diamond-encrusted K medallion. Karl never worked an eight-to-five job. He took his money from other crooks, a dangerous enterprise, one without workman's comp if he made the smallest misstep. At six foot three and three hundred and fifty pounds, no one messed with him. He'd been shot, stabbed, and bludgeoned, and those were just the injuries he'd sustained helping me. Why he showed up with a smile every time I called spoke of a deep loyalty rarely seen—one I did not take lightly.

He sensed I'd entered the lobby, stood, and turned. With a huge smile he hurried over, his hand extended. "Well?"

"Well, what?"

"Come on, tell me."

"What?" He'd caught me off guard. I took his hand, which dwarfed mine. In his excitement he'd squeezed too hard. He never worked out with weights. He kept ten fifty-five-gallon drums filled with used crankcase oil at his place where he picked them up and moved them around three to four times a day. He said that "work strength trumped pussy gym muscle every time."

He looked around me trying to see. "Where's Marie? She didn't make the trip?"

"Oh, right. Man, I am so sorry. I should've called. Yes, yes, she had the baby. A boy. A healthy baby boy. Yesterday. She had him yesterday."

Talking about the birth brought it all back, the heavy emotions, the overwhelming love I had for both Marie and the baby.

What the hell was I doing back in California? My place was at home with them.

His smile got wider, if that was possible. He slapped me on the back, knocking all the air out of my lungs and eliciting a small cough.

"Damn, that's good to hear." His smile tarnished a little. "I guess it wouldn't be right for her to travel then. I mean, if it was just yesterday and all."

"She sends her love." He still had not let go of my hand. He pulled me in closer.

"Well? Where's my cigar? You owe me a cigar, my friend."

"You're right, and I promise to get you an entire box as soon as things calm down."

His smile went to full power. His other hand appeared with a wooden box of cigars, Cuban Cohibas, expensive and illegal. He let go, opened the box, and took two out. He stuck one in my mouth, the other in his. He tossed the box on the couch where he'd been sitting and produced a cigar clip. He clipped my cigar and then his, letting the butts fall to the floor.

He took out a lighter just as a florid-faced man appeared wearing a nice suit and a nameplate that read MR. HERBERT, MANAGER.

"I'm sorry," he said, "but I'll have to ask you gentlemen to please step outside to smoke those."

Drago stared at him as he continued to light his cigar, puffing big billows of blue-gray smoke that filled our area and floated up into the high ceiling. "Bruno, you ever notice that all hotel managers are named Herbert? Must be some kind of gene, don't you think?"

Mr. Herbert squirmed. "You are going to force me to call security."

Drago handed the lighter to me, reached down, opened the box, and took out another cigar. "Here. My friend just had a baby. Tell him congratulations." Drago gave him the evil eye.

Herbert took the cigar. "Congratulations." He spun and fled.

"Come on," I said. "Let's go outside. We don't want the police breathing down our necks."

Drago shrugged and puffed. He led the way, lumbering out the front doors. Outside, the blue sky didn't compare to the one in Costa Rica. The noise from all the cars going by, the buses, the people, raised my anxiety level. I briefed Drago on Alisa, what happened at the airport, and what I found on her cloned text message. I didn't tell him about good ol' Mom. I was too ashamed over how I'd let her con Dad. She'd conned him right under my nose.

When I finished, Drago chuckled and puffed. "I thought when you left you said you were never coming back. What was that, six weeks ago?" His chuckle turned into a full belly laugh.

I wanted to get mad but couldn't. Instead, I laughed right along with him. His mirth was contagious and diminished the rising anxiety, the need to drop everything and run for home.

My cell phone buzzed.

I checked it. Alisa. I hit the "Answer" icon.

"Bruno! Bruno! I gave them the money, and they didn't give Layla back. They want more. They want more money. I don't have any more money. Help me. Please help me."

I ground my teeth trying not to get angry. "Come to the hotel, and we'll talk about it." I hung up.

CHAPTER THIRTEEN

I USED THE card key to open the hotel room door to the two-bedroom suite. The desk clerk had remembered me and apologized for the new manager's rude demeanor. He sent up a fruit basket and a bottle of champagne. Our two-month bill last time was in the tens of thousands of dollars. The room matched all the others in floor plan and decor and brought back a flood of memories from six weeks ago.

Six weeks?

Seemed like more than a year. Our stay had not been a happy time.

Drago plopped down on the couch as my phone buzzed.

Marie.

I answered it. "Hello, babe, I already miss you and—"

"Bruno, what are you doing in California?"

Uh-oh, she was angry. I took a step over to the wall and put my forehead against it and closed my eyes, prepared to weather the storm rolling in. "I'm here to help out Aleck and Alisa." She didn't remember; she'd been too exhausted when I told her. I didn't think she'd wake up before I got back.

A quiet sob came over the phone. "You said you'd never go back there. Bruno, you promised me."

"I know. I love you, babe."

"Then why did you go? You should've at least told me about it. Kissed me goodbye. You should've kissed me goodbye, Bruno."

She sobbed. I *had* kissed her goodbye while she slept. She was supposed to sleep for a couple of days. Her entire demeanor was out of character. She was the strongest woman I had ever met. She'd be back to her old self soon.

"This is just a quick turnaround trip. I'm escorting Alisa and their daughter, Layla, back to Costa Rica. That's all. This is not a big deal, I promise."

I shouldn't have made that last promise—the situation with Layla was already spinning out of control.

"And Dad asked me to do a favor for him, escort Bea back here. This is no big deal, I promise."

I could picture Marie taking in this information and processing it.

"Bruno, we have a new baby."

"I know, sweetie. I know. I want to be there more than anything in the world, but we owe Aleck a huge debt. And Dad—"

"Yes, yes, that's true. We do owe him. I don't know what would've happened had he not been here. And your dad . . . whatever he wants. He wouldn't have asked if it wasn't important."

I didn't reply and let sink in what she'd just said.

"Bruno?" she finally said.

"Yeah, babe?"

"I was thinking about naming our son Tobias. What do you think?"

I chuckled.

"What?" she asked.

"Nothing. Tobias is a wonderful name."

"You really think so? I know you were thinking Xander but, that's kind of . . . I mean, it's an outdated name."

"Tobias is great. I love it."

"Good. Let me think about it, okay?"

"Of course."

"You going to call me as soon as you get on the plane? I'm going to worry until you walk in the front door. You said just a couple more hours, right?" I had not said that; it was wishful thinking.

"I'll call you."

"Thank you, Bruno. I love you and thank you for putting up with me. I know I'm not myself right now. You're a prince, really."

"Hey, Karl's here. He's doing great. Looks great. You want to talk to him?"

"Yes, please."

I wiped my eyes and sniffled as I walked over to Karl. He took the phone with a huge smile. "Hey, Marie, congratulations."

I moved back to where I had stood and watched him talk to my wife.

Dear Lord, I wanted to drop everything and head back to her and . . . and Tobias. I chuckled again. I cried too often lately.

In a few minutes Karl walked the phone back over after saying a final goodbye to Marie.

"I'm here," I said.

"Bruno?"

"Yes, I'm here."

She hesitated on the other end, putting her next words together.

"Bruno, I think we should adopt Eddie. It's the right thing to do. I know you're going to say it won't be fair to the other kids, but it's the right thing to do. What do you think?"

"I think it's a great idea."

"Good. Is it okay if I tell him?"

"Of course it is." I'd tell her about adopting the rest of the kids when I got home.

"You come home soon, you big lug, you hear me?"

"I'll be home soon. I love you." I didn't want to hang up but did anyway.

The silence rang loud in my ears and filled the room. Without her sweet voice, the empty square footage turned desolate.

Someone knocked at the suite door. The racket broke the short peace.

Drago muscled me out of the way. The man tended toward over-protective. He looked in the peephole. "Some Mex chick. Not bad on the eyes."

"That'll be Alisa, let her in."

Drago opened the door. Alisa rushed in and didn't stop until she was in my arms, clutching, hanging on as her metaphoric *Titanic* went down with all her worldly possessions. Her face buried in my abdomen, her words coming out muffled. "Bruno, they still have her. I did what they wanted—and they didn't give her back. They want fifty thousand dollars. We don't have it. We don't."

I guided her over to the couch, peeled her off me, and sat her down. Black eyeliner ran down her cheeks, her face pale with fear. I held her hands. "Start from the beginning and tell me everything this time. And I mean everything."

Alisa had lied to me and now jeopardized my chances of getting back to Marie and Tobias in the few hours as promised.

Maybe I should have more empathy for her. I'd only met her daughter, Layla, once when she came home for a school break, a very nice young woman, lithe and cheerful like her mother.

Alisa was sobbing and hiccupping, trying to get enough air to breathe.

"You have to calm down if you want me to help."

All of a sudden, she sat back and cringed. She'd spotted Drago. He had that effect on people.

"It's okay, he's with me." Turning toward Drago, I said, "Get some water, would you?"

He hesitated and then moved to the kitchenette.

Alisa looked at me with big eyes. "He doesn't look real."

The way she said it made me want to chuckle. "I know what you mean. Now tell me what happened."

Drago returned with the water and handed it to her. She stared up at him.

"Back up, big man. Let the woman breathe."

He did.

She nodded. "Okay. I . . . I got this text two days ago that said they had Layla and not to tell anyone, especially not the police. To get a hundred thousand dollars and bring it to the States—that's today— and that I'd be given further instructions."

"You did that. Then what happened?"

She gulped air. "I got here with you—I mean, at the airport." She nodded again. "And I texted them. They called and told me to bring the money to the parking lot at Atlantic and Century Boulevard."

"Taco Quickie."

"Yes, that's right. How did you know?"

"I grew up in the area. Then what happened?"

"Well, I took a cab to that parking lot, paid the driver, and as the taxi drove away, the trunk of a car in the parking lot popped open. I looked all around and didn't see anyone, not even by the car. My phone rang. I answered it. The voice said put the money in the trunk and close it, then leave.

He said within fifteen minutes Layla would call me and tell me where to pick her up. I did what he asked and left."

I asked, "What did the voice sound like? Did you hear any background noises? Was the person old or young? Did he have an accent?"

She shook her head a little too adamantly. "No, it was one of those synthesized voices, mechanical, you know?"

Drago asked, "What kind of car was it?"

"White," she said, as if the color alone might help.

"No make or model?" he asked.

She shook her head. "I'm no good with cars. A white one, a Nissan or Toyota, you know. Oh, wait. Wait. I took a photo of the car."

Drago grunted.

He couldn't believe she hadn't led with that information. She pulled it up and handed me the phone. Drago grabbed it. "This isn't a Nissan or Toyota, it's a damn Maserati, a two-hundred-thousand-dollar car."

"Is that bad?" she asked

"It's not good," he said. "No one with a two-hundred-thousand-dollar car does a hundred-thousand-dollar kidnapping." He tossed me the phone as he pulled out his and stepped away to make a call.

Alisa leaned in and whispered, "I don't like him. He's mean."

While I looked at the car in the photo, I said, "Don't worry, he'll grow on you."

The picture showed the rear of the car, including the license plate. The car had to be stolen, that or at least the plates swapped out. It was new and well kept, and like Karl said, not the typical car used in a hundred-thousand-dollar kidnapping. Something wasn't right. "Hey?" I said to Drago, who now spoke quietly into his phone. "You want me to call and run that plate for registration?" I still had friends in law enforcement. He shook his head and pointed at his phone. He had friends with the DMV.

Karl clicked off. "Bruno, can I talk to you?"

I patted Alisa's hand. "I'll be right back." I stood, but she grabbed on and pulled me back down.

"No, I have a right to know. She's my daughter."

Drago looked at me. I nodded for him to get on with it.

Drago shook his head, "You mean, like Bruno had the right to know this was a kidnapping you were pulling him into when he has a brand-new baby at home?"

Her body shook as she started to cry all over again. "I'm so, so sorry about that. But what else was I supposed to do?"

"Friends tell friends the truth," Drago said.

"Take it easy, big man. Go ahead, give us the scoop."

He glared at Alisa a moment longer. A beautiful woman in distress cut no soap with him, not when she messed with his friends.

"The car is registered to a used-tire shop called 'Don't Tread on Me,' on Long Beach Boulevard in Compton."

"A Maserati comes back to a used-tire shop?"

"I know the place; it's owned by Johnny Fillmore. Johnny Ef."

"Shit."

The word slipped out all on its own.

An icy chill shook my backbone, and I suppressed the urge to check to make sure the suite door was dead bolted. That had never happened before. I had chased hundreds of violent men and had never been outwardly afraid. I feared pain like anyone else but never the debilitating fear that had just crept into my bones. In my world it equated to an incurable and fatal disease. Taking down a violent criminal to me was like a lineman working on a high-tension wire— it was dangerous, but if you did your job right, no one got hurt but the bad guys.

Back in the day—hell, just six weeks ago—had you told me I had a shot at the most vile and despicable creature that ever terrorized Los Angeles with rape, robbery, and murder, I would've said, "Suit up and let's go." Not now. Something had changed inside me, something deep down at my core. And I didn't like it.

"Who's Johnny Fillmore?" Alisa asked.

CHAPTER FOURTEEN

IN THE HOTEL suite, I answered Alisa. "His people call him Effin Johnny behind his back."

Drago said, "Johnny ever heard them talk that way you'd never see 'em again. The guy's a freak of nature."

"And a man like that has my Layla. Oh my God, what are we going to do? Bruno?"

I shot Drago the stink eye that meant: can it with the stuff about Johnny Ef.

Drago shrugged. "I say we go right to the source. We gun up, go to Johnny, and ask him straight on."

Classic Drago: if it doesn't fit, use the biggest hammer you can find and pound the square crook into a round hole. I envied his fearlessness, his selflessness.

The thought of going up against Johnny Ef brought on that same fear, one that chilled my bones and caused me to shudder. What the hell was going on? I got up and paced, trying to think of our next move, trying to figure a way to shrug off this debilitating ailment. If it came down to it, would I freeze in the middle of a violent confrontation?

Whenever Johnny Ef took a hand, someone died. Usually, multiple *someones*.

I came out of my horrid thoughts, still pacing faster and faster. Karl and Alisa watched as if I'd lost my mind.

My cloned phone buzzed at the same time as Alisa's. I watched her expression to see if she understood the meaning. She didn't. I ignored my phone and continued to watch her. She swiped at her face to clear away the tears and frantically started to type a reply to the incoming text message.

She wasn't paying attention to me at all. I pulled out my phone and read her incoming message from Layla: *Mom, I'm all right. Just give them what they want.*

Alisa: *Baby, I gave them all I could lay my hands on.*

Layla: *What about the Chalice?*

Alisa sobbed, and a little wail slipped out as she typed. *Your dad doesn't know I came here with all our money. He doesn't know what's going on.*

Layla: *Fifty thousand dollars isn't a lot, Mom, please.*

Alisa: *I gave them the money they asked for. What's to stop them from asking for more after I give it to them again? Where are you? I'll come and get you.*

A long pause in the texting. Drago's head had shifted back and forth from me to Alisa. He'd figured out what I had done. I put my phone in my pocket, moved to the couch, and sat next to Alisa. She put her phone to her chest, her face wet with tears. I reached up and gently took the phone from her. I didn't want to reveal I'd cloned her phone, not yet. I read the messages and handed the phone to Drago.

He read it. "This is good." He typed a message on her phone.

Alisa jumped to her feet. "Hey. Hey, what are you doing? Give that to me."

Drago held the phone up so she couldn't reach it. She tried jumping, her long black hair doing a dance.

Typing a message without first consulting me was typical Drago. He didn't see anything wrong with his actions. In his mind when the right answer presented itself you don't hesitate, you leap. Even if the chasm is too wide to reach the other side, you take a running start and give it your all.

But this time it was a long way to the bottom.

He pulled the phone down and checked the new message that came in. He again replied and put the phone in his pocket. Alisa flew into a frenzy, pounding him with her small fists, a gnat pestering a rhino.

He said, "Let's get crackin'. I told them we'd have the money and set the exchange in one hour. This time, *I* picked the drop site."

Alisa stopped her ineffectual onslaught and stepped back, her mouth gaping. "You did what? How dare you!"

She looked around for a weapon and picked up a decorative bowl sitting on the table, one made of thick green glass. She went at him again and the heavy bowl thudded off his bulk. He casually said to me, "You think she's gonna wear herself out anytime soon? Like I said, 'we gotta get crackin'.'"

He reached under his football jersey with her still banging away at him, each blow growing weaker as her strength waned. His hand came out with two Model 66 Smith and Wesson .357 Magnum revolvers, my weapon of choice. He handed them to me stocks first.

Alisa stopped and stepped back, breathing hard. Her eyes grew large at the sight of the guns. She must've just realized this wasn't a game and people were going to get hurt. People were going to get dead.

I'd lived with a gun in my hand for close to thirty years—and for the first time—these two weapons felt alien to me. The touch of the warm steel caused a fearful shudder to roll through my body, one that shook me right down to the bone. I looked up and caught Karl's eyes—pleading with him to help me.

"What's the matter, boss man? You just went pale as a ghost." He chuckled as if something were funny about my icy fear. But he didn't know the problem churning up my guts.

I shook my head, too ashamed to explain the dilemma. What the hell was I going to do? I looked down at the guns in my hands and tried to imagine the situation where I would have to use them, imagine a situation where it came down to them or me.

Could I pull the trigger?

Or would I drop the gun and curl up on the floor with my hands over my head? On three occasions in my career, I'd seen deputies let fear rule their lives. After the incidents were over, two of them walked in and tossed their badge and gun on the watch commander's desk. The third one couldn't do that—instead, he was fitted for a coffin and carried by six of his peers out to a vast lawn to start the beginning of a long dirt nap.

Maybe it wouldn't go to guns. Maybe we could bluff our way through. But a fellow predator would be able to smell the stink of fear that hung on me like a cloak and exploit the advantage.

That's it then. What I thought could never happen, just happened. I'd made the transition from predator to victim. I had championed the rights of victims all my life and now I *was* one. Who was going to take care of *me*? I didn't like this new disability. I hated it. But who could I talk to about it?

Dad.

I needed to talk to Dad. He'd know the right things to say, words that would fix me. He'd always been able to help when I needed it most. I'd call him first chance I got.

*   *   *

Ten minutes later we headed out, Alisa drove the crossover that I'd rented. I sat passenger in Karl's truck, a one-ton dually. Karl had set the meet in the parking lot to the upscale Westfield Culver City Mall. We followed close behind Alisa as she wove in and out of traffic, too nervous to drive like a normal human.

The one-ton truck was Karl's favorite vehicle. He used it as a partner in his capers or what I called "his crusade." He was wanted by the police in three different jurisdictions at least; "The *Holy* Man" was wanted for murder. He had a burning hate for all outlaw motorcycle gangs. He takes by force all of their ill-gotten gain that the bikers derived from rape, robbery, murder, and the sales of crank—meth. He doesn't do it out of desire to make the world a better place. He was once an outlaw biker who'd been banished from his crew—a move he made them regret any chance he gets. He works alone and is methodical in his attacks because nobody else was crazy enough to join him.

After days of surveillance and after he has determined no civilians to be in the target location, he backs the truck up at high speed and rams his way through the front wall. Fortified doors and windows became inconsequential to such destructive force. The diversion gives him the seconds of confusion needed to take control of those inside—people he refers to as "sketchy assholes with guns." He then loads all the guns and dope and money into the truck bed. He leaves the occupants duct-taped together with a large *hole* gaping in the front of their house.

On three occasions out of many, he had to shoot his way out of a heavily populated gang area. Karl called the downed gang members "the *low* cost of doing business," and claimed that they had "lost their license to breathe."

The police had yet to get enough information to identify Karl and link him to the killings.

Now, he parked fifty yards away from Alisa in the Westfield Mall parking lot. We sat back, watched, and waited.

CHAPTER FIFTEEN

ALISA CALLED ON the cell. I spoke to her in low tones, trying to console and relax her. I explained that we would handle everything once the kidnapper showed. When I clicked off, I wasn't sure about the "we." I wasn't sure I could handle anything other than a babysitting gig at a preschool, with naps and graham crackers served with cartons of milk.

I kept one of the .357s tucked away in my waistband. The other I held in my lap. No matter how hard I concentrated, I couldn't stop opening the cylinder and checking the loads and the firing pin. Emotionally, I was a total mess.

"You okay, boss man?"

"Not sure. You might have to take up the slack on this one. I got a bad case of nerves and I don't know why." Had I not known Karl the way I did, I would have never admitted even that much. "Talk to me, would you, boulder head?"

"Sure. What do you want me to say?"

"Doesn't matter. First thing that pops into your head."

He sat back and thought for a second.

I found it difficult to believe that six weeks ago, given the same circumstances, I would've been sitting back, calm, cool, and collected like my big friend. I needed to talk to Dad. Even saying that in my head sounded juvenile. I was forty-nine years old and should no longer be dependent upon Dad for support. *Forty-nine years old.* I just realized I'd be pushing seventy by the time Tobias graduated high school.

I said, a little too harshly, "Talk to me. It's not that difficult. First thing that comes into your head. Make some noise with words, would you please?"

He shrugged. "I think Darwin got it all wrong."

The randomness caught me off guard, and I wanted to chuckle but couldn't. I smiled. "Is that right?"

This was going to be good.

He nodded with a straight face. "Yeah, if he was right, then the way we, as Homo erectus, evolve, or is it Homo erecti, plural?"

"Doesn't matter, go on." I had to hear this one.

"Well, it's been proven that since we erecti are using our brains more, our heads are getting larger to contain greater brain function, right?"

"Okay, I'm following you, I think. But you wouldn't be a sterling example of that theory."

"You want to hear this or you wanna start slingin' mud?"

"Sorry, carry on, Jeeves."

He gave me the stink eye and continued. "Every time we do something long enough, I mean, for a sustained period of time, our bodies adapt to that environment, right?"

"Sure, okay."

"Right. So, the way I see it, any day now our bones should start to grow hollow and we should sprout feathers out our asses."

"*What* are you talking about? This is really what you were thinking when I said talk to me."

"Well, yeah. It's not so weird. Us erecti have been flying in planes for a hundred years now. I'm talkin' millions and millions of people have flown for the last hundred years. Millions of hours in the air. Tens of millions. So, if Darwin's theory is correct, shouldn't we be like turning into birds?"

The serious look on his face struck me as funny and coupled with his inane statement, I started to laugh and couldn't stop. He broke up too. We laughed and laughed until tears filled my eyes.

He put his thumbs under his armpits and flapped his arms like a bird. We laughed harder.

He wasn't that ignorant—he was only trying to cheer me up in a way only Karl Drago could.

We finally started to settle down. I wiped my eyes. "Thanks, big man, I needed that." My body, purged of anxiety, hung loose and easy. The quip wasn't all that funny but, in my condition, I had not needed much to set me off.

There wasn't time to relax too long. A white Maserati pulled into the south parking lot, as instructed, and made slow turns through the rows of cars checking for cops. Johnny Ef's sleek white Maserati with its limo-tinted windows swung around to the less populated southern end, and as luck shone down upon us, it parked one slot over from Drago's beast of a truck that also had tinted windows.

While we watched, the trunk popped open.

We waited.

No one exited the car like they should have. A normal kidnapper who didn't want to be caught would have left the car and entered a second one where they would wait for the drop. Without discussing it, Drago backed up, pulled forward, and blocked the Maserati from backing out, trapping it. My heart rate jumped to a thousand beats a second, something that never used to happen.

My mind knew what to do, but my body didn't respond with the old speed and confidence that came with years of training and experience.

I bailed out, moved around pointing my gun at the tinted window of the Italian sports car's passenger side. Drago didn't have a gun; he carried a twenty-inch length of galvanized pipe wrapped at the end with duct tape for a handle. He didn't hesitate, not afraid of the devil himself. He swung the pipe, shattering the driver's window. The window shattered into a million bits of cubed safety glass that skittered across the asphalt as the quiet afternoon fragmented into two distinct pieces; the peaceful and the violent.

A woman screamed. Then a second one screamed behind us.

Alisa.

Drago reached in and yanked the driver out of the car through the broken window.

I hurried around to his side. "Wait. Wait. Don't hit her."

Drago held the young woman in a fist full of her bunched-up shirt and bra, the twenty-inch pipe pulled back to club the daylights out of her.

"Drago, that's her. That's Layla."

Drago checked his swing. His gaze jumped to meet mine, his eyes fierce, ready to take on all comers. He looked back to the woman in his grasp. She'd fainted, her body limp.

Alisa violently bumped me out of the way and pounded Drago with her small fists before taking hold of her daughter. "Let go, you animal."

Drago let go. Alisa eased her to the hot asphalt and broken glass, tears dripping from her face onto her prostrate daughter's. I came out of my trance created by the confrontation and looked around. Twenty or thirty yards away, several shoppers stood by their cars and looked on, their mouths agape, their cell phones to their ears waiting for the 911 operator to come on the line for the police.

"Big man, we gotta roll—and I mean right now."

I put my gun away in my waistband, scooped up Layla, and climbed back in the dually. Drago grabbed Alisa around the waist with one arm and lifted her off the ground, a halfback with a football ready to run to the goal line.

She fought back, kicking, clubbing, and scratching. He tossed her in the back seat of the dually and slammed the door. He climbed in behind the wheel and roared off.

Alisa reached over the seat punching Drago in the head, his ear, and jaw. I put a hand on Alisa's face and shoved her back out of the way. "Stay there or next time I'll sock you." My harsh words and treatment shocked her. I turned to Drago. "They're going to have an airship up. We need to get undercover, now."

"I know. I know. I'm working on it."

He drove fast and loose for five blocks, making three separate turns. He slowed to normal speed and turned into the stacked parking structure that belonged to a high-rise building, an HMO. He pulled a ticket from the machine that raised the entry arm and then drove deep into the cool, dim parking area. He found a spot on the third floor and pulled in.

This was a risk. If spotted, we'd be trapped.

Out on the street, sirens zipped past.

Alisa recovered from all the excitement and regained her composure. "Here, hand her back here."

I picked up the still limp Layla and handed her back to Alisa.

Alisa glared at me. "I can't believe you," she said. "We are no longer friends."

Drago said, "Fine by me."

I put my hand on Drago's arm. "Take it easy, she's just upset. Anyone would be after what happened."

"What the hell?" Drago said. "If anyone should be mad, it's you. This little girl and her ignorant mother pulled you away from your newborn child. Pulled you away from Marie when she needs you the most."

Layla came to and startled at the new environment populated by Drago's large head peering down at her. Her eyes turned wild.

Alisa cooed and stroked her hair, moved it out of her eyes. "It's okay, baby. You're safe now."

"Safe now?" Drago said too loudly. "Your daughter just ripped you off for a hundred grand and tried to rip you off for another fifty."

Alisa's fierce expression softened then shifted to anger as she realized the truth in what Drago said.

Layla pulled away from her mom, moved, and put her back to the door, the flat of her hands up, ready to fend off the good spanking she deserved. "Now, just wait, Mom, let me explain."

Layla took all her traits from her mother; she was lovely, with the added benefit of youth. Smooth skin, brown eyes, and long black glistening hair. Another Aztec princess.

"Karl," I said. "Would you mind getting all of us something to eat and drink? We're going to be here a while until the heat cools off."

He glared at the two women a moment longer.

He finally cracked a smile. "I kinda wanna stick around for the fireworks." I gave him the eye. He started to get out. I said, "Hey, big man, could you get me a couple of Yoo-hoos and some Sno Balls while you're gone?"

Before he closed the door, he looked back in. "Marie's not going to like that."

"What she doesn't know isn't going to hurt her. Besides, she *expects* me to stray from my diet when I'm away. It's an unwritten rule. It is, really."

"I'm not going to help you cheat on her like that."

"You girls want anything?" I asked.

Drago slammed his door before they could reply. He'd didn't take to folks who messed with his friends.

Alisa took hold of Layla's hand. "Where's the money? The hundred thousand dollars?"

Layla didn't answer.

"If you needed money, all you had to do was ask. We have never left you wanting."

That was maybe part of the problem. Spoiled.

Ten minutes passed, Mom coddling her daughter.

My place in the truck shifted from friend to interloper. I wanted to step outside to give them time alone, but venturing out in public after what had just happened wasn't a good idea. With each passing minute our margin of safety grew, so why risk it.

Alisa finally said, "Let's take the money and go home."

"Mom." Layla pulled away from her. "You don't understand."

"What?"

"He has Sonny."

Alisa's expression shifted to confusion. "Sonny? Who's Sonny?"

"He's my baby. He's your grandchild."

CHAPTER SIXTEEN

"You . . . you had a baby?" Alisa asked. "His name's Sonny? How did I not . . ."

Layla was now crying freely. She nodded, unable to speak. Alisa took her in a hug. "Oh, baby, I'm so sorry. I didn't know. You should've come to us."

Alisa pulled her away and looked into her eyes. "Who has the baby? Who has Sonny? We'll go get him right now. No one is going to stop us from getting him back."

Layla looked to me as if I were something a cat buried in the cat box. Then looked back at her mother.

"It's okay," Alisa said. "He's with me. I brought him to help."

"But this is Bruno, Marie's husband, right? The guy with the orphanage? What can he do? He's a bartender at a cabana bar. You have no idea who we're dealing with, Mom."

"Johnny Ef," I said.

Her head whipped around to look me in the eyes. "How do you know that?" Her eyes lost focus as she went over all that had happened. "The car?"

"That's right. Where's Sonny, right now?"

She hesitated as if unsure about giving out information that might jeopardize Sonny's well-being. "I'm not sure. Johnny moves around a lot; he has five houses. He never stays in one place very long. He has people after him all the time. It's very dangerous for Sonny."

"Why did you need the money?" I asked.

Alisa snapped, "Ransom for Sonny." She said it as if I were a fool without a brain.

"Let her tell it," I said and watched Layla's expression—her eyes—for the lie.

"I thought that if I could raise enough money, he'd give my baby back."

Alisa looked confused. "He . . . he didn't ask you for a ransom?"

Layla shook her head, her eyes locked on mine. She knew I'd figured her out.

Alisa spotted our silent exchange. "Wait, what's going on?"

I said, "Tell her."

Layla shook her head, no.

"Tell me what? Layla, tell me. What is he talking about?" Alisa suddenly sat back in the seat, her hand flying to cover her mouth, her eyes going wide. "You mean Sonny . . . He belongs to this Johnny Fillmore character. The gangster? You fucked this Johnny Ef?"

The vulgar word coming from Alisa didn't match the woman I knew. The stressful situation had caused her to slip several rungs down her social station.

More tears. Layla couldn't answer and shook her head, yes—that she had, in fact, lain with the beast.

Alisa's jaw locked, her expression shifting to anger. She slapped Layla across the face. The sound cracked loud in the close confines.

"Hey!" I yelled and reached over the seat to put my arm between them to stop another attack. The sudden shift in Alisa's demeanor shocked me even more. This was no way to treat her daughter.

Layla put her face in her hands and wept. "That's why I tricked you out of the money. Because I knew how you would react." She pulled her hands down. "And you're true to form, Mother dear."

Alisa pulled back to slap her again. I leaned over more and caught her arm. "Stop it, the both of you."

Alisa said, "Drive us to the airport. We're leaving right now."

"Wait," Layla demanded. "What about my baby? What about Sonny? I'm not leaving him here."

Alisa rounded on her. "We want nothing to do with a child that has . . . that has this animal's blood. The child will be no good. He'll soil our good name. This whole sordid matter kicks dirt on our family. No, it's better no one knows about this. Please, Bruno, take us to the airport."

"Just like that," I said. "You're giving up on your grandson?"

"I know it sounds harsh, but Aleck will agree with me. We want no more to do with this matter. The more we push, the bigger chance it will come to light. Aleck has a reputation to protect. It's his livelihood. He's getting ready to announce his run for governor. There are important people behind him."

Layla folded her arms across her chest. "I'm not going. I'm staying. I'm going to get my child back whether you help me or not."

Alisa glared at her daughter. "You'll come with me right now or don't ever bother coming home."

I said, "Alisa, you don't mean that. Emotions are hot right now. Let's everyone just cool down."

"I do mean it." She stared at Layla. "Well, what's your decision?"

More tears streamed down Layla's cheeks. She shook her head, no.

"Fine. You will look back on this decision as the worst one of your life." She turned to me. "Bruno, please drive me to the airport."

I said nothing and looked at her.

"Fine, I'll find my own way." Alisa opened the truck door and stepped down to the smooth concrete of the parking structure. Layla had lied and stolen money from Alisa, but that wasn't enough to exile Layla and Layla's child.

"Mama, please don't go. Please don't do this."

Alisa slammed the door and walked off down the aisle of parked cars. She passed Drago coming back with two bags, one white with red lettering from a burger joint and the other a nondescript brown paper bag.

I thought I knew Alisa. I had no idea she could treat her daughter with such scorn. Alisa, not Layla, would be the one to regret it.

Layla held her hands to her face and wept.

Drago got in the truck bringing with him the heavenly grease-laden aroma of cheeseburgers and fries, a food staple I dearly missed. He tossed me the brown paper bag.

I found the Sno Balls and Yoo-hoos I ordered, the Sno Balls slightly mashed. He took out a fat cheeseburger and offered Layla one.

Through her fingers, she said, "No, thank you," and continued to weep.

Drago pointed with the burger toward Alisa, who'd just disappeared in the stairway stack that would lead down to street level. "That's one pissed-off broad. What'd you say to her, Bruno—that her hair needs a good shampooing?"

I shook my head indicating now wasn't the time to be glib. "You got another one of those burgers for me?"

"You asked for that crap. I got you what you asked for."

I gave him my best wounded puppy dog stare.

"Ah, man, I got four burgers for me, but I guess you can have one."

I smiled. "You're a true friend."

CHAPTER SEVENTEEN

I CHOKED DOWN half the cheeseburger. Couldn't eat the rest.

Drago reminded me of a steer in a field of fodder, grazing away on the greasy cheeseburgers and fries. He kept his eyes in the rearview, watching Layla as he gnashed. She was staring out the window, her expression pitiful and dejected, and Drago's expression softened.

I was wrapping up the uneaten half of my burger and putting it in the bag when Drago snatched the bag from me. "Here, gimme that if you're not going to eat it. Wasting perfectly good food."

His gaze immediately returned to Layla in the rearview. He nodded to me and whispered, "She gonna be okay? Man, does she have a look about her, you know what I mean?" He shook his hand, the fingers loose, and mouthed, "Va va voom." It was his personal expression in the rating of a woman who met his high standards.

The women he chose to rate were so far out of his range they might as well be on Mars. Maybe he chose instinctively knowing that any relationship mixed with his lifestyle was doomed to failure.

The anxiety suddenly returned in force. I had to get out. I opened the door and all but fell to my knees. I took hold of the truck bed and followed it to the bumper, where I sat.

I took out my phone and pushed the button to call Dad before I lost my nerve.

He picked up on the first ring. "Bruno, how's it going? You on your way back?"

"Dad I—" The words wouldn't untangle. I had too much respect for him. What would he think about his son's inability to handle himself?

"What's the matter, Son?"

"Dad, it's . . . it's nothing. I just called to see if you'd gotten out of that wheelchair and started to get some exercise, like you promised."

"Of course, I have. You at the airport? You coming home? The kids really miss you."

I smiled. "That right? How's Marie? How's Tobias?" Just that quick he let a little sunlight in an otherwise inky black cave.

"Both doing great. Sleeping a lot, which is normal. Doc Aleck is really looking after them. How's Bea? Is she there? Let me talk to her."

I stood up from sitting on the bumper as the bottom dropped out of my world. Knees wobbly. I had never lied to Dad; we always told each other the truth no matter how painful. The truth that his long-lost wife had taken it on the lam with all his money was one I didn't want him to know. At least not yet. It wasn't hard to hold back the words, a dirty lie to avoid that truth. That's what lies were all about—the suppression of the truth.

I closed my eyes tight and spoke low into the phone. "She's not here, she went out." That wasn't a lie, but he'd taught me a long time ago that *omission is the same as a lie, only one that's wearing a hat and fake mustache.*

"That right? Where did she go?"

The obvious follow-up question, one that put me in a box without an exit. Then I remembered the app I'd loaded on her phone. "Hold on just one sec, would you, Dad?" I didn't wait for an answer and pulled up the app.

My shoulders drooped as all the air left my lungs.

The little blue locator dot said Bea Johnson currently occupied a seat at the Gardenia Card Club, frittering away Dad's life savings at a poker table. I turned angry at the thought and my backbone stiffened. I wanted to drive over there and yank that woman by the hair out of the gambling house.

Dad's small voice penetrated my anger. "Son? Son, are you still there?"

"I'm here, Dad." I put the phone back to my ear.

"Well, where is she?"

My answer was going to crush him. "Truth?"

He hesitated, then said, "I wouldn't want it any other way."

"She went to a card club, Dad. She's at a card club gambling."

"Oh, is that all. For a second there you had me worried like there was something wrong."

He knew she had all his money. Of course, he did, he had to go to the bank to get the cash. Was he losing his faculties? Did he have Alzheimer's? "So, it's okay that she's at a card club gambling?"

"She's a grown woman. She's allowed her entertainment." He chuckled as if he agreed with the vice.

In all my life Dad had never played a game of chance, never bet one dime on anything. Now he goes along with Bea sitting at a poker table. Dad will always have that perpetual burning ember, a belief that there is good in everyone no matter how they act to the contrary.

I could only shake my head. Did he really think she was going to go back to him? Maybe if she lost all the money she'd have nowhere else to go. She was wanted for absconding on her parole, which severely limited her options.

Dad said, "Son, are you there?"

"I'm here, Dad."

"There's a tone in your voice, what's the matter? Something's bothering you."

Dad always possessed an eerie ability to read me, see right to the heart of the matter without the need for words. He did that now through the phone from thousands of miles away.

I squirmed.

I didn't want to tell him about this new issue, my inability to deal with violence, even though that's what I'd called him for. I was about to put a hat and fake mustache on the truth. "I . . . I ran into some trouble with Alisa and her daughter, Layla."

"Oh?"

"Alisa is on her way home. I have to stay here a little longer to help Layla."

"With what?"

"It's a family matter, the kind Alisa would rather not have aired."

"I understand. You be careful and get back here as soon as you can."

"I know, Dad, and I will, I promise. I gotta go now."

"Okay, Son, I love you. Keep your head down."

That last part was something my old boss Robby Wicks and I said to each other. Dad understood that what had to be done to help Layla was going to take a little *blood and bone*. Another term used in my past.

Dad was an oracle of knowledge and experience. He always knew the right words to say. I just couldn't tell him my problem.

CHAPTER EIGHTEEN

I CLIMBED BACK into the truck parked in the HMO's stacked parking lot. Drago had that rare sappy expression he used when trying to woo women. What was he thinking? He didn't have a chance with a girl like Layla.

He was talking about his tattoos with her. Why, for the most recent one on his back, he chose a warrior woman with a sword. A picture first painted by Frank Frazetta, the guy who did all the art for the Edgar Rice Burroughs book covers. Karl said he believed in strong women and had liked swords when he was a kid.

Layla stared out the truck window, her focus diffused, not listening. No doubt distraught over her son in the hands of an evil man. I couldn't imagine someone taking my son Tobias. My heart went out to her.

Drago never talked that much to anyone, a trait he should employ now.

I closed the truck door and the vacuum pressure pumped my ears. Drago continued to describe his tattoo in great detail. I play-slapped his cheek. "Hey, you in there? What are we going to do about finding Sonny?"

Layla came out of her trance, now paying attention.

Drago smiled too broadly. He was smitten for sure. Marie would be sad. She liked being the center of his attention. But at the same time, she'd be happy for him. To survive in this world, life required dreams, attainable and the unattainable. Unfortunately for Drago, Layla fell into the latter category.

Drago noticed Layla perk up when I asked the question about finding Sonny and said, "Oh, well, I know a guy."

"Well, of course you do," I said. "Can you call him?"

Layla put her hand on his arm.

She said, "Can you please call him?"

His expression melted. He said, "Yes." He continued to nod, not taking his eyes off hers.

"Drago?" I said.

"Huh? Oh, right." He fumbled with the door latch and stepped outside. He moved around to the front of the truck and spoke into his phone, his back to us as if we could read lips and spy on his confidentiality.

I turned to Layla, who continued to stare at Drago. "Can you tell me everything you know about Johnny Ef?"

"Huh? What? Oh. Yes, what do you want to know?" She finally tore her eyes away from Drago and looked at me.

"Everything. Start from the beginning and talk. I'll tell you when to stop."

Her eyes went back to Drago outside the truck. She wanted to hear what he had to say—more importantly, who Drago talked to—what *he* had to say. She needed to know where Johnny had Sonny.

"Sure, okay."

She'd met Johnny at a club her friends took her to in Hollywood called THB—Two Hours Before—located on Sunset Boulevard. A trendy, upscale bar with a small dance floor, lots of retro chrome and black leather, dim lights, and a white smoke machine. She'd never been there before and rarely went clubbing. She had too much homework. She wanted to be a psychologist. That was part of the reason Johnny initially intrigued her. She sensed his dangerous component, saw how other people treated him like a vicious fanged animal from a zoo, now at large in the public. She'd convinced herself her interest was merely the desire to write a paper. She'd call it "A Predator Living Among the Victims: An Inside Examination of a Criminal Alpha Male Lacking Social Conscience."

I had never heard of the THB, but clubs in Hollywood rose and fell as often as some people changed their underwear.

She said that Johnny Ef had a way about him—the way he looked at her. He made her feel like the most important person in the room, made her forget *he* was the topic of the paper.

Layla should've known better. A boa constrictor does the same thing, hypnotizing its prey before pouncing, taking its prey in unrelenting jaws then squeezing the life out of it.

Looking back on how the relationship started, Johnny had worked her perfectly. The first night she saw him in the club he introduced himself and bought her a drink, one she pretended to sip without the liquid ever touching her lips, deathly afraid of a date-rape drug.

Johnny flashed a white smile as a weapon, knowing just when to use it. And his eyes . . . he had these blue-gray eyes that worked hand in hand with that smile. He looked like an old-time actor she had to look up that first night when she got back to the dorm. A young Robert Mitchum, right down to the dimple in his chin. He spoke smooth and easy, comfortable around women.

Next, she bumped into him at the coffee shop she frequented—spent hours there doing homework and drinking double espressos.

He pretended the meeting was purely accidental. Again, he did not ask for her phone number. He bought her a coffee, flashed that smile, and kept her talking about herself. She soon forgot that he was on the prowl and she was the victim of the hour. The flavor of the day.

Three days later while she was walking to the coffee shop, a sleek white Maserati pulled to the curb. The window whirred down and there was Johnny with his smile. He asked if she wanted a ride. Getting in the car was a big mistake. But she'd already started writing the paper and even told the class PA about it. He thought the topic a wonderful idea that would guarantee her a good grade for the class.

She could handle Johnny like a lion tamer with a chair and a whip and still get the information she needed. She took a deep breath and opened the car door. For one last time she thought it wasn't too late to turn back.

Instead, she took the plunge and got in.

He made her laugh as he drove for hours around LA and stopped at three of his many businesses, drove up to them never getting out of the car. His employees came out running to see what he wanted—a cell phone store, a commercial real estate office, and a used tire shop. As the sun started to set, she wondered what he'd do next. He pulled up and stopped at the entrance to her school. She'd not been paying attention and was surprised the impromptu date was over.

She got out, a little dazed at the abrupt ending to a wonderful day. She closed the door. The window whirred down. He leaned over. "Layla, would it be okay if I got your phone number and called you?"

She smiled. "Of course." She gave it to him. He thanked her for the "magnificent day" and drove off. She stood there and watched him go. She remembered thinking later that was the turning point, the place where she made the big mistake, giving him her phone number, and thinking that maybe she'd been wrong about him, that maybe he was just misunderstood.

CHAPTER NINETEEN

DRAGO STAYED ON the phone for thirty minutes, making several calls. He stood in front of the truck and turned every now and again with scowl lines marring his expression. Apparently, finding Johnny Ef wasn't going to be as easy as he thought. Meantime, Layla continued to drone on about Johnny, their first kiss, his romantic moves—all roses and chocolate until it turned sour.

Johnny's interest waned once he made the conquest, and like a bee, he flitted to the next flower to pollinate.

She spoke using her hands. On her right wrist she had bruises that matched fingerprint impressions from someone jerking her around. I reached up and gently put my hand on her chin, moved her head to the side to see the faint shadows on her neck. More fingerprint bruising. Somebody had throttled her with one hand.

Some misogynist asshole.

Johnny Ef.

Her expression shifted to anger and she knocked my hand away.

That's when Drago finished his last call, came around, and opened his door. He didn't look happy. The humongous truck leaned to his side when he climbed in, the suspension compressing.

"Well? Well?" Layla asked. "What'd you find out?"

"No soap."

Layla sat back, disheartened.

"That's okay, big man, we'll work our way in. We'll find Johnny."

"What?" he said. "No, I know where Johnny's going to be at nine o'clock tonight. I just couldn't get a line on where he's hiding Sonny. It's like it's some kinda national secret. Damn that little weasel, Stank, he's never let me down before. I'm gonna skin him next time I see him."

"I guess we're going to talk with Johnny, tonight. Where's he going to be?"

"The LaRue, in Santa Monica."

Layla wrung her hands, worried. "You two are fools if you think you'll get within thirty feet of him, let alone get him to tell you where he has Sonny hidden. He has people, you know. People who will chew you two up and spit you out. I know, I've seen it firsthand."

Drago's jaw muscle bulged. He didn't like being told he couldn't do something. I only half-paid attention to his reaction.

My mind all on its own flashed back to another incident that happened in a restaurant. Back when I worked on the violent crimes team when I chased a murder suspect through a neighborhood and into a family restaurant.

The suspect, Little Genie, had cut off a woman's head in front of her five-year-old daughter and he was death-penalty eligible. He'd escaped from the jail, and his only way out of the restaurant was to go through me. I had never gone up against a more determined suspect. And like all previous violent confrontations when they flashed back, the experience was the same as if I stood right in the moment.

All of a sudden, I was again running in the street, chasing violence—the sights, the sounds vivid, the acrid smell of gun smoke, the thrill of the chase.

My heartbeat throbbed behind my eyes, the memory all too real. Blood and Bone.

Johnny Ef was ten times more dangerous than Little Genie. Johnny Ef commanded a platoon of Little Genies.

Something Dad had told me in the past echoed in my ear: "When you're dead, you don't know you're dead. The pain is only felt by others. The same thing happens when you're stupid. Son, don't ever be stupid."

Everything about dealing with Johnny Ef sounded stupid.

Drago brought me out of my thoughts by shoving my shoulder. "Hey Bro, you got a fever or something? You're sweating like a pig and your eyes are glazed over."

"What? Ah, no. I'm good. We have some time before we have to be in Santa Monica." I pulled the door latch and stepped out of the truck. "I've got something I need to do."

Layla said, "What about the Maserati? Johnny's going to kill me when he finds out about the broken window. He doesn't know I took it. He loves that car more than anything in this world. We left it in that shopping center parking lot. Someone's going to steal it."

I looked at Drago, who said, "I'll take care of it. You go do what you gotta do. We'll meet back at the hotel at eight."

Layla didn't argue about being left with Drago. Maybe she sensed she was safer with him than a crime figure like Johnny Ef. I closed the truck door, walked to the stairs, and took them down to the street while ordering up an Uber ride that would take me to Mom at the Gardena card club.

CHAPTER TWENTY

I STOOD IN the parking lot of a card club in Gardena looking up at the bright neon lights glowing in the moonless night, creating ominous shadows. Anyone could be hiding among the shrubs or behind pillars and cars out there.

The Uber driver, a young Iranian who spoke with a thick accent, talked nonstop the entire trip even though I never once said a word in response. I was too wrapped up in my thoughts.

Heading toward the entrance, I passed two uniformed security guards stationed outside the front door. I wasn't worried about them. I had a California driver's license and a passport in a different name. I had the PI license to give me cover.

When I opened the card club door, I was assaulted by the acrid reek of tar from a million cigarettes smoked there over the years. Tar permeated the carpet, the wallpaper, the cloth material in the furniture, and the clothes of everyone inside.

The worn red carpet had a floral design and led to an expansive sunken room three steps down. Round tables filled every available space in the card room. Someone sat at every spot at the tables, most all of them smoking and drinking from sweaty highball glasses. Many others congregated in a lounge off to the side, standing or sitting at high-top tables, watching the play, waiting for their names to be called after someone else lost everything they had—anxious for their chance to throw away their money.

This den of iniquity catered to three of the most vicious vices: alcohol, gambling, and smoking. Two of which crushed and ruined families and yet they waited in line—couldn't wait to give away their lives.

I stood on the top step looking down at the tables. Bea wasn't hard to spot. She sat in a wheelchair all the way over by the wall where two tables accommodated the handicapped. The card club had no scruples; they'd fleece any and all comers, which included the infirm.

The club took a percentage off each pot. The owners gladly raked in the tax-sheltered dough.

A man in a dark-gray silk suit came up to me, his hands crossed at his waist. "Can I help you, sir?" He put the emphasis on "sir," as if I needed to come in the back door, the servants' entrance.

I didn't want to cause a problem. I still had the two .357s in my waistband under my shirt. "No, I'm cool. I'm just here to pick up someone. Are you the manager?"

"Yes, I'm the floor boss. My name is Manker." He offered his hand to shake. I gave him back his attitude, looked down at his hand then back up at his eyes. I took his hand and shook. I lowered my voice. "Is there somewhere we can talk?"

"What's this about?"

I stepped to the side to let in three well-dressed Asian men who did not head over to the lounge to wait their turn. They were shown to a door that opened for them when they approached. They disappeared inside. High rollers. The whales.

Manker said, "We can talk right here." He'd pasted on a fake smile. I wasn't exactly dressed like an optimum client. I looked out onto the floor and realized very few blacks had been allowed to play.

The ones that did wore new clothes, their fingers, necks, ears, and teeth adorned with gold and diamonds. All "players"—gang members throwing away their easily earned rock coke money. Violent men by definition. The kind I used to chase.

I crossed my hands at my waist, leaned over, and said, "See that woman over there in the wheelchair?"

"Yes, that's Ms. Hamilton. She is a very good customer."

"You sure you want to discuss this here?"

"If you insist, then come over here. I really don't have time to play petty games."

He moved over to a Ficus plant that looked sick from breathing too much secondhand cigarette smoke. I took out my flat badge in a worn leather wallet, a holdover from when I was a detective in the sheriff's department, flipped it open and closed, but not too fast. Just fast enough for him not to recognize it. "State Tax Franchise Board," I said. "I've been tracking that woman in the wheelchair and her name isn't Hamilton. She owes back taxes, and the money she's gambling was embezzled from the retirement home where she resides. I really don't want to cause a scene and—"

"No, I understand and thank you for your discretion in this matter. I will have her escorted over here so there won't be a scene on the floor."

"Thank you, I appreciate your assistance."

Anytime you mention the IRS or a tax board around a gambling establishment, they piss their pants and bend over backward to make you go away. If I pulled out my badge, flipped it open, and yelled into the poker floor, "State Tax Franchise," half the players would stampede out. I stepped back to the edge of the steps without going down on the card room floor. I wanted to stay high enough to watch.

Manker pulled out a cell phone and spoke quietly. Part of the wall opened and expelled two thugs in suits that belonged on men two sizes smaller. They walked over to Mom's table. One leaned down and whispered to her. She looked at her cards and shook her head no. She flapped her hand at them to leave her be.

He put his hand on her cards and yanked them away. She made a grab, the cards fleeting as butterflies and her without a net.

The man took hold of her chair.

She grabbed onto the table edge and held on. Other players at other tables stopped playing, pulled out their cell phones, and snapped some shots. They immediately sent the photos over social media.

This wasn't the best plan of attack. Now she could be recognized by law enforcement. The odds were low; she was only wanted by parole. At least that's the only agency I knew about.

One of the thugs pushed down on the wheelchair handles, tipping her back. The other tried to pry her hands off the table's edge.

A woman employee in a faded mustard dress slipped in and scooped all her chips into a large bowl and slunk away.

Mom yelled, "Hey. Hey, that's my money. Bring back my money."

She pulled back and punched the guy who pried her hands loose and who was about to pick up the legs to the chair and carry her out, chair and all.

She caught him with a roundhouse right to his mouth. His lip split and instantly started to bleed.

He let go. The front of the wheelchair hit the floor.

Now everyone in the place stopped to watch.

Mom jumped to her feet.

A collective "Oh!" came from the crowd.

She took off running after the woman with the bowl. Mom could really move for an old gal. I chuckled at the spectacle. Another security guard headed her off. She changed directions and wove in and around the tables on the dodge. The players cheered at the game of keep-away.

Now I was glad it wasn't me making an ass of myself chasing an old woman.

More gorillas piled out of the hidden door in the wall. Mom reached down on the closest table, grabbed someone's highball glass, and threw it at the closest thug. The glass bounced off his forearm; sweet liquid and ice sprayed other players.

People cheered louder.

Mom threw her head back and cackled. She'd have been more at home flying around the room on a broom.

She juked around another table, did it with the agility of a sixty-year-old instead of someone who had to be seventy-five plus.

Players started to hand her their drink glasses to throw as she passed them.

Everyone cheered.

She threw the highball projectiles with surprising accuracy as she dodged and wove her way around the tables.

Until she finally spotted me up by the entrance chuckling.

She froze, shocked that her son had caused her to lose her place at the table. To lose her money.

That one-second diversion allowed the pursuers to close in. They scooped her, one taking her legs, the other her body. The other players booed and threw wadded-up napkins.

They didn't boo so much because Mom was an old woman railing against the establishment, but more because one day they knew it would be their turn to dodge and juke and throw highball glasses when *their* luck ran out.

The two thugs brought her over and set her down in front of me. I said, "Hi, Mom."

Manker moved his face up close to mine, angry. "*This* is your mother? You said she . . . that she . . . Get out, the both of you, and don't come back. You are both permanently 86'd. You come back, you'll be arrested for trespass. You understand?"

Mom's breath came hard from her Olympic tryout on the poker floor. "Oh, don't get your panties in a wad. Where's my money? I want my money or I'm calling the police."

An empty threat. She couldn't call the police—not without being discovered.

The mustard woman appeared, the one who'd scooped Mom's chips. She handed Manker a check. He handed it to Mom. "Here's your cash-out. Now go."

I snatched the check from her hand: thirty-two thousand dollars. She was pretty good at cards, that was ten thousand over the twenty-two she started with. Card clubs only drew the pros. The semi-pros and all the others were victims who only thought they knew what they were doing and easily parted from their money.

She snatched the check out of my hand as one of the thugs set her wheelchair down. She sat, brought her arm back and then forward. "Wagons Ho."

I gladly pushed her out of the establishment, a little sorry I had interrupted her lucky run at cards.

CHAPTER TWENTY-ONE

OUTSIDE THE CARD club, I pulled my phone to call an Uber. Two thugs followed us and stood by in their tight suits and sunglasses even though it was dark. They waited to make sure we left the premises.

Mom said to me, "What are you doing? Why did you stop moving? Come on, get going, my van's over there. Mush. They'll have the cops on our ass before too long."

I put the phone away and followed her hand as it signaled to go left over to the row of handicapped parking slots. She pushed the fob as we approached; the side door to a dark-blue van slid open. I pulled up and waited for her to get in.

"Son, would you please help your poor crippled mother into the vehicle?" She shrugged toward the van but didn't leave her seat.

"*You* have got to be kidding me. I just saw you run an evasion pattern the Green Bay Packers would be proud of."

"Son, please? The longer we dillydally, the longer we're bait for a cruising cop car."

Her stubbornness won out again. I picked her up and set her in the van. That strange tingling sensation rolled through my body—touching her reminded me this was my mother.

She patted my cheek. "You're a good son." I set her on the seat, a little befuddled with conflicting feelings. I fumbled trying to get the wheelchair folded and stowed. I came around to get in the driver's door and found her sitting behind the wheel. She'd crawled between the seats. The window whirred down. "Come on, get in."

I shook my head in amazement, came around, and got in the passenger seat. She took off using hand controls instead of foot pedals. I couldn't believe it. She'd even rented a handicapped van to maintain her con.

We drove in silence. I was angry. She had again buffaloed me into picking her up and for continuing to play this silly charade.

She was angry I'd burned her favorite card location. She finally broke the silence.

"You know, you put me in Dutch with that card club. They're serious about arresting me if I come back. Now I'll have to go all the way to Vegas. Son, that was mean. Just plain mean."

I didn't bother giving her the satisfaction of looking at her, let alone throwing insignificant words her way.

After a pause she said, "You know what your dad says about gambling?"

"Yes, as a matter of fact I do."

We again rode in silence. I never thought being born to Dad was a biological accident, a random spin of the wheel of fate. Dad could've only been *my* dad. No other explanation made sense. We fit together with a natural bond of love that couldn't be broken.

I hoped I could have a similar relationship with Tobias. I would try my damnedest.

"Your dad says that anyone with the three vices, drinking, gambling, and smoking, has a black rot on their soul and deserves to be forgiven for forsaking their family."

I turned to look at her. "He never told *me* that. And no, I will not forgive you."

She shrugged and drove on, headed to the hotel in Glendale. She knew the way.

Finally, she said, "You know, I had three aces when you rolled up on me. I was about to grab that fat pot and finally crush that crazy Asian broad with her smug smile. I would've ruined her."

The image of her jumping up out of the chair made me chuckle all over again, the look on everyone's faces. "You really beaned that guy with the highball glass."

"I did, didn't I?" She laughed.

I said, "Did you hear them when you stood up from your wheelchair?" My chuckle turned to a laugh.

"Yeah," she said. "Those pogues will be talking about it for weeks." She laughed. "They would never have caught me. I was rounding third coming home when I looked up and saw you."

Her expression shifted from mirth to seriousness. "That shocked me, kid, really threw me off my game. Why'd you do it?"

"If you don't know, then it's too late to explain it now."

She was gambling with Dad's savings.

"It must be nice to know everything about this world and to be able to judge like you do."

We rode in silence the rest of the way. She'd called me "kid." I yearned to be loved by a mother, a desire that rose up from a childhood need never fulfilled.

I was an old fool. How could I accept her in that role, not the way she conned Dad? What she said about Dad forgiving folks with three vices, the ones who forsake their families for those vices, sounded like something he'd say.

First and foremost, he was a forgiving person. I wanted to be like him and be able to forgive, but sneak thieves, embezzlers, and con men—con women—in my book go right up there with murderers, child abusers, and elder abusers. In fact, I can almost understand heat-of-passion murders, where the suspect is out of his/her mind with emotions and doesn't know what he/she is doing. Sneak thieves, embezzlers, child abusers, and elder abusers know better and do their heinous crimes with impunity and forethought. There's no excuse. None.

Mom had taken all of Dad's money.

Anger rose up inside me, shoving out all other emotions. I clung to that anger.

Dad had forgiven her for taking his money.

I wasn't going to.

She pulled into the parking structure for the hotel in Glendale, found an empty handicap spot by the elevators, and turned the van off. We sat in the uncomfortable silence.

She finally said, "Son, you have to be careful with hate, it'll bite you back. Now be a love and come around here and put me in my wheelchair."

CHAPTER TWENTY-TWO

DRAGO MADE ONE pass of the LaRue restaurant that sat on Pacific Coast Highway facing the Pacific Ocean, prime-plus real estate worth a fortune. Cars packed the small parking lot and side streets. Two men in white shirts, red waist-jackets, and black pants stood at the ready to valet cars for the arriving guests. A short line snaked its way down the sidewalk in front of a real estate office called "Homes by LaRue."

Drago dumped the truck five streets over and we walked back. He dressed for the occasion in his best Raiders jersey, freshly pressed, and a red ball cap with two letters—BK—a throwback to "Blood Killers" when the Crips took over the BK brand from Burger King. Five thick, braided rope necklaces of gold, all different lengths, hung from his neck. On one hand, he sported a gargantuan diamond-encrusted ring from an NBA championship; on the other a similar style ring from the NFL. He bought them on the open market for a price pushing 20k per and they almost looked normal-sized on him. He thought the extra bling created camouflage that would allow us to slide into the restaurant/club unnoticed. Yeah, right, a meteor the size of Texas trying to slip unnoticed into our atmosphere.

I dressed in chic Smith and Wesson under my long-sleeve blue shirt, though I did add a black bolo tie with a fake piece of turquoise I purchased from a kid on the sidewalk outside the hotel. Gave him an extra ten to boot.

Two tatted thugs stood at the door in black tee-shirts and black pants. Both carried portable radios clipped to their belts with a wire up to their headsets. Their shaved heads flashed and gleamed in the reflection from the soft neon sign on the roof that bleated Chez LaRue. The faux restaurant/nightclub front mimicked a French château.

We walked past the line and up to the door thugs. With the threat of a violent confrontation, sweat started to break out on my forehead and run down into my eyes. A cool breeze off the ocean made the air brisk.

Drago tried to walk in like he owned the place. He wouldn't be afraid even if thrown into an arena filled with man-eating lions.

I wished there was a blue pill that'd give me back one iota of his confidence and fierceness. I'd be okay once the action started. I had no doubt.

One thug stepped in front of Drago. "Ho there, dump truck, where do you think you're going?"

Drago furrowed his brow and glared, trying for silent intimidation. The door thug said, "Get in the back of the line, tubby."

The door thug should've been quaking in his black sneaks with the likes of Drago scowling at him, but he had to be more afraid of the consequences if he let Drago pass. Another point for the other team, an "X" marked in the "violence and mayhem" box.

Drago shifted his weight and took a half-step back, righting his balance in a horse stance. I'd worked with him enough to know he was about to go to war.

Not something we wanted.

Not yet.

I reached up and put my hand on his shoulder and gripped his deltoid as hard as I could to get his attention, his body stiff as a wound spring. I whispered, "Not the time or the place, my friend. Step back and let me have a go."

He hesitated, then did as I asked. I stepped around him. "Would you please tell Mr. Fillmore we'd like to speak with him?"

"He's not here."

Drago bumped into my back with his chest, ready to mow these two over. Without turning, I put my hand on his chest. I was caught between a bull elephant and two rhinos.

"Please tell Mr. Fillmore that we'd like to talk to him about Sonny."

The door thug took a couple of steps back, keyed the radio on his belt, and spoke quietly.

Cars on Pacific Coast Highway zipped past. The line of people had gone silent, wanting to hear the drama as it continued to unfold.

The door thug listened to the reply, gave a one-word response, and then stepped forward. He said nothing and just stood there. The door opened and out stepped two more thugs dressed exactly the same. The door thug said, "Mr. Fillmore can give a shit less about anything you have to say. He said to get away from his club, and if you don't, we are to assist you in that endeavor."

Drago smirked. "*Endeavor*. I can't believe he just said that. What, you got some of that toilet paper that has the word of the day on it?"

"Hold it." I held up my hands to keep World War III from kicking off.

A few weeks ago, four against two might have been a dog fall. But that night standing in front of the enemy camp, with others inside, we were grossly outnumbered. I had to think about Marie, Tobias, and the other kids who all expected me to come home in one piece.

My guts churned, tying me up in a knot. I swallowed hard. "Tell Effin Johnny that Bruno Johnson wants to have a word."

The door thug took a step back. "You're Bruno Johnson?"

"That's right."

"I don't believe you. He's dead."

"I've been getting that a lot lately." I unbuttoned my shirt, let my two dinner guests in my waistband be seen, then pulled my shirt off my shoulder, pulled up my tee-shirt sleeve, and showed him the "BMF" tattoo. A mistake from a bygone day when youth and testosterone ruled over common sense.

The door thug's expression shifted to fear. He again spoke quietly into his radio and nodded to himself. Now sweat broke out on his brow. Good, let a little fear work in our favor.

He held out his hand. "He'll see you. But you gotta give up your guns."

I pulled the two .357s and handed them to him, barrel first. I leaned in and whispered, "I'll be wanting those back." I started to walk by, then paused, and again looked into his eyes. He squirmed. Fear, an edge I'd exploit until I couldn't.

Drago followed me into the arena with the starving lions.

CHAPTER TWENTY-THREE

DESPITE THE LINE outside the door, the place wasn't packed. Soft music played, patrons slow danced and drank in the bar area, the noise level tolerable, sedate. More than anything else, the environment projected a sense of total control.

The shaved-head door thug had moved in around us. He led the way through the well-heeled patrons to a part of the restaurant all the way in the back. It was dimmer than the rest, lit only with the occasional guttering candle.

The delectable aroma of fresh-baked bread, cheese, and wine wafted in the air; the motif tasteful, understated French café. We passed tier-one LA folks having a quiet dinner, noshing on small salads, French cheese-encrusted onion soup, and entrées with rich white sauces.

We found Johnny Ef all the way in the back in the corner booth, one upholstered in soft red leather and a polished brass rail on top. He sat quietly next to a beautiful woman clad in a nightclub dress composed of near-invisible silver spangles that made her body shimmer when she moved. Sleek like a beautiful fish. Her eyes were at half-mast and glassy from drugs and made her seem even more youthful and vulnerable.

I didn't know Johnny Ef by sight but recognized him from Layla's description. In a weird sort of way, he did resemble a young Robert Mitchum, replete with the deep dimple in his chin and perfectly coifed hair. Smug and confident. He wore an expensive blue dress shirt with white French cuffs and gold cuff links stamped with "JF." He only wore one ring, a tiger's eye with diamonds on his right pinkie finger. He saw us approach, picked up a crystal flute filled with champagne, put his arm around his date, and eased back in his seat in an air of fearlessness.

We stopped in front of the table. He nodded for his thug to take a powder.

We waited while Johnny sipped his bubbles.

I'd too often seen the kind of light bruises on his date, the ones on her wrist and on her neck covered with light foundation makeup. Fingerprint bruising. Johnny Ef was abusing her. Treating her like chattel just like he had Layla. Anger flushed my face hot. Johnny Ef, a coward of a man who bullied women. He could do with an intense lesson in blood and bone from a card-carrying BMF.

He said, "I don't like that name you used at the door. You of all people should know better than to call me by that hateful slur. I'm a respected businessman."

I stood still and stared and said nothing.

He smiled and finally said, "You really Bruno Johnson?"

I slid into the booth and pulled over in front of me his scantily clad date's plate filled with exotic cheeses and grapes and strawberries.

Her movements were lethargic; she wasn't even sure someone had sat down next to her. I picked up a crumbling piece of cheese and took a bite.

Drago knew enough to wait to see how things played out. He stood in front of the table blocking the view to the rest of the establishment, his hands crossed at his waist. The diamonds in his championship rings flickered in the candlelight. Johnny Ef didn't give him a look. He shot his cuffs while staring at me. "I guess," he said, "you wouldn't be sitting here like that if you weren't Bruno Johnson."

I tilted my head to the side with indifference, picked up a grape, and popped it in my mouth. I took up her champagne-filled flute and sipped the dry bubbles. She tried to recover her glass from me. I gently patted her hand, her skin fiery hot. She nodded and went back to staring into the big nowhere.

Johnny guffawed and slapped the table. "Okay, you're Bruno Johnson. What are you doing in my fine establishment ruining a nice evening out?"

"I want Sonny. I'm here to get Sonny."

He instantly lost his smile. He brought his arm down from around his girl, who flinched from his quick movement. "I don't know what you're talking about," he said, gritting his teeth. "I don't know any Sonny and if I did, I don't like being strong-armed in my own place."

I stared at his eyes. Marie said that if a person is truly evil, you can smell the brimstone on them, a throwback belief from her semi-religious upbringing. I slowly took in a whiff. I didn't recognize the scent of brimstone, but his eyes were wild and unpredictable. I'd seen it before in some of the murderers I'd chased.

It no longer mattered. Johnny Ef needed to be taken off the board. I slugged down the rest of the champagne in the flute. I said, "You sure you want to play it that way?"

He raised his arm and snapped his fingers. Two thug-uglies appeared. I partially stood, leaned over the table, and took up the bottle of champagne from its silver bucket. I handed it to Drago. He smiled, took it by the neck, tipped it back, and glugged. I sat back down and leaned past his girlfriend—who smelled of lilac—and over close to Johnny Ef. "If you know of me then you might know what happened at that family restaurant called Mel's a few years back."

He let an evil grin slither onto his face. "You try that here, pal, and you'll end up the loser, big-time. I'll lose a little money in repairs, but patrons will flock back to this place to see where it happened. Where two thugs came into my place, tried to strong-arm me, and got their asses handed to them. You two will be in the hospital for months, guaranteed." He paused and then shrugged. "Or worse."

"I guess you want to play hardball."

"You picked that up from our conversation? You're not as dumb as you look."

I couldn't afford to break the place up. He was right—in the end, we'd probably be the big losers. At the moment he held the high cards. That would change.

I slid out of the booth. "Thanks for the chow." I stood. "But don't say I didn't warn you." I stopped and stared down at him a second longer, then turned and made my way through his restaurant with his two dogs following close on our heels.

Drago walked, tilting back the bottle, drinking. He brought it down and burped, one loud enough to echo in the quiet that settled while everyone paused to watch our retreat. The nicely dressed diners looked disgusted. Drago smiled, put one hand on his stomach as we continued to walk, and said loud enough for all to hear, "I told you this stuff makes me gassy."

Outside in the cool air, the door thug handed over my .357s. I checked their loads and put them away. We walked toward the truck five blocks down.

Behind me, Drago tossed the empty bottle in the street. It clattered without breaking. "Now what, boss man?"

"I don't have the first clue."

"What?" He took a longer step to get up beside me and used his knuckles to knock on my head. "Where's Bruno? What did you do with him? Give him back."

He was absolutely right. A younger Bruno would've torn down Chez LaRue, right then and there.

I asked him. "What would you do, big man?"

"I say we burn him down until he cries uncle."

What Drago said made perfect sense, and a distant memory of the old Bruno agreed. "All right, let's go find us a couple of torches." I'd said it metaphorically and should've known Drago wouldn't take it that way.

Drago smiled hugely and clapped his hands together. "Now you're talking, my man. Now you're talking."

CHAPTER TWENTY-FOUR

I WOKE TO sunlight filling the room, only I didn't know which room in our Costa Rica home; nothing looked familiar. The air even tasted different. I reached over to pat the bed, feeling for Marie.

She wasn't there.

My heart leapt up into my throat. What happened to her? Where was she? Where was Marie?

Then the past two days flooded back. An involuntary gag reflex made me choke. What the hell was I doing back in Los Angeles?

The suite bedroom in the Americana Hotel in Glendale brought back memories of physical and emotional pain like I'd never experienced before. This was where Marie and I hid out for two months while I recovered from a truly awful event on the freeway, and the one in the garage where people lost their lives, where I'd been shot multiple times.

The physical pain was easy to overcome compared to the depression. An emotional blackness that never dulled or went away until I forced it behind a door in my mind and locked it there never to see the light of day. Why was it flooding back now—the shame and regret too heavy to deal with? Why not back in Costa Rica? Marie had said something about delayed post-traumatic stress. I should've listened to her.

I swung my legs over the edge of the bed and put my head in my hands. I'd let my guard down and allowed the door in my mind to ease open just enough for Bosco to slip out. Bosco was a son that I'd never known I had—until that day on the freeway I'd killed Bosco with my bare hands. I continually see his pleading eyes as I flipped him out into traffic.

Alone now in the hotel bed, I shifted my torso and dropped face-first into the closest pillow. I screamed. And screamed some more as I tried to get that door in my brain closed—to force out those horrifying images.

His eyes, his words begging me not to do it.

I should never have come back to this hotel. Why did I? Was this self-flagellation for penance?

I punched the mattress again and again as slobber-laden screams filled the down pillow.

The suite door opened, and Drago's voice boomed, "You okay, boss man?"

I froze. Shame had me by the throat for killing Bosco. I didn't need more from Drago seeing me in a state—the spoiled child screaming into a pillow and attacking a helpless mattress. I slowly sat up and swiped the tears from my eyes and runny nose. "Yeah, fine, why?"

Drago looked confused. "Nothing, I just . . . I mean, I thought I heard something."

"What? Oh, that? It's this new Zen thing where every morning when you wake up you purge your soul. It's very relaxing, you ought to try it sometime."

I should've owned up to it, right then and there. Maybe by sharing, some of this heavy burden would ease. Just one iota was all I needed.

"No thank you," Drago said. "Every morning I get up, Waldo is hiding from me. I have to find him, and when I do, we tussle."

Drago's tussle at the very least entailed broken furniture and dented drywall. *Tussle* equaled chaos.

Waldo? I'd forgotten all about Waldo. "Well, let's not bring Waldo into this ho—" A black and brown torpedo ran from the living area of the suite into the bedroom. He leapt up on the bed.

Waldo bowled me over, put his huge paws on my chest, and stared down at me with demon eyes. Drool from his floppy jowls dripped on my chin. I didn't move a muscle.

For some reason, Waldo didn't take to me.

"Lookie here," Drago said. "Waldo remembers you."

A low rumble of a growl emitted from his entire body and vibrated through his paws into my chest.

"And he likes you."

My voice came out cracked. "Call him off. Please call him off."

Waldo could remove my face with one chomp. His eyes told me he was ready to if I so much as twitched.

Waldo was Drago's 130-pound trained Rottweiler. Smartest dog I had ever seen. Drago could give Waldo verbal, multifaceted tasks and somehow the dog understood what to do— almost as if Drago and the dog had some sort of Vulcan mind-meld.

One time I had tried to give Waldo the exact same tasks. He turned his head one way, then the other, and looked at me like I was ten pounds of uncooked pot roast.

Waldo always wore a spiked dog collar and never barked. Not so much as a growl while on alert, ready to devour. Drago called it "silent death."

I was nervous around him even with Drago's assurance that Waldo wouldn't maul me unless Drago gave him the word. Maul. Most dogs bit people, but apparently not Waldo. He mauls.

"Waldo, out," Drago said, and snapped his fingers down by his leg.

Waldo gave me one last grunting growl and retreated off the bed. He sat on the floor next to where Drago stood. My heart rate came down slowly. I sat up. "What's going on? What time is it?"

"It's after three in the afternoon, bro, you slept the day away. Everyone's been waiting for you."

My body and mind still needed to recover. It had only been three and a half months since the horrible incident on the freeway and the one in the garage. Time healed all, but in this case, I didn't think there was enough left in the hourglass, not for me.

I stood, knees a little wobbly, along with other achy body parts— hips, shoulders, neck. Waldo let go with a rumbling growl.

I held up my hands flat. "What's with Waldo?"

Drago let a grin fill his expression. "If he didn't like you, you wouldn't hear him."

I asked, "Who's in the other room?"

"I called Simon to come give us a hand."

"Simple Simon?"

"Yeah, it's a perfect job for him. He's gonna drive your moms to Vegas and stay with her. I didn't think you'd want her to go alone."

I headed for the door. "She's *not* going to Vegas."

"That's what I said, but your moms is stubborn like you. So, I called Simon. They're waitin' on you. She wants to talk to you before they head out."

On the way past Drago, I said, "The hotel doesn't allow dogs, especially dogs like Waldo. How'd you get him in?"

"Through the kitchen and up the freight elevator. I know a dude who works the kitchen."

"Of course, you do."

I have found that when he says he knows a dude, it also means he found someone to bribe. Not necessarily with money but with whatever gets the job done. Drago has one of those minds that remembers everything, and the guy in the kitchen, whether or not he was before, was now a dude Drago knows.

Today Drago wore his Rams football jersey, blue, white, and gold, with an OH Kruse Feed and Grain ball cap. In his hand, he carried a length of one-half-inch galvanized pipe he had painted brown and added a handle to make it look like a cane. He was never far from a piece of pipe or rebar. What a world he lived in.

In the big room to the suite, Layla sat on the couch, Mom in her wheelchair. Simon stood over by the bar drinking a fifteen-dollar can of beer from the mini-fridge. He was skinny and wore his brown hair shaggy. Simon had an Adam's apple the size of a walnut. Probably not that big, but in comparison to his pigeon chest and stick arms it looked larger. He was five foot six and weighed in at a buck ten. Not enough stature to knock back an attacking raccoon. But he was reliable working as a bird dog and would do what he was told.

Mom saw Layla look my way and pivoted her wheelchair. "Oh, good morning, sleepyhead. Did the bed finally kick you out?"

"You're not going to Vegas."

"Yes, I am. And Drago was kind enough to find me a companion. I'll be fine."

I wanted to pull the wheelchair in the other room and scold her, tell her that she was ahead financially, and at the very least to give back Dad's original 22k. But I didn't have the energy to battle her and knew I'd lose.

Waldo walked over, sat next to the wheelchair, and let Mom pat his head. One evil recognizing another. The perfect picture of the two, the new American Gothic.

My cell phone rang. I checked the screen. Alisa Vargas, Layla's mother. "Excuse me," I said, "I have to take this."

On my way out, I caught Drago staring at Layla with that same sappy expression. He had it bad for her. I stepped back into the bedroom and eased the door closed. At the last second Waldo tried to nudge his way in with his nose and a growl. I gently pushed the door closed and kept him out. He continued to growl on the other side, one that sounded like the rev from a distant Harley-Davidson.

What was it with that darn dog? I never did anything to him to warrant that kind of treatment. How come he didn't know I was a dog person?

I answered the phone. "Hello, Alisa."

"Bruno, I'm so glad I finally got you."

"I haven't gone anywhere, and you have my number." I was a little rude. I still couldn't get past the way she scorned Layla and little Sonny, left them to fend for themselves with the likes of Johnny Ef.

"Bruno, I deserve your tone. I was absolutely horrible with Layla and I regret it terribly. She won't answer my phone calls. I don't blame her. I acted like a spoiled little brat more worried about Aleck's reputation than what our precious daughter was going through. More worried about money. Is she okay? Can you please have her call me. We are worried sick."

This was not what I expected after the way Alisa had acted. She'd had time to figure out what was truly important.

Family.

Now I felt sorry for her grief and her need for forgiveness.

"Alisa, there was a lot dumped on you in a very short time, a new grandchild, the money . . . the fraud."

"You're very kind to defend my behavior, but there was no excuse. I promise that if she forgives us, we'll do everything in our power to get our daughter through this. I'm on my way back to the airport right now driving from Tamarindo to San Jose."

The last thing I needed was Alisa coming back, someone else to keep track of and deal with when I already had too many balls in the air.

"Please don't come. It'll just make things worse right now. Her emotions are hot and need some time to cool off. I'll take care of her, tell her you called, tell her you apologized and that she's welcome to come home."

A long pause where only her heavy breath came over the phone line.

"You really think that's for the best?"

"I'll take care of your daughter and not let anything happen to her."

"You'll bring her and her baby home safe?"

"Of course, I will. I promise."

She whispered into the phone, "Thank you, Bruno."

"I'll have her call you as soon as I can."

"Yes, yes, please do. Thank you."

"Goodbye, Alisa."

Out in the living area, Drago's words made it into the bedroom, a conciliatory tone I'd never heard before. "Layla, while we're out, can I get you anything? Anything at all?"

I didn't hear a reply and came out of the bedroom. Mom and Simon were gone. Drago saw me looking around for them. "They left."

I gritted my teeth. "Perfect. Just perfect."

I tried to cool off and level out my tone. "Layla, that was your mother on the phone."

Her neutral expression turned to anger. I couldn't blame her, not after the way her mother had acted, but at the same time Layla wasn't without blame. What a mess.

And I was caught in the middle.

"She says she's sorry and that you and Sonny are welcome to come home. She wants you to call her."

"Yeah, if she calls you again tell her not to hold her breath." Her eyes filled with tears and her chin quivered.

She'd come around soon enough.

CHAPTER TWENTY-FIVE

DRAGO DROVE THROUGH an In-N-Out Burger to get me two double cheeseburgers, fries, and a chocolate shake. He got his usual five 4x4 burgers—burgers with four meat patties on each—three orders of fries, and three strawberry shakes. He gave one of the 4x4 burgers to Waldo in the back seat. Just tossed it in the back, wrapper and all. Drago put a handful of fries in his mouth and said, "Hey, listen to Waldo get after that burger. Sounds like sloppy sex, don't it?"

No matter the situation, Drago could always make me smile with his unique perspective on life.

I said, "Don't you think this truck kind of stands out in a mobile surveillance?" He'd pulled up and parked on a residential street just outside Brentwood. Beverly Hills was its own city, Brentwood was the "Beverly Hills" section of Los Angeles with huge expensive estates.

He took a large bite out of a burger with one hand and with the other he opened a laptop on his console. The screen came on with a city map that had a flashing blue dot.

I chuckled. "You put a GPS on Johnny Ef's car?" Drago must've done it while I slept.

I'd slept too long.

What else had he done while off the leash?

He nodded. I tried to imagine someone of his size sneaking up on a house in Brentwood and attaching a GPS to an expensive car without getting the cops called on him.

"So," I said. "I guess your plan is to wait for him to move and hope he leads us to Sonny?"

He shook his head and spoke around burger mash in his mouth. "That's pie in the sky. If he moves today in daylight, I'm hoping to identify other targets of opportunity that we can attack."

It worried me that he spoke more like a general briefing his soldiers: *targets of opportunity* and *attack*.

I said, "Like drug houses and safe houses and the like."

He shrugged, took a pull on the strawberry shake. "Sure. But that's not going to hurt him as much as hitting him in his wallet in his legit businesses. After dark I'm hoping we can flush him out, make him go where he doesn't usually go."

"How are you planning on flushing him out?"

I really didn't like the sound of what he was describing and cringed waiting for the answer.

He winked and continued eating. I lost my appetite at the thought of turning Drago loose on anyone, even Effin Johnny.

In previous times when we worked together, I kept a tight control on Drago and used him more as a guided missile in surgical strikes.

On his own he was more about shock and awe released upon the axis of evil.

Now he even had me thinking military.

I tossed my second burger in the back seat, wrapper and all. I didn't look, just listened. I shuddered; sometimes Drago took me down the wrong path. He was right about the sound.

"Aren't you worried about Waldo eating the wrapper?"

Drago shrugged. "Why? He'll just crap it out. I do it sometimes, doesn't hurt me."

The interior of the truck filled with a godawful reek. Waldo had let one go.

Drago chuckled and waved his hand. "Man, that's one for the books." He tossed a full strawberry shake back to Waldo with the lid still on.

I rolled down the window and stuck my head out. "He's going to make a mess out of that shake."

"So? It's not my truck."

"Of course, it's not."

*   *   *

We sat in silence for a few hours, Waldo spread out in the back seat of the truck snorting and farting, his legs sometimes running after fleeing 4x4 hamburgers. The strawberry shake had burst open from his earlier onslaught. Dried strawberry shake crusted his mouth and jaws. He'd licked up the mess until he tired and lay down for a nap right in the middle of it. One side of the back seat looked like an aborted Jackson Pollack painting.

Drago kept checking his phone messages for Layla, which were not forthcoming and probably wouldn't be. We'd told her under no circumstances was she to leave the hotel. I pulled my phone from my pocket and checked the app that showed Mom's and Layla's locations. Mom was about to cross the California border into Nevada in her beeline for the Vegas poker tables.

Layla was also on the move after hours of static activity. She'd left the hotel and got on Interstate 5 headed south toward Los Angeles. What the hell was wrong with that girl and following orders?

I showed Drago the phone. "Come on, let's go check this out." He instantly understood and started up. Waldo heard the engine. He jumped up and shoved his strawberry shake–covered muzzle over the seat in my face. I raised my hand to push him out of the way.

He growled.

I held my hand up. "Okay, take it easy. I gave you a burger, remember?"

Drago took my phone and set it on the console where he could follow Layla's blue dot. He stared at the dot for a long moment, as if it might speak to him. "You think that maybe she and I . . ."

He didn't finish what he wanted to say. I knew him well enough to know where his mind went. "Big man, she just had another man's child."

He took his eyes off the blue dot and looked back at the road. He nodded. "Yeah, you're probably right."

Not to be antiromantic, but Drago and his world would never work with Layla in her world. Even though there were mythical stories about it working like *Beauty and the Beast*. Fiction, all of it, that had no place in reality. I found out a long time ago the difference between real life and fiction: fiction has to make sense. And you can't always make sense out of what life throws at you.

I didn't want to hurt his feelings and didn't say more.

He drove on shrugging and nodding to himself, his lips moving without sound as he played logic against far-fetched fantasy that danced hand in hand with romance.

Drago jumped on the San Bernardino Freeway headed east. If Layla stayed on her current course, we could head her off. She had a red line of traffic coming up that would slow her down about nine minutes.

Perfect.

He stared at the road when he spoke next. "I know you're a lot smarter in things like this and I respect your opinion, I do, but—"

He didn't finish.

"Big man, look—"

He cut me off and looked over. "She kissed me."

I sat back in the seat stunned.

"She what?"

"Yeah, she did. She kissed me. I didn't dream it. I know she did it, I mean, I was right there. It was wonderful. Absolutely wonderful. Best thing that ever happened to me."

Drago never opened up emotionally, especially not about relationships.

"When?"

"Last night when we got back from the LaRue and you went to bed. Me and Layla stayed up late talking. Just me and her. She told me all kinds of stuff about herself. She's perfect. She really is the perfect girl. Kind, tender, the nicest girl I ever met. She really loves that baby. She's wanted one for a long time. She started crying when she talked about him. She's a great kid.

"Thank you for introducing us. Really, Bruno, thank you."

"What did you tell her about you?"

He looked back at the road and thought for a minute and shrugged. "I guess not very much, she did most of the talking. She has the most wonderful eyes. You ever notice her eyes?"

"Tell me about this kiss."

I wanted to know if it was chaste on the cheek or something more intense. I didn't have the heart to ask him the difference if he didn't volunteer such intimate information.

"Okay, look. She got up and went to get a glass of water. I did like you said and loaded that app on the phone she left on the table. Man, I felt like such a shitheel doing it, but you said it was for her own safety. And I get that, I do. It's just . . . anyway, when she came back, she sat *real* close. You know what I mean, like right next to me. Man, it scared the hell outta me. She sat right down next to me. Girls like her just don't do that.

"Not with me.

"I didn't know what it meant or what I was supposed to do next. Like you said, she just had a baby and all. Right? With someone else, right?"

"She kissed you?" I prodded him again.

"Yeah, I'm tellin' ya. She put her hand on my arm, then leaned up and kissed me on the lips. It lasted a long time. Four or five minutes. Or at least it seemed that long. She had her eyes closed and everything.

"I think this is the one, Bruno. I never felt like this with any other girl."

On the lips? She kissed him on the lips? What the hell.

"What about Cloe from the Waffle House?"

He waved his hand. "That was different. You think something like with Cloe is the real thing until something like this happens."

He'd taken his eyes from the road too long; the truck had started to merge into the adjoining lane. He jerked the wheel, pulling us back into ours.

Layla kissing Drago didn't make sense. She had to be working him, and Drago was too lovestruck to see it. I was going to have a serious talk with that girl. She just set up my good friend for a huge fall, and I wasn't going to let this messed-up relationship get any worse.

I burped burger and put a hand on my stomach. Marie was right, I shouldn't have gone off my diet.

CHAPTER TWENTY-SIX

LAYLA'S BLUE DOT on the app moved down the 5 freeway and got off in downtown Los Angeles. Drago drove without a word, trailing along but not too close. Waldo's big head rested on the seat, his eyes going from me then back to his master.

"Where do you think she's going?" Drago asked.

I didn't want to tell him what I really thought, that she was going to see Johnny Ef. Love did that to a person, blurred the lines of sanity.

The blue dot stopped near the Staples Arena. Drago pulled to the closest curb and waited, watched. Ten o'clock at night, prime clubbing hour, meant plenty of folks filled the streets on foot and in cars. Laughing, smiling, giving off an overall air of frivolity.

"There," Drago said. "Right there." He knew better than to point while on a surveillance.

Layla popped out of a black older-model Lexus at the curb two cars farther up. An Uber, based on the decal in the rear window. She didn't look around to see if anyone had followed her.

She beelined for the double glass doors to the Shimbuto Loft Apartments. She entered, waved at the uniformed woman behind the security desk, and went right to the elevators. She pushed a button and waited. Layla had obviously been there before. The security personnel knew her well enough to let her go up without calling ahead.

The interior was decorated in Asian reds, blacks, and golds with large bamboo potted plants.

One thing for sure, Layla was holding back information, which put everyone involved at risk.

Drago pulled on his door latch, ready to get out. I quickly reached over and put my hand on his shoulder.

Waldo growled.

"Where you goin', big man?"

"To talk to that woman at the security desk. See what this place is all about."

He wanted to know if Johnny Ef owned a place in the loft apartments. Drago didn't like the idea of Layla going to see him.

"Let's slow this thing down a little and watch for a bit. Huh? Whattaya think?"

If he went in there asking questions, he'd get burned. Especially if Johnny lived there. The security staff would be on alert for anything out of the ordinary, paid extra under the table to notify Johnny.

And Drago was anything but ordinary.

He hesitated, his foot out ready to go. He finally nodded and closed the door. "Yeah, okay. But we only got about two hours, then we gotta be set up on Johnny Ef's place in Brentwood."

"Why? What happens in two hours?"

"I told ya, I'm gonna flush him out."

"I know that's what you said, but how are you going to do it?"

"What do you think Layla is doing in there?"

"Drago?"

He looked over at me, scowled, and waved his hand. "You really want to know. I'll tell ya, if you really wanna know."

He didn't wait for an answer and went back to watching the Shimbuto.

I said, "Tell me all you've found out about Johnny."

He nodded, still watching the double doors. "He's shifted out of the crime game. He's all about his legit businesses. He doesn't touch anything close to illegal. He has two cutouts in between him and his criminal shit, dope, pandering, loan sharking, protection, you know the routine."

"Who's the first cutout?"

"This guy named Nick. Not a lot's known about him because Nick also uses a cutout. He only talks to Johnny on burner phones, and he likes to gamble, plays poker and pai gow in big games. He has one every week at the New Otani Hotel in Korea Town."

"And the second guy, the one closest to the street level?"

Drago took his eyes off the double doors and looked over at me. "The word is its Ennis Freemantle."

"He's a—isn't he a—"

"CCS, the Celtic Cross Syndicate," Drago said. He went back to watching the doors. The longer we watched with nothing happening, the angrier Drago became, his tone shifting.

I said, "Well, that explains why you never hear any problems on the street level in Johnny's organization. Ennis Freemantle? That's really something. That means he has the CCS to back his play and he's probably paying tribute to those white supremacist assholes."

The CCS was a cancer on the city that corrupted everything it touched. A gang that started in the state prison system and conscripted ex-cons on the outside. Scared the hell out of them. The conscripts couldn't say no to their demands. If they ever went back to prison, they'd get a shiv between the ribs in the shower or out in the rec yard. Tyranny in its purest form.

Drago grunted his affirmative, then pointed at the Shimbuto. "My guy doesn't know about this place, how it fits in. We need to check it out."

"How's Johnny cleaning his money?"

Drago spoke to the truck window as he stared out. "Real estate mostly. He invests and flips houses. McMansions. He has millions wrapped up in them right now, from what I can tell anyway. That real estate office called LaRue next to his restaurant is his and he runs all his transactions through it."

The elevator doors opened inside the Shimbuto. Out popped Layla walking with a woman at least twenty years older but well put together and dressed in custom designer clothes. Layla smiled and talked and looked happy.

So did her older friend; all was right with their world. They came out onto the street, turned, and headed away. They didn't go far and entered The Coffee Hut, an upscale coffeehouse.

Drago started the truck. "Well, we better get back to Brentwood before the witching hour."

He sounded relieved Layla was with a woman and not Johnny.

"Just hold on. I want to wait on this a little longer. You got a ball cap and some sunglasses?"

He tugged open the console and pulled out both. I took them and opened the door.

"She'll recognize you."

"I'm not getting that close. I just wanna take a look, that's all. Then we can go."

I eased the door closed, put on the hat and sunglasses, and moved down the sidewalk. Behind me, Drago opened his truck door. I didn't turn, just kept walking.

Waldo appeared at my side. "Perfect," I said sarcastically to the dog. "He sent you along to keep me out of trouble, right?"

Waldo looked up. "Grrr."

A couple of men walking arm in arm enamored with each other walked past. One of them said, "That dog should be on a leash."

"I agree with you, he's not my dog. You want him?"

The man harrumphed and kept walking.

I stopped short of the window for The Coffee Hut and as a diversion knelt down to tie my shoe. Waldo stuck his mug in my ear and growled. He smelled of strawberry meat.

"I'll give you two burgers if you go back and wait in the truck."

He understood and stayed just to spite me.

I looked up in the window. Layla and the woman sat at a high-top table right next to the window. Layla had her back to me. I pulled out my phone and pretended I wanted a photo of my cute little Waldo and snapped a couple of pics of the woman who faced me. I pulled the phone down.

The woman only had eyes for Layla. She looked Eurasian with jet-black hair and clean facial angles.

Breathtaking.

She reached across the table and laid her hand onto Layla's. Layla turned her hand over and took the woman's hand in hers.

Uh-oh.

CHAPTER TWENTY-SEVEN

AN HOUR LATER we'd set up on Johnny Ef's house, which I'd yet to see. We waited in a residential area parked at the curb under an ancient elm, many blocks south of his house. The night quiet, sedate in the rich part of town.

The pulsating blue dot to Johnny's car sat in the same place on the city map. I'd been mulling over what I'd seen in the window of The Coffee Hut, Layla with her Eurasian friend. Something about the way they held hands bugged me. Women were definitely more comfortable in their sexuality than men, and friendly public displays of affection like holding hands were not uncommon. Was it the way that woman had looked at Layla? Was that it? Or was I imagining it, my instinct barometer on the fritz due to the stress of being held over in the States longer than the promised twelve hours?

I turned to Drago. "Okay, I've decided I want to know how you intend on flushing out Johnny Ef."

He'd been quiet thinking about his newest true love, one he intended on turning into his soul mate. A smile broke across his face. He pulled out his cell phone and cued up a photo.

He handed me the phone and said, "I'm calling them Fat Man and Little Boy."

"Oh my God," I said. "You didn't."

The photo depicted two of what Drago had long ago tagged as "Belly Busters." Something I had inadvertently told him about. I really had to be careful around Drago; his mind worked like a sponge soaking up everything and remolding the information to work in his world.

I originally came upon the information after an unfortunate incident—a pursuit of a federal fugitive named Jimmy Suggs. Suggs fled from us driving a jeep that carried four five-gallon jerry cans of gas across the dry lakebed in the Mojave Desert. The department decided the violent crimes team needed remedial training in some "impromptu barbeques," as Robby Wicks called it. Whenever I thought about that day, I could still feel the heat on my face combined with the sound of Jimmy Suggs shrieking.

The department sent me and Wicks to remedial training with an arson bomb guy named Harry Baumgartner who had a perpetual wild look in his eyes.

Out in an open field, the arson bomb Baumgartner put a one-gallon jug of gas wrapped in det cord inside a stack of car tires. The result made a believer out of me. The tires all disintegrated in a thirty-foot-high ball of fire that shook the ground. The memory still brought back the warmth and concussion that hit my face.

I'd made the mistake of telling Drago about the destructive power of gasoline.

Now he'd made up two one-gallon incendiary bombs. What was worse, he'd snapped a photo of them and kept it in his phone. Perfect evidence if his phone fell into the wrong hands.

The entire visit back to the States for an overnight escort of a young girl now spun wildly out of control.

CHAPTER TWENTY-EIGHT

"KARL, WHAT DID you do with . . . with Fat Man and Little Boy?" We sat in the truck's front seat in Brentwood.

He didn't answer just as the blue dot that indicated Johnny Ef's car started moving. Karl checked the time on his phone. "It's too early. Johnny's doing something else." He started up and moved out through the residential mansions with their tall privacy hedges, black automatic gates, and long, shaded driveways.

He kept glancing at his watch.

He still had not answered my question about the belly bombs he'd planted. I held onto the door, the other hand on the dash as he drove too fast.

Waldo sensed the excitement and barked, a woof close to my ear that startled me. Just what I needed.

Drago counted down, barely audible over Waldo's heavy breathing. "Four, three, two, one. Mark, fire forward torpedo tube."

He turned and smiled.

Nothing happened.

But we would be too far away to see the results of Fat Man and Little Boy.

Drago liked old black-and-white movies, and now he apparently was making believe we were in a submarine. I needed to retake control, or the situation would only get worse.

The blue dot on the app wound its way through the streets. I said, "Looks like he's headed back to the LaRue." I switched over to Layla's phone tracker. She was now almost back to the hotel in Glendale, the opposite direction. I switched back to Johnny's; at least he wasn't going to meet her.

Johnny didn't turn left on Pacific Coast Highway; instead, he made a right. He wasn't going to the LaRue. His speed hadn't changed, so he wasn't anxious about an expensive possession of his burning to ash.

He pulled into the parking lot to a public beach, drove to a spot wide open without any parked cars, and stopped. Drago pulled over and parked on PCH. He stuck his arm over the seat, his hand going into a gear bag on the floor. He came out with an ancient Starlite scope that wouldn't work all that well with the streetlights and passing car headlights. He rolled down his window, leaned back toward me so the scope didn't protrude out the window, and watched. A green light escaped between his eye and the scope.

"Look," I said. "A white newer Jag just pulled into the parking lot. It's heading over to Johnny's Bentley. Can you see who's driving?"

"Naw, the ambient light is washing out the scope. This thing really only works in the bush."

"You got any binoculars?"

"Yeah, in the bag."

I reached over, shouldering Waldo out of the way, and found a large pair of Marine binoculars.

Before I got them up to my eyes, Drago said, "Doesn't matter. Johnny's on the move."

I trained the glasses on the white Bentley. Johnny was really moving out. Drago chuckled and made a fake explosion noise with his mouth.

"What did you do?" I said, while trying to get a make on the driver of the Jag. It had started to move out of the parking lot but at a more sedate speed. The dark tint on the windows hid the driver.

Drago messed with his cell phone. "Here, look." He'd pulled up a photo depicting a southern-style McMansion with the tall white pillars, manicured grass, and shrubs—very elegant.

He said, "It's Johnny's, he's got it for sale. It's one of five he's flipping in Beverly Hills. It's paid for and in his name. He's selling it to launder money, listed for 3.2 mil."

Drago made a fist and sprung his fingers open while making an explosive sound with his mouth.

I subconsciously knew this was what he had in mind as soon as he showed me the photos of Fat Man and Little Boy, but his words, the way he said it so cavalierly, shocked me. My friend Drago had a little Harry Baumgartner from Arson and Bomb in him.

"The house, it's empty?"

"Of course. You know me better than that. But look, here's the best part." He thumbed the screen to the next photo.

I chuckled at first but immediately stopped. Drago had painted a huge target on *our* backs with black spray paint. That's the way he liked to play the game, them chasing us instead of the reverse.

Not me.

He'd used black spray paint on the sidewalk in front of the now torched estate. He'd written only five letters: "Sonny."

"Ah, man," I said. "You should've asked me first. You just kicked over a hornet's nest. Ennis Freemantle and the entire CCS is going to be gunning for us now."

He smiled. "Yeah, I know, ain't it great?" He checked his watch. "Three, two, one. Fire two. Second torpedo in the water."

He made the explosive sound again.

He laughed and slapped me on the back. He started up. "Come on, let's go get something to eat. Playing *Run Silent, Run Deep* gives me an appetite."

I didn't know what to say and was still a little stunned. "We just ate."

"That was three hours ago. How's Mex sound? You good with some chalupas and enchiladas? I think Johnny's going to be busy for a while. Then we'll see where he goes after he watches his money go up in smoke."

He drove on without an answer from me, a huge smile on his innocent mug. He didn't care who he pissed off, not even Beelzebub or the four horsemen of the apocalypse. He reached over and slapped my leg. "Come on, boss man, cheer up. Ol' Johnny's going to talk to us now. Don't you think? He'll give us Sonny, or we'll load up Das Boot and ride on him again." He laughed harder at his own analogy.

I stared at him as the passing streetlights made his face into a kaleidoscope of light. "I think he's going to do more than talk to us."

"All the better. Either way, we get what we want, right?"

"Yeah, we get what we want," I muttered silently to myself, all the blood and bone we can handle.

CHAPTER TWENTY-NINE

DRAGO PARKED IN the parking lot of Carlito's Tacos, an insanely popular roach coach that moved around during the day to service the commercial areas of LA and then at night stopped on Sunset Boulevard close to the nightclubs when they emptied out. Drago opened his door and got out. Waldo came over the seat and jumped to the ground. "Come on, let's grease. I'm hungry enough to eat the ass-end of a Clydesdale."

"You go, I'm going to stay here."

"You sure? They've got the best chicken mole in the city."

"You go. I'm good." I waved him away. Just the thought of Mexican food made my stomach churn, burp, and rise up into my throat. I lay back in the seat afraid to close my eyes but did anyway. Bosco and the freeway incident jumped into my thoughts like they automatically had for the last couple of days. I closed my eyes tighter and let Bosco come back into my world. Maybe if I confronted him, let him have his say, he'd leave me alone. Or at the very least back off a little. Just a little, that's all I asked.

* * *

The way the incident on the freeway started was happenstance; fate came hunting for me. I'd been on my way to a meeting ten minutes farther down the freeway in a mixed-use industrial area when I ran into some of the same people en route to the same meeting.

That kind of luck no one wished for.

A young, inexperienced Highway Patrol officer had pulled over three outlaw motorcycle gang members looking for trouble. The officer was in way over her head. I stopped to help.

The incident went to hell, a fight and shooting occurred. In particular the part with my son, who I'd never met before, who I didn't know was my son, will forever remain emblazoned on my memory, never to be erased. A moment in time I'd give my life to reverse. The clip of memory on a continual loop always started and ended the same:

I struggled to my feet, looked left to the gun on the ground. I didn't have time to make a move toward it. The redhead biker crouched and sprang at me. I let him come, grabbed onto his denim vest, and fell backward as I stuck my foot in his chest. His eyes went wide as he saw the move unfold. He said it fast, pleaded with me, "No, mister, please don't. Don't."

Three against one didn't make a fair fight. I had to even the odds or die. I flipped him high overhead, right out into traffic.

A black Honda Accord took him. Snatched him right out of the air. He smashed the windshield, flew in the air again, and landed on the hot concrete. The Honda with the shattered windshield skidded out of control and crashed into the three motorcycles on kickstands parked on the shoulder.

I didn't find out until later that same day that I even had a son and that he'd been the one I'd flipped out into traffic.

His words a perpetual echo in my brain, "No, mister, please don't. Don't."

CHAPTER THIRTY

DRAGO OPENED THE truck door. Waldo hopped in, a large furred beast with fangs coming right at me and disrupting my fugue state. I jumped back in the seat, sweat dampening my shirt and running down my forehead into my shock-widened eyes, my breath coming fast.

I had not been asleep, not completely, more in a trance with sights and smells, violence and pain. I had yet again relived the incident on the freeway that had now taken over my entire life.

Marie had said to be prepared for an emotional response after my body had physically healed. She was right as always. This time, more so than others, I wished she hadn't been. I'd take the worst kind of physical pain over this anytime. The shame, the regret, the dark depression that perpetually clouded the sky, tainted the very air I breathed and caught in my lungs hindering my heartbeat and making it ache for relief.

Waldo jumped the seat into the back and Drago got in on his side dipping the truck with the weight exchange. "Whoa, there, old hoss, you'll give yourself a heart attack if you keep waking up like that."

With him, the aroma of savory spiced chicken mixed with warm grease tagged along, filling the truck and masking the reek of dog eau de strawberry shake. He tossed me a bag. "Here, got you some chicken mole, anyway. You're welcome. Has Layla moved from the hotel?"

"What? Ah, I don't know." I looked at the phone app. "No, I don't think so."

"What do you mean you don't think so?" He grabbed the phone from my hand.

I rubbed my face hard. "Her *phone* hasn't left the hotel."

"Oh. Yeah, I see what you mean." He started up and headed toward Glendale. He'd been away too long from his one true love.

Thirty minutes later, we pulled into the stacked parking garage for the hotel. Upstairs in the suite we found Layla asleep on the couch. Drago got a blanket from one of the bedrooms and covered her. He sat down across the coffee table and stared at her angelic countenance. She was a beautiful young woman far too vulnerable for this violent world in North America.

I moved in close and whispered to Drago, "She wakes up and sees you staring, she's going to think it's creepy."

"Yeah, you're right, thanks." He grabbed the hotel magazine from the end table and held it up pretending to read, looking over the top at her.

"Oh, yeah," I said, "that's so much better."

He put the magazine down, picked up the controller, and turned on the TV, his attention still on the sleeping Layla. A rerun of news came on a local channel. As coincidence would have it, the lead story was a video of a house fire, a large stately manor fully engulfed.

Drago pointed and whispered too loudly, "Hey, hey, that's what I did. That's mine. It's a work of art, don't you think?" He made a fist and opened his fingers while making a hushed exploding noise with his mouth. He slapped his leg. "Hot damn, that house was in escrow too. Was gonna close in a couple of days. Not anymore, boyo, not anymore."

I eased down into the seat, stunned, and not because he used "boyo."

The house had been beautiful. An inanimate victim caught in our crossfire. In the front yard in the foreground of the shot stood a real estate sign that said, "Homes by LaRue."

The newswoman on scene stood in the street with the blazing fire behind her as she spoke to the camera. "The fire captain said he has never seen anything like this. They arrived minutes after the call and found the entire house fully involved. He says it has to be an arson on an extraordinary scale. There is no other explanation for such a massive spread so quickly. This had to have been a well-engineered firebomb. The house is a total loss."

"Did you hear that? A well-engineered firebomb. That's me. I'm the engineer."

Drago never talked this much; he never acted like such a kid. Love had different reactions, this one out of character for my large and normally quiet friend.

The TV commentator put her hand to her ear and listened. "I'm hearing now that there is a similar fire of a house in Brentwood.

"Is someone torching these lovely homes on purpose? Fire-bombing them? Is this an act of domestic terrorism? Thank God this home was vacant. Channel Four News will keep you updated on further developments as they unfold."

My stomach clenched, bile rose up in my throat. I'd been the cause of this. I'd lain down for a nap and let Drago's mind run amok.

On the screen a man in a gray trench coat, deep in the background, flashed by behind the reporter. It happened fast but I still recognized Johnny Ef with his hand up to his face trying to mask his identity. The tiger's eye ring with diamonds gave him away.

He wasn't happy.

I stood. "We gotta move. It's not safe here, not anymore."

Drago lost his smile and looked down at Layla. "Yeah, you're right. But we gotta little time. We'll let her sleep for a bit while I get things set up someplace else, then I'll move us."

"Yeah, okay. I'm going to get some air."

I needed to clear my head, think over the predicament Drago had thrust upon us.

"Take Waldo with you." Drago said something in German to his faithful sidekick.

"No, that's okay, I—"

Too late. Waldo came over and stood at my side ready to go. "Okay, I guess I'll take the damn dog."

"Don't talk like that. You'll hurt his feelings."

"You're right. I'm sorry." I patted Waldo's head and pulled my hand away as he snapped at me.

"See, I told you. Dogs are people too."

I whispered so only Waldo could hear, "Devil Dog."

Waldo followed me out the door, down the hall, and into the elevator. We didn't talk on the ride down; he must've been mad about the Devil Dog comment. He stayed at my side as we crossed the lobby headed for the front doors. A man in a blue blazer with "Manager" on a nameplate hurried over. "Excuse me, sir, but dogs are not allowed in the hotel."

"He's not my dog. He's just following me around."

"Oh, I'm so sorry, I just assumed."

I stopped. Waldo sat next to my leg as if he were my dog and stared up at the man. Waldo pretended the encrusted strawberry shake on his shiny coat didn't make him out a fool.

The man looked uncomfortable looking into the eyes of the beast. "Yeah," I said, "he makes you feel like a six-pound pot roast, right?"

"I'll call animal control and have him carted off."

"I don't know if that's a good idea."

Waldo growled a low grumbler.

The man raised his elbows high, as if that would forgo a mauling, and hurried away.

I started for the front door and said to Waldo, "You ever read the book *How to Make Friends and Influence People?*"

He kept walking and turned his head up to me.

"Yeah, I didn't think so."

We came out the doors and turned right, headed down the street. The cool night air did wonders. Waldo's claws clicked on the sidewalk next to me. I guess it was nice to have him along after all. I didn't want to be alone.

A long black limo pulled to the curb. I stopped, put my back to the wall, and slid my hand under my shirt gripping one of the .357s. This was Johnny Ef or Ennis Freemantle coming to get even, catching me with my back against the wall and nowhere to go.

An old man dressed in a livery exited the driver's door. He came over to the sidewalk, not projecting any kind of threat.

"Sir, Mr. Wilbur Wentworth the III would like to have a word." He extended his hand toward the limo. His tone was nasal and haughty.

"I think you've made a big mistake, pal. I don't know a Mr. Wilbur Wentworth III."

The back window whirred down. "Bruno, get in the car."

It was Dad.

CHAPTER THIRTY-ONE

THE DRIVER OPENED the door.

Uninvited, Waldo shot into the car, self-assured and imprudent, the same as if he jumped into a limo every day. I stood too shocked to move. Dad wore a black top hat five or six decades out of style and an expensive black suit coat with a gold ascot and cravat peeking out the top of a black vest. He looked nothing like my dad, more like the little man in the Monopoly Game.

If the Monopoly game had been designed by African Americans.

He leaned his head out a little and lowered his voice. "Close your mouth, you're going to catch flies. Son, get in the darn car."

My legs had more experience obeying Dad's commands than I had and all on their own carried me over to the door. I climbed in. The driver closed the door, came around, and got in. The partition slid down. "Where to, Mr. Wentworth?"

"Just drive around, please, Howard." Dad took off the silly-looking hat.

"Very good, sir." The partition whirred back up.

I sat opposite Dad, facing him. Waldo took a spot right next to Dad in a reclining position. Dad patted Waldo's head. "What a nice dog, where'd you find him?"

Dad pulled his hand away and looked to see if any of the crusty strawberry shake stuck to him.

Nice dog, yeah, right. Waldo stared at me, acting smug over having the seat next to Dad when I didn't. I'd get even.

"He's Drago's beast."

The passenger compartment had a chrome and crystal decanter bar, the leather seats soft and comfortable enough to sleep on. In his other hand, Dad held a black cane with a brass head depicting a bird of prey, maybe a Maltese falcon.

"Dad, what the hell is going on?"

"I wish you wouldn't use such language. Tobias will pick it up sooner than you think."

"Tobias? How is he?"

"Cute as the dickens. I'm so sorry you are up here dealing with this when you have a new child at home."

"How's Marie?"

"Up and moving around. She's a wonderful mother. How much longer do you think you'll be up here? She misses you. We all miss you."

His words made me yearn to be home.

"I'm not sure."

I didn't know how much Dad knew about Sonny and Layla, or Johnny Ef, for that matter. I didn't want to worry him with the details.

"Dad, let's not ignore the huge elephant in the room. What're you doing here and why are you dressed like this? It's too big of a risk you coming to the States. There are warrants out for your arrest."

If he ever went to prison, at his age he'd never come out. He'd been named in the indictment, the kidnap of the children we smuggled out of harm's way down to Costa Rica. I'd made him a criminal and would have to live with it to the end of time.

He broke into the biggest smile I had seen in a long time. His eyes glimmered with excitement. He held his arms out wide. "I'm a whale."

"You're a what?"

He'd lost it, gone over the edge, old age having pulled him down into the horrible depths of dementia, and I'd somehow missed the early signs.

"A whale," he said again. "After I get done talking to you, Howard's driving me to Las Vegas.

"You know, in all the years we've lived in Southern California, I've never driven the four hours to Vegas. And as far as the warrants are concerned, how many police officers are going to pull over a limo? If they do, how many are going to arrest a man named Wilbur Wentworth III, who's dressed like this? It's really the perfect cover, don't you think?"

"Dad, you don't gamble."

"I know, and I don't intend to. I'm also going for the shows. I've always wanted to see the Blue Man Group."

I chuckled at the thought of Dad watching the Blue Man Group.

Bea was in Vegas gambling his money away, and now he was going out to meet her. It was his life and his money. I had no right to intervene.

He continued. "I'm going to pull up in front of Caesars Palace and Bea is going to be out front waiting. She wants me in this getup so I'll look like a whale. That's a big gambler who loses a lot of money. She said it'll raise her profile with the hotel and help her get into a big game that they've excluded her from. Anything to help, you know."

For him to involve himself further in Bea's scandalous activity caused a pain deep in my chest. I wanted the best for him. To sit back and watch him travel down this path was wrong.

But I knew him well enough to know to say anything further would only get his back up. I should be thankful he was happy, dressed like the Monopoly man, and headed to Vegas for the first time.

Had things been different I might've gone with him just to see his expression the first time he drove down the boulevard and witnessed the massively gaudy and ostentatious hotels.

But a thought niggled at the tip of my brain. Dad had cared for me all these years; now, in the twilight of his life, wasn't it my turn to care for him? That's the way family was supposed to work. Should I insist he get right back on a plane for Costa Rica? I was going to be nervous every minute he stayed in jeopardy.

"Dad, why did you stop here to talk to me?"

Dad lost his smile, his expression turning somber. "The way you sounded over the phone, I know you're in trouble and that you need to talk face-to-face."

A lump rose in my throat. I loved him so. He was still taking care of *me*. He could tell just by the tone in my voice that I was in trouble.

I stared at him.

The buildings zipped past outside the car. We stopped for an occasional red signal with other cars all around, life going on for those folks who had no idea of the emotional pain that filled the limo that sat beside them.

"Bruno? Talk to me. What's going on?"

"You need to get to Vegas. It's a long drive."

Shame had clogged up the real words I wanted to use. I needed to tell him about the shift in my emotions, the way I now felt about violence, the sudden lack of intestinal fortitude.

But couldn't.

I respected him too much to tarnish his image of me. Just thinking that way made me out a narcissistic, selfish oaf.

"We are going to drive around this town until you tell me, so you might as well get to it or hunker down for a long nap."

I couldn't look at him and instead watched the world go by out the window.

"Bruno, you're about to make me angry. There's nothing you can say that will make me think differently of you. You're my son."

When I looked back at him, tears jumped to my eyes and blurred my vision. "That's what this is about," I said. "Fathers and sons. Bosco was my son."

"Ah, damnit."

Dad never used those kinds of words.

CHAPTER THIRTY-TWO

IN THE BACK of the limo, Dad leaned forward and put a hand, now gnarled with time, on my knee and gently squeezed. He waited for me to tell him.

"I . . ." The words started and stopped, a jumble on my tongue, afraid to slither out.

He gently squeezed again.

"Dad, I'm . . . I mean, I've turned into an emotional mess, a complete and utter mess. I'm scared to death of my own shadow. I can't live this way. It's tearing me up inside." The words came out in a rush and maybe a little exaggerated.

Dad sat back in his seat, relief obvious in his expression. He didn't exactly smile, but his expression no longer showed concern.

"This is serious, Dad. I've never experienced anything like this."

He stared at me, thinking, I was sure, on how to tell me in a nice way that I was a damn fool.

He said, "This came on sudden, didn't it, like overnight?"

"Yes, exactly." He'd said it like he knew something about this evil affliction.

I leaned forward. I needed to know what he knew. Maybe he *could* help me after all.

"Son, this isn't about Bosco. It is, but not entirely."

I leaned back, stunned. Of course it was. "What are you talking about? That's all I can think of right now. I can't close my eyes without seeing Bosco's eyes. With him . . . with Bosco begging me not to toss him out into traffic." I choked on the last words.

"At the time, you didn't know he was your son."

"That excuse doesn't carry any weight and you know it." I said it too harshly to this gentle soul dressed like the Monopoly man, who in the board game was called Rich Uncle Pennybags. The thought of that moniker suddenly took the heated edge off the emotion. Dad was Rich Uncle Pennybags sitting there in the limo trying to decipher my screwed-up emotional ailment.

What an odd situation.

Dad lowered his voice. "The same thing happened to me. But in a lesser degree. Yours is just exacerbated because of what happened with Bosco."

"What are you talking about? You never—" I caught myself before I said something I'd regret, telling him he was *only* a mail carrier who delivered mail for forty years without missing a day of work.

How could he possibly think he'd experienced anything close to what I had in a life of violence that left a wake cluttered with broken bodies, blood and bone.

He shook his head. "Bruno, you don't know everything about me, about my life before you were old enough to remember."

"What are you talking about? You told me about Bea."

I sat back as my mind raced. I had not known the story about my mother, Bea, until recently—a story that stunned and shocked me. I was a forty-nine-year-old man and I had not known about my mother and her scandalous past. I had not even laid eyes on her until two months back when she showed up in our suite at the very same hotel in Glendale.

Was there something else I didn't know about my own father? I naturally assumed I knew about Dad's past just by the way he carried himself, the way he acted, his strong moral fiber that guided me so well in life.

No, Dad couldn't have done a better job raising me.

"Bea was a part of it, sure," Dad said. "But back then I was bold and brash and invincible, I too had the devil sitting on my shoulder the same as all young men. I fought the devil and won. *Most* of those arguments."

"Most?"

I had never seen my father question his own judgment or ever have a problem deciding right from wrong. He'd been a rock, a solid immovable rock, one that I always knew where he stood on any topic. Life for him was always black and white with no in between. For me that same in between the black and white was a chasm filled with gray, a color I never ventured away from. I'd lived in the gray doing what was right when the law wouldn't.

Dad said, "I'll tell you about it someday when we have more time."

"You can't open a hot topic like that and then just drive off into the sunset. No, I'm sorry, Dad, I have to know what you're talking about right now."

He looked out the window, his expression wiped clean as he ventured back to a time he didn't want to remember. "There are events in my life that I would rather not dredge up. One of them involves Casandra." He turned and looked at me. "I always think of it as the Summer of Casandra."

"Casandra? You've never told me a thing about Casandra. I mean, nothing at all."

Rich Uncle Pennybags was turning into an enigma. I really didn't know my father after all.

"I'll just tell you that she was a blind woman who lived on my mail route, and I involved myself in her problems when I shouldn't have. Bold and brash and a little testosterone doing all the thinking led me down the wrong path. We'll leave it at that for now. I promise when we get back to Casa Bruno in Costa Rica, I'll tell you all about it. We'll go for a long walk."

I recognized his tone as being the final word. "Then tell me what you meant, about going through something similar. How did you get through it?"

I knew exactly what he meant about feeling bold and brash and most of all invincible. I'd lived it working the streets as a patrol deputy in South Central Los Angeles, never once feeling vulnerable like I did at this moment.

"Son, when you have a child, there is a huge emotional response that comes with the birth that I believe is inborn to our species, a protective mechanism. The male shifts in his thinking so he's not as bold and brash. In this way he'll stay closer to the female and the new child to help protect them."

Huh, what he said actually made a little sense.

Dad continued, "You're not only afraid for yourself, you're also worried about what would happen to your family, who'd care for them. It's absolutely a natural response."

"I didn't feel this way with Olivia when she was born."

"You weren't there for the birth or the pregnancy like you were with Marie. Sonya knocked on your door one day, and when you answered, she handed you Olivia. Then Sonya just walked away. That's how you got your first child. You were also starting a new job, your first day as a detective, your mind was focused on getting through that part of your life. When you were handed Olivia, you were involved in a serious life-or-death investigation."

"I loved Olivia like nothing else in this world."

"I'm not saying you didn't. I'm just saying the circumstances are different this time. Tobias was placed in your arms moments after he was born. You lived the pregnancy with Marie. There's a huge difference."

"Okay. Okay. All this makes a lot of sense, but I can't live this way. How do I deal with it?"

"You have to fight it. I felt the same way. I was scared to death, especially after Bea was gone and I was all you had to take care of you. If something happened to me, you'd be all alone. The government would've dumped you into the Child Protective Services system. I was careful when I crossed streets—I watched for that phantom bus that tends to take people out when they least expect it. I became afraid of all the dogs on my route, scared of my own shadow." He patted Waldo's head again.

Waldo licked his hand.

The little suck-up.

"Dad?"

"Okay," he said. "What I did to feel better about the situation? I simply talked to you. Even when you weren't there. When that overwhelming fear came on, and it did come in waves, I pretended you were there with me and I talked to you. It was comforting. I drew strength from you."

"Are you serious? That's how you got through it?"

"Yes, but you—"

"What about me?"

"You have the added issue of Bosco. I've been waiting for what happened with your son to manifest into something else, and to tell you the truth, this emotional response of yours scares the heck out of me."

"What are you talking about? Speak plain. Please."

"Son, you're a good man, an upright, moral man. That's why it's taking so long for you to go to the next step in grief."

Wait. I'd learned about grief in the academy all those years ago—a one-hour block on how to recognize it. There were stages of grief people work through.

"Tell me."

He lowered his tone. "You were the mechanism that killed Bosco, but by no means were you the cause. That's all on Sonya. She was the one who let Bosco run with that outlaw motorcycle gang. Not you. You had nothing to do with that decision. In fact, you didn't even know you had a son."

"You're saying that anger is the next step in my grief? Anger over what happened, what I had been forced to do? Anger focused on Sonya?"

Sonya was dead.

He nodded. "And now, coupled with Tobias . . . well, you have a lot going on. What I'm scared most about is when you come out of this regret phase . . . what your anger will do to you when you have nowhere to focus it.

"I've seen you angry before, really angry. And this has all the potential to be off-the-scale violent. Don't let anger get a foothold, it'll rot your soul. You have to wait for time to heal. If you're not careful, time will stand up and gallop away from you. And as you get older, it happens more often than you think.

"Be careful, Bruno. Please be careful. When anger takes you by the throat, remember what was said here. Talk to Tobias—he'll help you through it."

CHAPTER THIRTY-THREE

I CLOSED THE limo door and watched Dad/Rich Uncle Pennybags drive away, leaving an emptiness in the hollow of my chest.

I already missed him.

Had he taken Waldo with him? Wrapped up in the surreal event I'd just lived through in the back of that limo, I hadn't paid any attention to the dog when I got out of the car.

I started to smile and wave to the limo. Drago was going to be mad Waldo caught a free ride to Vegas.

But with my kind of luck, Waldo was probably one of those miracle dogs who would run the thousand miles back to Glendale just to be with his master and to menace me.

Behind me the devil dog growled.

Ah, damn.

I slowly turned.

His growl had shifted into a snarl with teeth showing on one side. I let out a long sigh at the sight of him. "Yeah, I know," I said. "Playtime is over, and you want to go back upstairs."

He turned and headed to the hotel's double doors.

I followed along and opened the door for him. The manager was nowhere in sight. He probably saw us coming and preferred to keep his bum free from fang scars. He made himself scarce rather than confront the hotel pet violation named Waldo who again walked into his lobby.

Upstairs, I used the card key to open the door and stepped in. Then stepped back out to look at the number on the door. Our hotel suite was empty. Drago had taken off without telling us.

Waldo walked in and moved around. sniffing the couch and carpet, unperturbed that his master had left him in a lurch.

Now was my chance. While he was busy sniffing I could hurry out the door and close him in. I'd be shed of him. For a while at least.

I moved quickly to the door, opened it, stepped through, and almost made it out. Waldo grabbed onto the back of my pant cuff as my second leg tried to make it out. He dug his paws in and pulled.

"Okay. Okay," I said. "I was just checking. I thought I heard the door, you know room service with some hot tomato soup and grilled cheese sandwiches, BLTs for you. Hmm hmm."

He let go and walked past me out of the suite, disgusted with my lack of creativity. He continued to sniff the carpet. He went to the door across the hall and slightly offset from our suite. He scratched at the door.

It opened.

He entered as if he owned the place. Drago's large head stuck out past the door into the hall. "Hey, bro, we're in here now."

I walked over. He had to step out of the doorway to let me in.

I said, "I see you decided to move a long way from our last room. This is really a nice safe distance. Karl, we're right across the damn hall."

This had been another strategy he'd learned from me during one of our earlier capers, but back then we didn't have a young woman's safety to consider, or my emotional dilemma.

He closed the door. "Yeah, I thought about it and realized the reason I torched those two houses was to get them to come after us, right?"

"No, that was *your* strategy, remember?"

I moved deeper into the suite. Layla was asleep on the couch with a blanket covering her just like she had been in our other suite. I lowered my tone. "Did you pick her up and carry her in here, while she was asleep?"

He smiled that sappy lovesick smile as he nodded. "Yeah, I did. She's light as a feather. I can't believe how light she is."

The meeting with Dad and what he said weighed heavy on my mind. I needed time to process it. I didn't need Drago running the game while my mind checked out for a bit.

"So," I asked, "you're going to watch the peephole in the door until some emissary from Ennis Freemantle knocks on the other door, and then you're going to ask him not so nicely where they're holding Sonny?"

He nodded again. "Yeah, great plan, ain't it?"

I threw my hands in the air. In my confused state, maybe it was better if he did run our plan to recover Sonny. I seemed to be two steps behind everyone.

"You need to wash your dog. People are starting to talk."

"You gonna watch the door in case someone comes around and steps into our little trap across the hall?"

I needed some time to process Dad's theory. I trusted him implicitly but needed to apply the pieces to the puzzle to view the whole picture. This before I was ready to meet street-hardened thugs sent by Freemantle.

"Karl—?" I said. "All right. I'll put Waldo in the tub and start the water, but you have to tell him to mind his manners."

"I don't need to do that, he loves you."

"Tell him."

Drago spoke German to his devil dog covered with strawberry malt and followed me to the bathroom.

He stood by watching me fill the tub.

I turned the water off. "Come on, get in." Why was I thinking I could give a hundred-and-twenty-pound beast a bath?

"Come on, Waldo, get in the tub. I'm not kiddin' here. Please?" I put my hands together in a mock strangling.

He wasn't even my dog *and* I wasn't the one who gave him the strawberry malt.

I wiped my damp hands on my pants. "Now you be good." I reached down, took hold of his front legs, my head right next to his choppers, and lifted, dragging him toward the tub's edge.

He had bad halitosis.

Had Drago not given Waldo the command to be good, there wasn't a doubt in my mind Waldo would've chomped my face off. I got his front legs in the warm water and grunted when I picked up his back legs and set them down in the tub.

He stared up at me like I was crazy. "Go on," I said. "Soap and water. Chop chop." He didn't move.

"Yeah, I figured I'd have to do this." I rolled up my sleeves, soaped up a washcloth, and lathered up the dog. When I got to his chest we again came eye to eye. I stopped for a second and looked at him.

He leaned in. His wide pink tongue shot out and licked my cheek.

It startled me. A dog's kiss. I kind of had the same reaction Drago did with his description of when Layla kissed him.

I said, "You're welcome."

CHAPTER THIRTY-FOUR

WHEN I PULLED the stopper, the pink-tinted water in the tub swirled down the drain. Waldo took his cue and jumped out. He shook off, spattering the walls and toilet with dog water. I used one of the big fluffy towels to dry him.

He didn't growl once. Was that all it took to turn Mr. Hyde back into Dr. Jekyll, a semi-intimate bath?

As I came out of the master bedroom, I met Layla coming from the little kitchenette area with a cup of tea; her long raven hair hung down past her waist, the sheen reflecting the light.

"Oh," she said. "I didn't know anyone was here."

I looked around. Where had Drago gone?

I followed her into the living room and sat in the chair across from the couch. Waldo sat at my feet, put his head down on my sneaker, and closed his eyes. Baths relaxed him, it seemed.

"So," I said to Layla. "You going stir crazy sitting in this hotel room?"

She'd put the blanket around her shoulders and sipped her tea as if we were in the Alps with eight feet of snow surrounding the building instead of balmy Southern California. Costa Rica didn't have air conditioners; people kept their windows and doors open to the warm breeze.

She blew on her tea and sipped. "No. More than anything else I'm worried about Sonny. I'm going crazy sitting here not doing anything to find him."

"I know and we're working on that. Have you been outside at all?"

She shook her head in the negative looking down at her tea. "You told me to stay here."

She lied.

She'd gone out and met the woman from the Shimbuto. Why had she lied? Was it because she didn't trust me?

I didn't want to show my hand just yet, not about the cloned cell phone, and said, "How did you keep your pregnancy a secret from your parents?"

"Is that information really necessary?"

She'd just woken up after a long nap and looked beautiful, her skin glowing, her eyes alive with unmatched exuberance and an innocence I was finding difficult to believe. The wonderous advantages of youth.

I didn't answer and stared her down.

She nodded as if she understood. "I found out I was pregnant and flew home. I was about three months and not showing very much. I was able to cover it with the type of clothes I wore. Then I came back here and had Sonny at the County Medical Center, LCMC. It's not uncommon for me not to see my parents for months at a time. They're busy and I had to study for school."

That made perfect sense and probably happened just the way she said.

"Why didn't you want your parents to know about Sonny?"

She sipped and watched me over the top of the cup. She didn't answer.

I said, "Because the father is Johnny Ef?"

I mentally clocked an interrogation error: Interviews 101, you never lead the interviewee, you want *them* to reveal the information.

She looked away and didn't answer.

"What places did you go to with Johnny Ef?"

"He doesn't like that name."

She was a baby lamb trying to survive among the wolves, Johnny Ef and men of his ilk that populated his orbit.

"I know," I said.

"He took me all over the place. I'm his girl. *Was* his girl. He loved me." Her voice dropped off with the last part. She said, "I can make a list if you like."

"Please, it would help a lot. You have any idea at all where he might be keeping Sonny?"

Her arm came outside the blanket and set the cup down on the glass coffee table, the little clink loud in the quiet suite. She retracted her arm under the blanket, her black eyes alive with vitality. "If I had to guess I'd say . . . I guess I would say the Comstock Hotel. He owns the entire building." She reached out and took up her teacup again, blew on it, and sipped, as if stalling to see if I'd buy into the dog biscuit she just tossed me, expecting a woof.

I sat forward in the chair. "Why didn't you tell us about this place before?"

She shrugged. "I didn't know about it. Before I fell asleep, I called a friend and she told me about this hotel Johnny owns. I was asking around, you know, about Sonny. None of the rooms are rented out. But people still live in them—Johnny's people. He put some money into it and fixed it up a little. He lets people who work for him live there so he can keep an eye on them. He's a real control freak."

I fought back the urge to pull my phone to see if I'd missed a call she claimed to have made. I'd cloned her phone and the call should have registered. Unless she'd gotten the information from the

Eurasian woman at the Shimbuto. I needed to track that woman down and have a heart-to-heart talk with her.

I pulled my phone and manipulated the screen. "You sure it's called the Comstock? I can't find it."

I used the search as a ruse to check the calls. There *was* one call that I had missed; it lasted fifty-seven seconds and ended about the time she left the hotel and Ubered down to the Shimbuto.

"It's old, and from what I'm told it's a real dive used by whores and crackheads."

She said the words *whores* and *crackheads* with hubris as if she stood up in the clouds far above people who'd fallen on hard times and who did what they needed to do to survive and feed an addiction they never asked for.

The street people coming and going from the Comstock added a layer of cover from law enforcement, kind of a brilliant idea. Johnny Ef was cunning. I needed to keep that in mind.

She said, "It's on Alabama just south of the 105 Freeway. It wasn't torn down with the rest of the houses and businesses when they built the thoroughfare to LAX. One side is right up against the freeway. From what I'm told you can open a window on that side on the fifth floor and can almost touch concrete. The noise of all those cars and trucks is supposed to be horrendous. I don't know how anyone could live there. And the reek from all that exhaust." She puckered her face. "Ew."

She had too much information in her description. She'd just lied again—she'd been to the Comstock.

I knew the place she was talking about from when I worked patrol in South Central LA. Back in the day when they were building the 105 freeway, it was called the Fernwood Corridor. I knew the Comstock, but that wasn't its original name.

It used to be the Regal, a sixty-year-old dump that had been moldering away for the last two decades. Back then it had been condemned by the health department and red-tagged for demolition. Johnny Ef had to have paid someone off, or several someones.

I said, "How can we identify Sonny when we find him? I mean, if you're not with us?" Many babies, especially if they weren't yours, all looked alike.

She nodded, stood, gently set down the teacup, turned to the side, and delicately pulled down the top of her flora-colored house pants exposing more hip and butt cheek than I was comfortable seeing. A wine-colored birthmark high on her buttock resembled a very small boot of Italy.

Had she pulled down more of her pants than necessary—playing some kind of dangerous game between me and Drago?

"Sonny has one of these on his right foot. His looks like a happy face, though. Kind of, anyway."

Birthmarks were like navels, most all kids had them. This wasn't proof, Sonny belonged to her if that's what she was implying.

The suite door burst open and in walked Drago.

Layla startled and pulled up her pants.

Drago paused as he came in, his mind trying to justify why his girlfriend, the newest love of his life, had her pants pulled down next to my face.

She sat on the couch, pulled the blanket around her, and picked up her tea mug. She shot Drago a coy half-smile and came up short of batting her eyelids.

Layla came from a good family and had a staunch Catholic upbringing. The way she pulled down the top of her pants to me, though, did not speak well for her recent street education in the underworld.

Drago moved into the kitchenette and with a clang dropped a long piece of bloodied rebar in the sink. When he spoke, his tone had left behind the giddiness of a lovestruck puppy and returned to Drago pre-Layla. "I got a lead on where we should look."

He had his back to us as he rinsed blood off the rebar and his hand. While I was giving Waldo a bath and talking with Layla, Drago had been across the hall dealing with the prey caught in his trap. I didn't want to go over there and see the aftermath: "pile-o-thug," with blood and bone in the mix.

I needed him to know that what he saw when he walked in on me and Layla wasn't what he thought. I loved him too much for him to be angry with me. Jealousy was insidious, quick, and sometimes deadly. "The Comstock," I said.

He turned around slowly, the only sound the hiss from the water in the sink. His expression spoke of a friendship betrayed. Layla hunkered down into her blanket, her eyes on me as she gave an indifferent little shrug.

I tried to recover. "Layla just remembered that the Comstock might be a good place to start.

"Fine." He picked up the rebar and shoved it up the sleeve of his bomber jacket where he always kept it when he was on the prod. "Let's get this done."

CHAPTER THIRTY-FIVE

DRAGO LEFT A clean and fluffy Waldo on alert back in the hotel suite to protect Layla. He also told Layla not to open the door for any reason and to ignore any "ruckus" out in the hallway. One that would surely arise when housekeeping found the bloody thug-pile in the other suite.

Drago said nothing during the first part of the trip to South Central LA en route to the Comstock.

I broke the silence. "Look," I said. "It was totally innocent. I simply asked her how we could identify Sonny. She, all on her own, showed me a wine-colored birthmark on her hip."

In the hip area anyway. A little lower than the hip. Okay, lower butt cheek exposing the delicate cleave.

Yikes.

"She said Sonny has a birthmark on his foot that's similar to hers only it looks like a happy face, 'kinda.' Her words, not mine."

He drove while looking over at me, then back at the road, then back over at me. He watched my eyes for the truth. I'd never lied to him, but since *his* woman was involved along with the evil temptress jealousy, he now questioned my integrity. Not his fault. Jealousy with any normal human was an impossible beast to overpower and put back in the box.

"On his foot, huh? A happy face?"

"That's right. Like I said, it was perfectly innocent."

I wanted to slap Layla for putting me in the jackpot with my friend.

He shrugged. "Good. I mean, I knew that. Once I told you she was my girl I know you'd never . . . and . . . what am I talking about. I'm sorry, bro. She's just making me crazy. That kiss was like some kind of poison that rotted my brain. I'm not kiddin'." He knocked on his noggin with his knuckles. Lovesickness had him by the throat and wouldn't let go anytime soon.

I reached over and put my hand on his arm. He didn't like any sort of physical touching from men, but I wanted him to know I was there for him. Maybe it was from his time in prison, or maybe it was from how his father treated him as a kid. Long ago, I had pulled the reports that described his abuse—for long stretches of time his dad had kept him chained to a tree in the backyard—and he'd done worse to him.

Drago nodded and drove for a few more miles. I took my hand away and gave him some time to think.

After a while I said, "Do you have a guy who can run the number Layla called just before she Ubered down to the Shimbuto?"

"I've been thinking about that whole phone cloning thing and maybe we shouldn't be doing it. It's a big violation of her privacy."

"Your calling foul on *this* as being an invasion of privacy?"

He and I had done far worse in the past.

He jerked his head around to look at me with a confused expression.

I said, "You and Eve have picked the poison apple, and only you've taken a bite. Whether you like it or not, my friend, she's got you on a short leash."

"You think my logic is clouded over my . . . my *friendship* for Layla?" The word friendship didn't belong in his vocabulary and it came out a little jumbled. He only had two friends as far as I knew, me and Marie.

He was badly smitten, worse than I first believed. When Cupid fires his arrow, it's indiscriminate and rarely hits both parties at the same time.

Marie said that some people subconsciously fall in love with people they can't have because they are afraid real love, rather than unrequited love, would tear their guts out. The guts part was what I'd added.

One thing for sure, I felt sorry for my large friend.

"Yeah, I do," I said and stopped short of saying she was a liar and using us both for whatever game she had going.

He held my eyes a second longer and nodded as if answering a question he'd mentally asked himself. "Yeah, I can run that number. Give it to me."

I pulled out the phone and swiped the screen until the number came up. I fed it to him once. That's all it took with him—he had that kind of brain. He manipulated his phone with fingers from his free hand and texted the request to *his guy.*

With his mood I didn't want to think about what was going to happen when we arrived at the Comstock. More importantly, how I would react to the threat we'd walk into, a place bristling with security that didn't play by any rules.

I needed to keep talking as a distraction.

"Don't you think the way Waldo acts . . . I mean how smart that dog is . . . that his intelligence goes far beyond any other dog, that it's kinda weird?"

He looked happy to change the topic. "What are you talking about? Haven't you ever watched *Lassie* on TV?"

"Drago, those are not real scenes."

Lassie was trained for each individual act in a controlled environment and was given many tries to accomplish that act for the final product that went on TV.

He looked over and smirked. "What are you talking about? Of course, it's real. That dog ain't a robot."

I stared at him trying to decide if I wanted in on the debate over a TV dog's intellect as it pertained to the real world.

"Yes, you're probably right, Lassie's real."

He nodded and kept driving.

*   *   *

Thirty minutes later, we pulled up and parked on Alabama south of 117th Street. The Regal—now the Comstock—wasn't exactly where I remembered it. The building sat two blocks farther north of 117th. Sweat beaded on my forehead in anticipation of the guaranteed violent confrontation. I caught myself wringing my hands and did as Dad recommended—talked to Tobias in my head.

"You okay with this, old hoss? I can handle it if you want to hang back in the truck. No big deal and no judging."

He didn't say it with any sarcasm—he really meant it when he said he'd handle it.

For a brief second, I considered staying behind, but in all likelihood if this place did belong to Johnny Ef, he'd have more cronies than my big friend could handle. I had to go. Six weeks back, I would've been chomping at the bit to get into the action.

"No, I'm good. I'm going with you."

I gave my word I'd get Sonny back, and my word was my bond.

He leaned a big arm over the seat, his hand rummaging around in his war bag. "What do you prefer?" He came back with a long-handled carpenter's hammer and some wicked-looking custom-made brass knuckles. I took them both. Odd weapons to use on the human body. With all the modern weapons available, the tried and proven harked back to medieval times.

Drago smiled. "Now we're talkin'."

The cold steel of the knuckles and the wood handle from the hammer made my stomach twist into knots.

Entry into the Comstock would end in blood and bone, no two ways around it. I wanted to call Marie and would have had it not sounded too much like a kid on the playground confronting a bully and needing his mommy.

Drago started to slide out of the truck. I put a hand on his elbow. He stopped and looked back. He really did not like to be touched, even by a friend.

"Let's wait a minute and watch. And when we do go, we don't wanna walk too far. When we're ready, we'll drive up. If that's okay with you. It's going to burn your truck and you'll have to get rid of it."

He shrugged, looked over his shoulder into the back seat. "Don't like the strawberry smell anyway." He eased his door closed.

Drago got most of his vehicles with fake IDs. He'd go into a dealership, pick out a truck, and lease it under someone else's credit. He'd drive it for three months, the time it took for the owner of the credit to figure it out and file a crime report. The dealer would get his new car back now heavily used and smelling like strawberry Waldo.

I pulled out the binoculars and watched. Three skeevy hypes worked the street slingin' heroin. A car would pull up, the guy standing in the street would make contact, take the money, the dope guy would go to the other side of the hotel and come back a minute later to give the dope to the driver.

The third guy stood half a block south and worked as an advanced warning system to alert if the cops prowled up the street. We didn't care about the minor drug sales; all we wanted was Sonny.

After fifteen minutes a nice new Lincoln, black and sleek with tinted windows, crept up the street as if afraid to approach too quickly. The driver parked out of our view in the dirt parking lot on the north side under the Century Freeway. The car didn't match a street urchin hooked on tar heroin there to cop some dope.

Seconds later a man with gray hair in a nice suit came around the corner and disappeared into the Comstock. He didn't fit the picture at all.

Five minutes more and another man came out the front door, disappeared around the corner. He reappeared driving a Porsche crossover, a bronze Cayenne, and passed us southbound driving too fast.

Why hadn't the sheriff deputies been all over this place? It was ripe for the picking. I didn't want to believe the cops had been paid off, not the kind of patrol deputies I had once worked with.

I said, "They can't be just leaving their cars back there unprotected, not with all these street hypes coming up to cop some dope."

Just as I finished saying it, a thug in a suit stepped around the corner of the hotel to peep the street. He wore a suit coat too hot for the afternoon; he would be carrying a long gun underneath to protect the cars and the operation inside.

Drago said, "Good thing we waited. Not a problem though, we just need to fall on that guy like a ton of bricks. No sound. Hey, I can lie down in the back seat and you can drive up around the back like you're a customer. I don't fit the part like you do. You take the guy out and I'll back you up if there are any more. Whattaya think?"

I swallowed hard and my voice cracked. "Ya, we can do that."

CHAPTER THIRTY-SIX

DRAGO CARRIED A penchant for chaos around in his back pocket. He thrived when the world around him didn't.

When I sounded less than eager to execute his plan, Drago said, "Screw it." He slammed the gearshift down into drive and punched the accelerator driving into the breach without leaving any choice.

The truck lurched forward. The skeevy lookout who stood under the shade of a tree zipped by as we accelerated past. He whistled his alert loud and sharp.

Drago drove at the curb in front of the Comstock at an angle, the front tire bumping over the curb.

We stopped half in the street and catawampus to the building. Anything out of skew in Drago's world he described as catawampus, only he said it, "Cattywampus."

Drago didn't slow down; he jumped from the truck and rushed the building corner, moving quicker than a man of his size should've been able to move. I tried to stay behind him right on his tail.

The parking lot guard in his hundred-dollar suit came around the corner just as the rebar slid down out of Drago's sleeve into his hand.

He swung as the guard went for a sawed-off shotgun inside his suit coat, one that hung from his shoulder by a cheap piece of yellow nylon rope.

Everything happening too fast to intervene but vivid, alive, the threat a slithering animal that made my back itch.

I rode in Drago's wake and hoped he'd get there in time, ashamed of the unwanted feeling, the need to hold back a little instead of pushing Drago out of the way to be first.

The rebar hissed through the air and chunked against the side of the man's head. He wilted.

Drago caught him by the scruff and dragged him around the corner of the building. I looked back, the street empty, all the dope fiends had fled.

That always happened when a class-one predator arrived on the savannah, coming out of the tall grass to eat the weak.

A portable radio clipped to the downed guard's belt burped out dangerous words. "Sims? Sims? You down there? I heard the whistle, what's going on?

"Report.

"Report now."

My voice cracked. "Now we've done it. They're onto us. We've lost the initiative."

Drago's hands checked the guard's pockets, pulling out his phone and a wad of greasy U.S. currency the man had strong-armed from the addicts. Drago froze and looked up at me. With his eyes still on me, he picked up the radio, keyed the button, and said, "Roger, Wilco, ten-four, over and out."

"Sims, you piece of monkey shit, I warned you about screwin' around on the radio. Now I'm comin' down there to kick your skinny ass so hard you'll have to unzip your pants to eat a sandwich. You hear me. I'm fed up with it."

The man on the other end of the radio sounded breathy and on the move. He was coming down. There would be a confrontation. Drago was playing it just right.

He put his hand on my chest and eased me back against the wall. He raised the rebar, ready for the guy on the radio to come around the corner.

Sweat made the carpenter's hammer slick in my hand. I should've put duct tape on it, but I wasn't thinking straight, hadn't been since Tobias was born.

The sound from a shoe scuff on pavement made it to us around the corner. A second later a shadow appeared. Again, the hiss through the air. A chunk. The man hit the pavement. He'd wake up in the hospital after a two-week nap.

Drago dragged him the rest of the way around the corner and piled him on top of the other thug. He grabbed my shoulder. "Come on, and I can't believe I'm saying this, but you better have my back here, bro."

His shaming words snapped me out of the emotional funk, anger shoving in to take control. Friend or no friend, he couldn't talk to me that way.

I hurried around him. "I'll go first, you watch *my* back."

"Now we're talkin'. Bruno's back!"

Dad had been right about the anger; I wanted to crush the world. I stoked that fire thinking *my son Tobias is at home safe*. Nothing would get to him. "You're safe, Tobias. I won't let anything happen to you. I'll always be there for you."

"What?" Drago asked. "What did you say?"

"Never mind."

We moved around the corner headed for the door. On the sidewalk, a crow with a broken wing hopped in front of us and cawed, unafraid of foes twenty times larger and capable of crushing him with a boot. His feathers had a beautiful black sheen similar to Layla's hair. I didn't like crows and considered them a bad omen.

We came to the inset front double door of the Comstock that had been glass at one time and now had a piece of desiccated plywood painted over and over again with gang graffiti and hung haphazardly in the frame secured with rusted heavy gauge wire. I jerked it open and entered.

A large dollop of nostalgia slapped me in the face. Inside, the Comstock looked the same as it did twenty years ago when I drove a patrol car policing the area. Right down to the same threadbare carpet and fast-food wrappers and clumps of human feces.

The reek like no other.

Some of the food wrappers came from Stops restaurant, which had closed a few years back. Time had stopped in the hotel that should've been razed to the ground the way all the other buildings in the freeway corridor had.

We passed old doors kicked in too many times by the good guys—and the bad guys—the doorframes splintered and glued or nailed back together. All had hasps with padlocks, the doorknobs no longer viable. The importance of the occupant gauged by the number of locks; most had one, some had two, and one door had three hasps and three padlocks. He'd be the main heroin dealer, the shot caller for the two floors of mopes.

Another door painted a pastel purple opened. A sketchy woman with dirty hair and sores on her cheeks, missing front teeth, spotted us and jumped back into the gloom, back into a life long ago lost.

I headed right for the stairs. We hurried up the first flight, then on up to the third floor. We came out of the stairwell on the third-floor landing. Straight ahead a hard metal door stood ajar, an added barrier that closed off the floor. Beefed-up security.

A comfortable chair and table sat just inside, the table filled with cards in a game of solitaire. The player had lost and hadn't yet figured it out. That player now down in the parking lot lying on top of Sims with a similar furrow on the side of his head.

I pulled the metal door open and found a different world, the same as in *The Wizard of Oz* when the movie all of a sudden turned from black-and-white to color; Dorothy's sparkling ruby shoes an absolute marvel.

The third floor would've passed muster for any high-dollar medical office in Beverly Hills: plush carpet, wallpaper, and real potted plants—Ficus and figs. For a brief second, I felt the fool standing in this place holding a carpenter's hammer in one hand and brass knuckles on the other.

Until a door to the right opened and a thug in a cheap suit stepped out. His eyes didn't react. Pure professional. He went for a gun under his coat.

I skip-stepped over to him and used the hammer on his knee. He fell to the floor with a grunt, his kneecap shattered. He still reached for his radio to alert the others. Drago knocked me out of the way and whacked him in the head with the rebar.

"You keep doing that," I said, "and they're going to run out of ICU beds at MLK."

Drago didn't say anything. His hand went over the downed man's body and jerked out a Berretta model 92f from a shoulder holster. He dropped the mag, pulled back the slide ejecting the round in the chamber, and tossed the gun down the hall. Smooth, clean, efficient.

I peeked in the door the man had come from and found a control room with TV screens monitoring all the other rooms on floors three, four, and five.

I froze, horrified at what the screens depicted.

CHAPTER THIRTY-SEVEN

In a daze, I stepped out of the hall on that third floor of the Comstock and into the room with all the monitors—CCTV security screens. When Drago pushed in behind me, he saw the screens and blurted, "Sons of bitches. *Sons of bitches!*"

I grabbed his shoulder as he turned to go. "Wait. We have to do this smart."

He shrugged out of my grasp. "*You* do it smart. I'm gonna kick some ass."

On the monitors, perverse scenes played out with women, young girls, and small boys, all of these victims enslaved and sold. Commerce dredged up from the bottom of society.

The people involved, the deviant exploiters, could never be rehabilitated.

A seething anger rose up inside me. I wanted to crush them, my safety no longer part of the equation. I no longer needed Tobias as an emotional crutch.

Then I realized I had misinterpreted what Dad had been saying. He meant that when anger and hate took me by the throat, to think of Tobias, let Tobias guide me, tamp down the fire and brimstone.

But his advice didn't count in this situation. How could I let people like these survive in our world, how could I not—for Tobias' sake—purge them with extreme prejudice?

The anger continued to rise up and flush my face hot. I spoke through clenched teeth. "Drago!" I said. "Wait!" He froze halfway out the door and came back.

I said, "This is a complicated situation, and if we go headlong into it like a couple of blind bulls, it's only going to get more complicated."

He pointed his rebar at the screens. "You see what's going on here? No. I'm not slowing down until every one of these—"

"Look." I pointed to the top screen in the corner labeled "Floor 5 Rm 5." The screen depicted three small infants in bassinets with a nursemaid sitting in a chair by the door reading a magazine, a full-length shotgun close at hand propped against the wall.

Drago's mouth dropped open as he took several steps closer to the screen. He pointed with the rebar that now carried a bit of blood and scalp hair. "There's Sonny, right there. He's here. These dirty bastards are also running a baby farm, selling kids. Bruno, they're selling kids."

I didn't answer him, reached over, and one by one hit "record" on all the machines, recording a multitude of damning evidence. A taped record of a puzzle we were about to upset and scramble all the pieces.

Law enforcement could reconstruct the puzzle later.

Then I took out my phone. I dialed a number from memory: Helen Hellinger, a detective with the Los Angeles County Sheriff's Department.

"Who are you calling?" Drago asked.

"Hellinger."

He nodded and instantly understood. He paced the room staring down at the floor, unable to look at the CCTV screens, the vile activity too much for even Drago to tolerate. He slapped the piece of rebar in his hand harder and harder, the beast in him difficult to restrain.

Helen worked a kidnapping case with me six weeks earlier when I masqueraded as an authentic detective. She had discovered my real name and the warrants out for my arrest that guaranteed life in prison. She promised not to book me if I gave her one thing. She asked that Drago and I rescue her niece from an abusive and violent home. She couldn't do it herself because she was law enforcement and, more important, afraid of her own need to kill everyone involved.

We hit the house hard and fast and found her young niece huddled in a hall closet with a wire wrapped around her ankle and attached to a wall to keep her locked down. We smuggled her down to Costa Rica, where she now thrived with the other children, at the place that Dad now referred to as Casa Bruno. I'd never call in the marker owed by Helen for rescuing her niece, but Helen would want a piece of this in any case.

"Helen," I said when she answered.

"Brun—!" She caught herself before she said anything that might be picked up by intrusive law enforcement.

Just in case.

"It's okay," I said. "Your niece is fine." Out of an abundance of safety I didn't say Helen's last name or mention her niece's. "I'm up north again."

"I understand. What do you need?"

She was a no-nonsense type of cop and I liked her for it.

"I'm standing in . . . in a very bad place right now and it's about to go south in a big way."

"I understand."

"There are children and women."

Her tone turned terse. "Where? I'm coming. Tell me where?"

"On Alabama north of 117th alongside the Century Freeway."

"On my way."

I clicked off.

Drago whacked his hand with the rebar.

I used the claw end of the hammer and smashed just the CCTV screen that depicted the three infants and then smashed that particular recording device as well.

"Okay, look," I said. "I need you to cause a distraction down here on the third floor. There are bouncers on the landings of four and five." I pointed to the screens. "I'll take them out as I make my way up to the infants. I'll secure the infants."

"Yeah, that's good. Once it starts, all the pervs will have to go by me to get out. You're right, this is a better plan. You funnel those bastards to me and I'll spank 'em good."

He didn't ask if I could handle what was coming; he was a good friend.

"You ready?" I asked.

"Let's light this fuse."

"You heard it, the deputies are on the way. We don't have much time. Give me thirty seconds, then start the distraction. Go into the first room, take out the asshole, then get back out into the hall and wait. We don't want anyone getting away."

"I got it. Go."

I ran out into the hall headed for the stairs up to the fourth floor, the rage inside me finally unleashed. I didn't need Tobias for this. I absorbed every bit of anger and channeled it into the carpenter's hammer.

CHAPTER THIRTY-EIGHT

I BOUNDED UP the flight of stairs headed to the fourth-floor landing. I had told Drago to wait thirty seconds for me to get in position.

He only waited fifteen.

The violent sound of a door being kicked in rolled up behind me. In that same second, a woman screamed.

Then a man.

A window shattered.

The man's scream a dying echo in a deep cave.

Drago had thrown him, probably naked, out the third-floor window. Drago bellowed to me, "Send 'em on down, I'm ready for 'em."

Doors on the third floor—his floor—started opening.

More screams.

Drago stood at the confluence to the stairs and the hall on the third floor, not letting any of the disreputable escape down to safety. He'd cull the fleeing crowd, picking out the scandalous men with a long rod of punishing steel.

His muffled bellow floated up the stairs: "Let the Big Dog eat." Something he liked to say while at bat playing softball.

I'd been distracted by the sounds and images of Drago mowing through the men trying to evade his blood-filled wrath.

I almost turned back too late to find the guard on the fourth floor on his way down. Like a fool, he wore dark sunglasses indoors, and a shiny blue sharkskin suit.

His arm was extended with a large handgun pointed at my head. Another mistake. A professional doesn't extend his arm like in the movies.

In CQC—close-quarters combat—you're supposed to hold your pistol at your hip to protect it. You fire from the hip.

I knocked his gun aside with the carpenter's hammer just as the gun bellowed flame in a mind-numbing explosion inches from my face.

I stepped up and swung a left roundhouse with the brass knuckles, caught him on the jaw, shattering it. He wilted to the steps, out cold.

My ears rang, and my face burned, having been peppered with burnt gunpowder. I used the claw end of the hammer to catch the man's shoulder and pulled him out of the way. He tumbled down the stairs.

On that same floor, the fourth floor, the doors had already started to open. Men half-dressed with scared, guilty expressions lacking one iota of shame piled out into the hall, their eyes fixed on the hammer in my hand.

They carried their clothes doing a chicken-hop to put on pants or shoes. My anger wanted me to slow down and deal with these nasty excuses for humans, but I had to get to the infants.

The men and some of the women and children bumped past me headed for the stairs.

When they made it to the stairwell and saw the inert sunglasses man, they yelped and screamed again.

By the time I made it down to the end of the hall to the next set of stairs to go up, the fifth-floor thug had just stepped down into the fourth-floor hall. Still ten feet away, he had his hand inside his suit coat ready to draw from a shoulder holster.

I held my hammer up and shifted my expression from guile to scared and spoke, the words coming rapid-fire. "I was down on two fixing a doe, you know one a dem kicked in so many times—when all of a sudden these Crip gangsters come running in with guns. There's a real mess down there. You better hurry, mister."

I had moved toward him while talking. He figured out the ploy too late. I brought my hand up to show him the brass knuckles, the distraction. I swung the hammer from the other side and pulled my swing a little or I would've crushed his skull.

Even so, the mushy crack vibrated up through my hand and into my arm. He fell the same as if shot and didn't move. I stepped over him as a flood of people came down the stairs from the fifth floor.

Down the hall from where I'd just come, muffled screaming grew to a crescendo as Drago went to work with his rebar, reaping the poisonous crop, the cancerous part of mankind.

I put my back to the wall and slid past the folks in their downward flight.

The men gave me the widest berth.

On the fifth floor all the doors stood open. Pieces of abandoned clothes littered the plush hall carpet. I made it to the end and stopped. On the other side of the last door, the nurse was holding a shotgun. A weapon with that kind of devastating firepower did not mix with infants. No weapons did, for that matter.

I stood off to the side and knocked. I said, "Are you okay in there? Johnny sent me to get you out before the cops get here. Hurry, open the door."

"I'm not supposed to open the door for anyone but Ms. Chang, Nick, or Johnny himself. So piss off."

My face flushed hot with anger.

We didn't have time for this. I stepped in front of the door, rose up on one foot, and kicked beside the knob.

The woman had been foolish and stood in front of the door while talking to me. The door's edge caught her on the nose with a wet crunch. She went down, out of the action. The shotgun clunked to the floor.

The babies started screaming a riot of caterwauling. I picked up the shotgun, racked out the rounds, and threw it through the glass window.

Outside it banged against the side of the 105 freeway and fell to the ground. I came down out of my anger-fueled fugue state and realized I couldn't carry three babies, not all at once. I only had two arms. I looked around and spotted four baby carriers, the kind that strapped right into the back seats of cars. I grabbed three and set one in front of each bassinet with a baby. There were six bassinets, three of them empty.

We arrived too late for the other three. God only knew where they disappeared. I gently picked up the first warm, squirmy child and my heart swelled, I missed Tobias so.

I couldn't leave those children to the Los Angeles Child Protective Services, an organization overworked and desperately short of resources to properly vet prospective parents.

I'd give Helen some time to find the natural parents, if the parents had not sold the children in the first place. And barring their return to their families, I'd take all three of them down to Costa Rica.

Huh, what was Marie going to say? Tobias would have three more brothers and sisters to grow up with if Sonny wasn't in the bunch.

I didn't have time to check their feet for the happy-face birthmark. Sonny had to be there. It made too much sense for him not to be.

I stuck the hammer claw in a belt loop and the brass knuckles in my pocket. I'd have my hands full of baby and would be unable to defend us. I picked up two carrier handles in one hand, those carriers leaning into each other just a little, and picked up the third with my other hand.

I peeked into the hall. Empty of people. I hurried out just as sirens reached into the Comstock from several blocks over. Our time left to escape counted in seconds, not minutes. I hurried.

CHAPTER THIRTY-NINE

I came out of the stairwell on the third floor where Drago had been busy administering the penalty common in Jungle Law and was glad the infants were too young to register the carnage.

The pristine office building had been turned into an abattoir. Drago stood among the piles of men that lined the hall, men who squirmed and moaned and bled, a scene more from a Civil War aid station at Gettysburg.

Drago's face a mask of blood spatter along with his hands and arms and football jersey, the walls and carpet. His eyes were wide, the whites stark against all the red. His body shook with a palsy from adrenaline and unvented rage.

"Take it easy, big man, it's me, Bruno." I stopped ten feet from him until he acknowledged me.

The downed men were not from any one type—they came in all shapes and sizes and social cast. The truly sad part about it was that even with these thirty-five or forty men the number didn't scratch the surface to the depth of the cancerous cyst that their ilk formed in our society. They were the cause of the problem—and without the demand—there would be no need for the supply.

The broken and bloody men on the floor in the hall would re-member this day and still not be able to suppress their uncontrollable perversion that crushed so many other lives. Only one thing could stop them, and Drago had stopped short of meting out that coup de grace.

As I stood there, I realized there was a huge hole in my plan. All the victims who would eventually be listed in the criminal complaints to speak against the suspects had fled. But there had only been two of us, and we did what we could. Law enforcement could do the research and the tracking.

Drago bellowed, "We need to cut the head off this snake. I'm not kiddin', I'm gonna give Johnny Ef a visit."

I stepped over and in between the arms and legs and bodies, compound fractures, broken faces and skulls. "I hear ya, buddy, but right now we have to roll. The police will be here in seconds."

He came down off the ledge of rage, his eyes going back to normal. "Right—Let's roll." He turned and stomped hands and arms and legs, kicked a few torsos.

"Drago?"

He turned back.

"Take one of these, will you? And try real hard not to get blood on him."

"Hey? Hey, is this Sonny? Did we get Sonny?"

He hurried back to me doing the same with his size-sixteen feet kicking and stomping. He tossed down the piece of rebar and wiped his hands on his pants, an act of futility, before he took the carrier, marring the handle with blood smears.

With the small child in his hand, I couldn't help but envision the old American Tourister commercial with the piece of luggage in the gorilla cage, the gorilla doing its darnedest to damage it.

I said, "Now move. We have to move."

We hurried the best we could, negotiating the last two flights of stairs that now seemed endless.

Down on the first floor, spilling out into the bright sunlight, all the victims had stopped and crowded into each other for protection, herd mentality. They had nowhere to go.

Some had slashes of blood on them cast off from the rebar. The sight made me want to gently put the babies down and go back, finish the job we'd left undone, stomp those bastards in the ground.

But far off down Alabama, the first black-and-white cop car turned onto the street, red lights and siren blaring.

We hurried to the truck and got in.

We didn't have time to belt the babies to the seat. The cop car would cut off our only means of escape; we'd have to drive right past them to get away.

If they blocked the street.

Game over.

Drago slammed the truck in drive and drove over the curb while I buckled in the two babies in the back seat.

Drago tried to look back as the truck canted from side to side going over the curb and driving down the sidewalk. "We get Sonny? Is Sonny there?"

"I haven't looked. Pay attention and drive."

When I looked up to tell him not to hit anyone, the truck passed some of the victims.

A small fair-haired little boy raised his hand and waved, his blue eyes vacant without emotion. He'd only waved because of a past memory, one not used in a long time, a memory that told him this was what he was supposed to do. The sight of him broke my heart. I wanted to go back and rescue him, rescue all of them, take them all down to Casa Bruno.

I got the two babies in the back buckled in and leaned all the way over the front seat to buckle in the last one when Drago said, "Hold on."

I looked up.

The dirt parking area under the Century Freeway was filled with the thirty-plus cars from the slobs left piled up in the Comstock. The cars blocked our way out. Drago hit the accelerator and aimed between the two smallest cars at the end of a row, a BMW coupe and a Jaguar parked nose to ass-end.

"The babies," I yelled. "We have babies!"

"That's why I said hold on."

I clicked in the third baby's seat belt a microsecond before Drago hit the cars, shoving the cars out of the way, their tires on the dirt moving sideways easier than they would've on asphalt.

I flew forward from the back and slammed into the dash. Drago said, "Hey, bro, would you quit messin' around here, I'm tryin' ta drive."

"Yeah, yeah. Sorry." I righted myself and sat in the back seat between both babies, who seemed unaffected by their abrupt shift in ownership. My back ached from the impact.

The first thing Drago did when appropriating a new car was disconnect the airbags, in preparation for similar situations.

The two cars only moved half as much as we needed to get clear.

Drago hit the gas, the back wheels spinning, pushing the cars the rest of the way and gouging the sides of the truck with their bumpers as we passed through.

We were in the clear with only two chain-link fences and an open field between us and the street that led out eastbound. I didn't have to tell him to aim for the pole in the chain-link fence. He already knew.

You hit a chain link in between the poles and the links stretch and cause serious problems, most of the time not letting you get through. Hit the fence at the pole and the entire fence just lies down and you can drive over it.

The truck kicked up a plume of dust traversing the field and then went through the second chain-link fence with a loud thump. I looked back. No one followed. We'd made it. We were in the clear.

CHAPTER FORTY

I SAT ON the couch I'd pulled over to the open sliding glass door in the Summerset, a room on the second floor, and watched the parking lot down below waiting for Drago to get back with a cold car or truck. Waiting for Layla to arrive on foot after being dropped off by an Uber. I told her to be let off two blocks down and walk in, my anxiety rising by the minute.

The Americana Hotel where we had been staying was now too hot, nuclear-spill type hot with the pile-o-thugs in the room across the hall. Drago really didn't think that one through. We'd rented the rooms with fake IDs and stolen credit cards, not that it mattered.

The blue dot on the locater app showed Layla in an Uber headed south, but she got off at the wrong off-ramp. The blue dot continued to the address across from the Staples Arena, the Shimbuto.

The blue dot stayed there and continued to blip and blip.

What the hell was she up to?

We'd dropped the three infants off at Mrs. Espinoza's in Fruit Town, a section of Compton. I didn't tell her what was going on, but she knew me from around the neighborhood. And since I left the country, rumors were rife in the ghetto about rescued children and a black man acting the fool as some kind of "errant white knight."

More a court jester, truth be told.

While working uniform patrol I had found Mrs. Espinoza's daughter Carly after she went missing and brought her home.

Three times.

The fourth time no one could've brought her home in anything other than a pine box.

Crack ruined too many young lives.

I took photos of the infants and their feet. Sonny wasn't among them. No happy face birthmark. After all the trouble we'd caused, we still hadn't recovered Sonny.

I needed to see Tobias, hold him in my arms, kiss my wife, see her smile that lit up my world.

When I had called Layla and told her where to come, she immediately asked if we recovered her son. She took down the information for the Summerset—the excitement plain in her voice and the fear of a fretting mother.

I sent her photos from my phone of the three children. and she confirmed Sonny wasn't among them.

Two hours had passed since we fled the Comstock. My cell phone buzzed.

Helen.

I answered and waited for her to say something. Her breathing, a little rapid, came over the phone. When I didn't say anything, she said, "My God, Bruno, I've never seen anything like this."

"I'm sorry we left such a mess. How are all the victims?"

"The only thing that saved this whole clusterfuck was you pushing the 'record' button on all the machines."

The only way she could know I'd been the one to do that was if there'd been a camera in the CCTV room. Something I had not thought of and should have. What did a few more warrants for my arrest matter? A person had only one life to waste in prison.

Then my mind all on its own happened on another explanation. She could've assumed I'd turned on the recorders based on the time they were started. The time would correspond to the time I'd called her.

She said, "By quick count we only lost three of the older women, and by older I'm talking nineteen or twenty.

"It looks like a bomb went off on the third floor, assholes and elbows everywhere. Every one of those guys has to go to the jail ward at LCMC. Half are in critical condition."

I got up and moved to the kitchenette and used a glass under the tap for a drink of water, my mouth having gone dry as hot sand. I swallowed the water. "Only half of them?"

She chuckled. "Yeah, I wish it were all of them, too. But as is, this is going to put a strain on LCMC's jail ward. We're going to be paying a lot of overtime to guard them."

While she talked, I sent her the three photos of the babies. She paused and checked the incoming message. She whispered, "Those sons of bitches. Screw the overtime." Her tone turned harsh. "You're telling me these guys are also selling babies? You have a lead on who was running this place? I want a piece of him."

"Johnny Fillmore."

"Ah, man. Johnny Ef. Are you sure? He's untouchable. He'll have at least two cutouts in between him and the street. We'll never get to him."

"I can. I don't have to play by the same rules."

"It'd almost be worth it to take some vacation time to come out and play."

"It's probably better that you don't. It's going to get ugly before it gets better. Ennis Freemantle is the first-level cutout, and he's already made a run at us. He sent two guys."

"The thing at the Americana Hotel—that was you?"

"Yeah. Can you check on the three babies, see if there are any reports of missing children and if they match the descriptions?"

"If there aren't any deserving parents, are you taking them?"

"I don't have a choice. No, I didn't mean it that way. Of course, I will, they'll be better off with us."

"Marie know you're up here? She wasn't too keen the last time you . . . hey, she have that baby yet?"

I smiled into the phone. "Yes, we had a boy, Tobias, day before yesterday. And Marie knows I'm here but would rather that I wasn't."

Marie and Helen became good friends when Helen flew down on vacation time to be with her niece at Casa Bruno. Helen talked with her niece on a regular basis by phone.

I was back at the slider watching the parking lot as I drank the water.

"Bruno, the news crews are here, lots of them. All of them, in fact. This story is going international. Homicide is giving a statement right now. Turn it on, if you want to see it. Homicide is not getting anything good as far as descriptions of who . . . caused this mess."

"Naw, I don't need to see it."

"Homicide is figuring five to six suspects did all this damage. There wasn't five or six, was there?"

"No."

"You and Drago?"

I nodded as I said, "Yeah." That answer came out a lowball slider.

"Sweet Jesus, you two caused some mayhem." She chuckled. "Just two of you. I would've paid big money for front-row seats on this one. The department should recall our batons and issue us all rebar. Highly effective on perverts, I'd say."

"Homicide is on scene? Why?"

"One of the suspects took a flyer out the third-floor window and landed on the roof of a Mercedes, caved it in. I tried to talk

Homicide into believing it was a suicide, and they wouldn't have it. Two other guys outside, clubbed over the head, they're circling the drain. A couple more on the third floor, the same."

I said nothing.

I closed my eyes and put my forehead against the slider. Did those men deserve treatment that severe?

Six weeks ago, I would never have questioned it. I would've simply folded my tent and moved on without giving them a second thought.

They chose the game and with it came the consequences. My old boss Robby Wicks would've said that I was ruined, that I'd grown a conscience and no longer belonged on the street chasing violence. He would be right about the last part. Maybe even about all of it.

Helen said, "I'll get back to you. Gotta go. Here comes my boss." She clicked off.

The jackpot I put her in might be hard to explain to her supervisor. Sure, she could say it was an anonymous tip, but the kind of mess we left would sound questionable—discovered with just a phone call—and then worse, the call coming minutes before it happened. That would be the kicker, the time factor.

Forty minutes later, an Uber pulled up and let out Layla and her sidekick, Waldo. I had told her to get out two blocks down. She didn't seem to care about security, only about her baby, Sonny. I guess I'd be the same way if it were Tobias.

The Summerset in the city of Hawthorne was built in the seventies, in the old horseshoe configuration. She headed to the room where I'd told her to go, one across the horseshoe from where I stood. The room was used as a trip wire for anyone who came looking for us, the same tactic Drago had used at the Americana, only one with a lot more distance, an entire parking lot.

I wasn't sure anybody followed her. In a few minutes I'd have to walk over and take her phone away, yank out the phone cord in the room. She wasn't good at following directions.

I felt a bit guilty having her stay in that room as bait. Drago wouldn't like it. But this whole mess suddenly became less about Layla and more about Sonny.

CHAPTER FORTY-ONE

THE LIMO EASED to the red curb in front of the Shimbuto, the driver got out, ran around, and opened the door for me, the action in plain view through the glass wall. I caught a glimpse of the security man inside watching with interest.

I'd taken a page out of Dad's playbook. No way could Bruno Johnson walk into the Shimbuto and expect any kind of assistance, but Mr. Wilbur Wentworth IV could. I just needed to get past the front desk security without an alarm going out. I'd gone to Armani on Rodeo Drive in Beverly Hills and paid cash for a stylish suit cut to fit while I waited. A huge expense but something a good con required.

The small details made the con—this according to Mom.

The fit was tight and the sleeves a tad short. The tailor assured me this cut was "all the rage." An antiquated cliché. It might've been "all the rage," but I looked stupid and uncomfortable, like the whole getup had been left in the dryer too long.

Drago lent me some bling from his stash, a nice diamond Rolex and understated gold cuff links. He gave me money for the suit that I insisted on paying back later. Somehow.

The money detail was less important. Getting Sonny back was all that mattered now.

Drago didn't care about money; it was only one component in a life that facilitated his cause, taking down outlaw motorcycle gang members and what they represent. In his world nothing else mattered. He carried out his vendetta with cunning, creativity, and violence equal to what his prey perpetrated upon their unsuspecting victims. Drago often smiled and said, "Best job I ever had."

I'd done the research into the Shimbuto and its occupants online. Through social media, I discovered who had left the country to visit second homes in Switzerland, Italy, and France, who lived off a trust fund, who worked as CEOs and CFOs. Armed with intelligence was better than going armed with a gun.

The phone number Layla had called on her cell phone, the one I'd cloned to mine, came back to Aimee Langhari, top floor, penthouse 3.

The limo driver hurried over and opened the door to the Shimbuto. I ignored the front desk man and moved right to the elevators, my footfalls silent on the beautiful Asian carpet. The lobby walls were covered in butterscotch-colored hardwood and framed four-foot-tall hand-painted Geishas dressed in brightly colored obis.

"Sir? Excuse me, sir, who are you here to see?"

He was a big corn-fed white guy who probably once played pro ball, red hair and a big nose flattened at the top from violence.

I ignored him and pushed the PH button. Nothing happened. The elevators had to be released by the security man.

Damn.

I turned and with an expressionless face moved back to the front desk, a slightly elevated podium high enough that the security man looked down at me.

I took a business card from my pocket that just had my name on expensive cotton rag card stock. I handed it up to him. "I'm here to see Samuel Betts, in penthouse 2. It's a personal matter."

"I'm sorry, Samuel Betts is unavailable."

He was in Nice on his yacht for the next two weeks.

"Is that right? I came all this way and . . . wait, what about Ms. Aimee Langhari—she's also a good friend and can help me with my issue."

He picked up the phone and dialed. He spoke quietly into the receiver, his hand over it to keep undesirables from hearing, like the African American in a too-small Armani suit with a pompous name standing in front of him.

"Yes, I understand," he whispered into the phone. "He originally asked to see Mr. Betts. Sure. Black guy about fifty, dressed in stolen clothes. Yes, I understand."

He hung up. "Ms. Langhari is not in."

I wanted to pull the guy down off his pedestal and put the boot to him. "That was a long phone call with someone who isn't in."

"Get out, before I come down there and boot your raggedy ass out the door."

So much for Dad's ploy. I'd given it a go. I pulled one of my Smith and Wesson .357s and pointed at his freckled forehead. His eyes went wide, his mouth to a small O.

"Call her back and tell her to come down or I'm gonna air-condition your brainpan."

He fumbled with the phone and dialed. "Yes, ma'am, it's Jenks again. He's pulled a gun on me and it's pointed right at my face. Yes, ma'am." He hung up. "She said she's on her way down."

We waited. Sweat broke out on my forehead. I still had a little residual from that emotional issue hanging on like a bad ague. This was one of those awkward moments where neither party had much to say to each other, a fat, uncomfortable pause. I said, "And this suit wasn't stolen. In fact, it's all the rage."

He shrugged. "If you say so."

I gritted my teeth, the anger flushing out that last bit of fear residue. "Yes, I say so." I cocked the gun. "Tell me it's a very nice suit and you wished you had one."

He swallowed hard. "That's a very nice—"

The elevator door opened and out stepped Ms. Aimee Langhari, taller than I remembered, clad in a shiny silk dress, blood-red with Asian landmarks outlined in colorful thread—the Great Wall, the terra-cotta warriors, and the Forbidden City.

She moved with feminine ease, the dress a sheath that gently massaged her curves. Her skin smooth and perfect; the bright red lipstick made her lips lush and desirable and matched the color of her long fingernails. Her dark almond eyes held mine.

"The gun is not necessary, Mr. Johnson. Thank you, Jenks, and I'd appreciate it if you did not alert the police. I have this situation in hand. Come, Mr. Johnson, let's get a coffee."

She didn't wait for me to answer and headed toward the door, the dress alive the way it glided over her skin, the rise and fall of her bottom.

Jenks came down and hurried to open the front door, his eyes on Langhari even though I'd just aimed a gun at his forehead.

Sex has that effect, shutting down all common sense.

The whoosh from the door wafted her scent into her wake, sweet jasmine.

Out on the sidewalk heading south, she didn't turn to see if I followed. I put the gun away under my suit coat and caught up to her. "You know my name?"

She turned with a haughty expression and didn't answer. She had all the information, all the power, and wasn't going to turn loose with it if she didn't have to. I wanted to know about her relationship with Layla and what she knew about Sonny. I thought I knew but needed her to tell me.

We came to the door to the Coffee Hut; she waited for me to open it for her. She had two chopsticks in her hair holding a tight bun, enough hair that when released it had to hang down to her ass. Just like Layla's, jet black with a sheen that reflected any and all light.

I opened the door.

She hesitated and slinked past closer than she needed to, the air between us alive with unseen electricity, an unseen promise.

She knew exactly what she was doing, playing a much better game. I needed something to shake her up. She had to be Johnny Ef's organ grinder monkey. She possessed all the information about his operation, including where he held Sonny.

It was the only thing that made any sense. All I had to do was figure a way to get her to tell me.

Simple.

Drago had suggested that he could get the information if left alone with her for five minutes and a piece of rebar. I told him we would not resort to those tactics. He'd muttered back, "Not yet, anyway."

The Coffee Hut's motif mirrored a day at the beach, with posters of Hawaii on the walls, a red-striped sun umbrella suspended from the ceiling, and colorful beach towels framed on the walls. On the counters sat tikis and plastic leis, tiny surfboards, outrigger canoes—too much kitsch. Less would've been more.

At the counter she ordered an organic tea with almond milk and walked away, expecting me to pay. I ordered a seven-dollar coffee, black, and met her with the drinks at the high-top table by the window, the same one where she'd sat with Layla.

The glass window left me too vulnerable to the street and caused the back of my neck to itch.

Suspended from the ceiling, a television silently played the news from an LA station.

She added one packet of raw sugar and stirred while staring into my eyes.

I couldn't help it, I squirmed. I said, "What is your relationship with Layla?"

She continued to stare, took a dainty sip from her cup, and said nothing.

Outside, cars whisked past on the wide boulevard, and pedestrians walked by the window.

I sat on that high stool, an animal on display in a zoo, or an art exhibit in a posh contemporary museum, call it, The Death of a Foolish Man.

I said, "You know my name, which means Layla told you." I didn't want to give up that we'd tailed Layla to this exact location.

She sipped again and watched me. She set the cup down. "I met her here at university. We took abnormal psych together and hit it off. There is nothing odd or untoward about our relationship, we are simply good friends. She told me how thuggish you could be and to be prepared for you, as she put it, 'sticking your brutish nose into my business.'"

Langhari had said "at university" the way people said it in Europe.

"We just want Sonny back and we'll leave you alone."

A small smile crept across her face. "What in the world makes you think I would have that nice young woman's child?" Her smile completely transformed her face and turned her into a radiant woman who could conquer entire countries including the Troy of old.

"You work for Johnny Ef and he took Sonny. Give him back and we'll go away."

"I'm sorry, you have been misinformed. I don't know any Johnny Ef."

"How do you support yourself? How do you afford to live at a place like that condo? It has to be two and a half to three million-dollars?"

"That's none of your business, and you're turning into a nuisance."

Oh, and a black man in a too-small Armani suit holding a gun on the deskman wasn't?

"What I don't understand," I said, "is a woman of your . . . ah, standing, why a hundred-thousand-dollar ransom? It doesn't make sense."

"If you must know more about me, I'll tell you. My family back in Bombay owns a billion-dollar communications company. I am here going to school without the need of anyone's financial assistance. Especially from this . . . this man you call Johnny Ef."

"You're a little old to be going to school." She looked to be about thirty.

"Now you've turned tiresome and boring. I agreed to speak to you out of courtesy to my friend Layla. If you continue to harass me or my friend Layla, I'll be forced to notify the authorities."

I remembered the way Layla looked at Langhari the last time the two sat at the same high-top table by the window, the way they touched hands. "Are you two lovers?"

Her mouth went from a straight line to a little curved smile on one side, her eyes coy.

"Are you asking out of some perverted personal interest? I should take offense at the question, but since coming to LA, I have far too often come across men like you."

Maybe I was wrong about this woman. Maybe she was exactly what she appeared, a beautiful, spoiled trust-funder living in LA trying to push back encroaching age by hanging out with the younger set.

Someone like Layla, an innocent young woman, could easily fall in love with her, or what she represents: mystery, intrigue, beauty. Or was that just what I wanted to believe? That I really didn't want a woman like Langhari to be wrapped up in the ugly mess back at the Comstock.

She wasn't going to budge, and I didn't have anything to use, no leverage to make her tell me.

Up on the television screen, a woman reporter again stood in front of another burning mansion in Beverly Hills. The scrolling banner underneath said, *Three more firebomb arsons of expensive houses for sale. Police fear domestic terrorism.*

I'd told Drago to lay off the belly bombs and to stay in the room keeping an eye on Layla. He wasn't one to stay in one place when he had a mission.

Aimee Langhari followed my eyes and caught the news story. When she turned back to me, her calm demeanor shifted to anger, her face flushing with color.

"Aha." I pointed at her. "Gotcha. You almost had me. I'm getting too old for all this spy vs. spy shit."

She hissed. "You have no idea what you're messing with . . . who you're messing with."

"Oh? I thought you didn't know Johnny Ef? Those are his houses."

She should've been angrier about the take-down of her operation on 117th and Alabama, but that could be viewed as a minor setback in comparison. They could get another place up and running in a couple of days, if not sooner. Burning down money already laundered, now that hurt all the way down to the bone.

She leaned in over the table. "You're a damn fool. You've set in motion your own violent death. Not only yours but all your loved ones as well. There's nothing anyone can do to stop it. Not now. You're a sorry excuse of a man and—"

CHAPTER FORTY-TWO

IN THE COFFEE Hut my hand all on its own shot out and grabbed the lovely woman around the throat. Her skin soft and supple.

I squeezed. No one threatened my family. No one.

She slipped off the stool as I forced her up against the window, lifting her from her feet. From outside on the street it would look as if she had levitated.

She was accustomed to a violent life and didn't give in easily. She clawed at my arm with long nails lacquered red. When that didn't work, she slapped my face hard, sending stinging needles shooting into nerve endings and making my eyes water.

And still I held on, her eyes going from confident to scared, bulging.

People on the sidewalk on the other side of the window continued on by, too wrapped up in their own lives to see the real world.

The customers in the coffee shop, though, yelped and murmured. Then someone yelled, "I'm calling 911. Leave her alone."

Two men, out of place for the area, dressed in outlaw motorcycle garb, black leather with chrome zippers, and dirty denim pants, their hair long and greasy, walked in. Each wore a tattoo on his neck exclusive to the Celtic Cross Syndicate, a Celtic cross with *CCS* underneath. They stood still, their eyes glassy from meth as they quickly scanned the room.

Their eyes automatically came around to me, their hands going under their denim cuts to hidden handguns.

Langhari had called in support before she came downstairs to meet me at the Shimbuto, told them where we'd be, and then walked me right over to the killing ground.

I let her go.

She slid back to stand on the floor, bent at the waist, choking and coughing, her face turning back to its regular color. She held up her hand and stopped the two outlaw bikers from advancing. She wanted to get out of the Coffee Hut before the mayhem started so she wouldn't in any way be implicated in the sensational murder of a wanted fugitive.

Two more bikers came in the other door, cutting off any hope of escape. I had two guns, .357s, but against four unscrupulous men, I was still outgunned. The Coffee Hut was filled with college students and yuppies who would get in the way of the approaching violence as it blossomed outward. I wouldn't be a part of innocents getting hurt, not in order to save my own skin.

Langhari held her throat with both hands. She regained her voice, which came out in a rasp. "You're not some kind of invincible violent man like Layla described. You're just a silly old man who was brought here under the misconception that you could help. You're a fool. And a dead fool at that."

I'd set my cell on the table when I sat down just like anyone would. Now I pushed the "Call" button. But there hadn't been the need. Helen Hellinger was close enough to see the trap crimp down on me. Two black-and-white sheriff patrol cars, their overhead red and blue lights flashing, zoomed down the street, made a U-turn, and parked in front of the Coffee Hut. The four deputies jumped out, guns drawn.

The bikers chose to live and fight another day. They tossed their guns on the floor, obscuring their possession for the court case. They put their hands on top of their heads.

When it came to outlaw motorcycle gang members, especially ones who possessed guns, deputies tended to shoot first and ask questions later. An outdated cliché, when in reality it came down to shoot first and fill out all the paperwork later; no other questions needed.

The four deputies were from the elite SEB unit, Special Enforcement Bureau, with perfect uniforms and polished leather, Marine haircuts high and tight. They rushed the coffee shop and took the bikers into custody, recovering their tossed firearms all within seconds of arrival. Helen came in the side door dressed in black slacks and a white long-sleeve blouse. Her sheriff's star clipped to her belt, her gun in a shoulder holster.

She came up to the high-top table. "Ms. Aimee Langhari, you're under arrest. Please put your hands behind your back."

"For what? I've done nothing wrong."

Helen looked at me, waiting for me to comment. I said, "You're under arrest for mopery."

"Mopery, what kind of crime is that?"

Helen smiled. "It's a sandwich in both pockets refusing to eat."

"That's ridiculous, there's no such law. That doesn't even make sense. You'll hear from my attorney. What about him? This is Bruno Johnson. He has warrants out for his arrest for murder. He's a murderer."

"You're mistaken. I know this man—he's in commercial construction and his name's Wentworth, Mr. Wilbur Wentworth IV."

Langhari took in a deep breath and composed herself. "Looks like you won this one, Johnson. You won't be so lucky next time."

She looked at Helen. "Did you know he's the one burning down all those nice houses in Beverly Hills and Brentwood?"

I'd not told Helen about the houses. Her head turned a little too fast to look at me, at my eyes.

"Ah," Langhari said. "Looks like that was something your cop friend here didn't know." Langhari winked at me. "See you next time, cowboy." Helen took her by the arm and escorted her out.

My hands shook. That never used to happen. I wanted my old life back. I exited the Coffee Hut as all the cop cars with the bikers, along with Helen's plain-wrapped car, took off from the curb.

CHAPTER FORTY-THREE

I WALKED THE street for several blocks to calm down, then took two different Ubers for the ride back to the Summerset Hotel, walking several blocks each time to further throw off any manhunt.

I unlocked the second-floor hotel-room door and found Waldo waiting just inside on alert. He greeted me with a growl. "Oh, so we're back to that, are we? What did I do this time to make you mad? What are you doing over here? You're supposed to be guarding Layla."

I took a step deeper into the room and closed the door behind me, stunned at what I had walked into. Waldo had sensed the intimate situation and had been protecting his master.

Drago sat on an ottoman with his shirt off. He was a sight to behold with muscle and fat and all of those tattoos intermingled with a road map of ropy scars.

Every inch of skin was covered in white supremacist and outlaw biker tattoos that all came from a previous life, a life he regretted and now tried his best to rectify in his personal crusade to squash any and all biker gangs. For his trouble, all the different gangs had put a substantial price on his head. But no one came looking; his reputation was too fierce. And Drago knew how to hide in plain sight. Not hiding really, he didn't care if they found him. "Let 'em come," he'd say. "Best job I ever had."

Since the incident at the Comstock, I hadn't really seen him. I hadn't bothered enough to care about him, the sure sign of a grade-A heel.

I had wrongfully assumed the blood belonged to the suspects' injuries inflicted with the rebar.

My good friend Drago had been brutalized.

The pervs acting as rats fleeing a sinking ship had rat-packed him. A knife slash across his back gaped like an upside-down smile, one drooling, leaking blood at the corner that ran down to the top of his pants. A lot of blood. The wicked wound only had a couple of inches left to close. Too many sutures to count at first glance. The cut transected the tattoo of a big-breasted, topless Viking woman wielding a double-headed battle ax, and a big biker with a bandana across his forehead pointing a double-barreled shotgun.

Layla, who was supposed to be across the way in the other hotel room, sat on the edge of the coffee table sewing up the gash. She'd had plenty of impromptu medical experience growing up with her doctor father.

Her face slick with tears, she cried as she sewed. She turned to see me come in.

"You know, you're a real bastard for letting them do this to him. For letting him go this long without medical attention. Look at him. Just look at him!

"He should've been stitched up right after it happened, not hours later." She wasn't faking the sorrow and was truly upset. She did care for Drago.

I shouldn't have found that odd, but I did.

I took a closer look. He had three bumps on his bald pate, two of no consequence. The third one, large as a goose egg, required professional medical attention. He could have an interior bleed.

I hadn't seen him since the incident and when I did he'd put on a hat after getting cleaned up. His arms and hands had a myriad of scratches and bruises. But with all those injuries combined, what worried me the most was the deep bite mark on his shoulder.

One of the rats had jumped on his back and sunk his teeth in. A human bite was the worst for infections and could easily lead to sepsis and death.

I'd seen a deputy bit on the web of his hand by a coke whore; his hand blew up to the size of a catcher's mitt and he almost lost it.

"Ah, man, Drago, why didn't you say something?" I came closer, sat on the couch, and put my hand on his leg. He flinched. He didn't like that at all.

"About what? This is all about nothin'. I've been hurt worse mowin' my yard."

He didn't have any grass. He lived in a warehouse up in Cajon Pass in San Bernardino with dirt and weeds surrounding the five-acre property. All of it booby-trapped.

Layla continued to sob as she finished suturing and applied a bandage. She came around and put her hands on his cheeks. She sniffled. "You got this way because you're helping me get Sonny back. I won't forget it. I promise I'll make it up to you." She tenderly kissed his lips.

Drago swallowed hard, overwhelmed, the unfamiliar emotions plain on his face. He turned away, so no one could see. He said, "Hey, bro." His voice caught. "Would you take Waldo out? He needs to do his business."

"Sure," I said. I stood and moved away.

He stood and picked Layla up. In his arms she looked more like a large doll with perfect skin and makeup and beautiful hair. She rested her head against his shoulder, her forehead touching his chin. Her one hand still gently rested on his cheek. He said, "We can finish this later." He carried her into the bedroom and eased the door closed.

Seeing Drago's tender, loving care for Layla made me stop and take stock in the way Drago viewed life, his crusade, his violent lifestyle. Sad as it seemed, I had never imagined him possessing the simple ability to ever grow old.

CHAPTER FORTY-FOUR

IN THE ROOM at the Summerset, I took the long blue nylon leash off the counter and bent down to hook it to Waldo's collar. He growled. "Okay, take it easy. I was only trying to follow the law."

I opened the door and we slipped out to leave Drago and Layla alone. The Summerset welcomed pets, so Waldo wasn't as much of an outlaw. The elevator smelled of pet urine. When we strolled through the lobby, the clerk in thick black-framed glasses behind smeared bullet-resistant polycarbonate didn't even look up from his antique *Playboy*, the whole scene a time-travel throwback to a bad seventies movie.

Outside, the night air had cooled and thickened with moisture that rolled in from the beach. High above, the flyover for the Harbor Freeway, with its constant roar from cars and large semis, created a constant reminder of the tons of steel, black rubber, and concrete that had no business being so close to humans stacked in a decaying hotel. The whole place one good Southern California shake away from total disaster.

Just where did my obligation to Aleck and Alisa end? Was I supposed to intervene in Layla's relationship with Drago? A relationship that was doomed from the start? How could it work, her world and his?

I'd talked with Drago about finding a serious relationship, hoping that if he found someone, he'd find a path out of the violent life he'd chosen. At the time he'd looked at me and gave a classic Drago response that had nothing to do with my question; he'd said, "You know, humans are the only beasts that make love face-to-face."

The comment yet again proved his mind spun far out ahead, moving up and down on different planes playing tri-level chess in every part of his life.

I talked with Waldo as we walked in the bad part of town, past a check-cashing shop, two dive bars, and a topless girly joint called the Lusty Muff, the sidewalk grimy and littered with cigarette butts, empty Ziploc baggies, and discarded gum flattened out into black coins of different denominations resembling a galaxy of dark stars. The greasy concrete had been abused and was long past a good steam cleaning; it would have to be demolished, started over in order to wring out all the sorrow and grief.

Waldo didn't answer, somehow knowing I just needed to get a few things off my chest. The lower strata of humanity, the B girls, the dope dealers and petty thieves on the prod, moved out of his way.

"Do you really think Layla loves Drago? I mean talk about mismatches. And don't you tell him I said anything; he doesn't like anyone talking behind his back."

Waldo turned his head up to look at me. I couldn't read his expression, whether he agreed or not.

"If it's not some kind of ploy and she does love him, then I misread the relationship between her and Langhari. In any case I need to sit that girl down and have a heart-to-heart. She knows a lot more than she's telling. You know what I'm saying here? Hey, she took you over to Langhari's on her way down here. You stopped over at the penthouse apartment, right? What'd you think about it? What'd it look like inside? Real nice, I bet."

This time he didn't even bother to look up at me. He growled at a skeevy heroin hype who didn't move far enough away as we passed.

My phone buzzed in my pocket. I answered it.

"Hey, Dad," I said, "how are you doing?" Talking to him automatically brought on a warm glow. I put my hand over the phone and said to Waldo, "It's Dad."

"Just thought I'd call, tell you I made it to Las Vegas okay. This place, I'm tellin' you, Son, it's really something else. Who would've thought this . . . this kind of blight that promotes every human vice could sprout up in the middle of a sand pile? All the lights, the degradation. It ought to be illegal what goes on here, the women, the gambling, the smoking, and drinking, no wonder this country is going to heck in a handbasket."

Now *there* was the dad that I knew and loved. Not someone who happily went along with his demented ex-wife on her headlong rush to bankrupt him.

I chuckled into the phone. "I know, Dad, I've been there. Be sure to take advantage of the buffets. You could stand to put on a few pounds."

"Keno. They even want you gambling while you're eating. If a person isn't corrupted when they get here, they will be by the time they leave."

I shifted my tone. "How's Bea doing?"

His voice turned animated. "She's up a hundred thousand—can you believe it. A hundred thousand dollars?"

I slowed walking and stopped altogether. "Dad, that's great, really it is, but the way Vegas works, they'll give you free meals, and comp you a nice hotel suite so you'll stay and not walk out the door with their money and—"

"Oh, they've already done that. You ought to see the room they put us in, it's five or six times the size of our old house on Nord. Three bedrooms, a huge master bath with everything marble, and a bathtub the size of a small pool. The floor is heated, can you believe that? And the view—"

"Dad. Dad, listen. You have to get Bea to leave, walk away from the tables before she gives it all back."

"Why would she do that? She's on a hot streak. That's what she calls it. She said she's riding the wave. Isn't that cute? Riding the wave? And besides, she hasn't hit her goal. She has to hit her goal before we can leave. That's why we're here in the first place."

I could picture him standing in the casino turning in a slow circle marveling at all the people, the cigarette smoke, a fog bank hanging in the air, everyone with a sweaty free drink in their hands, handing over their money to the casino in games with odds heavily favored by the house.

My phone beeped. Helen was calling. I ignored it.

Dad said, "I can't believe all the money these casinos must take in. After seeing the size of these places, all the opulence, do people really think these places are losing money? That they have a chance at all of coming away winners? It's knucklehead logic."

What a contradiction. I wanted to ask him why he didn't apply this correct theory to Bea.

Waldo growled; he wanted to continue the stroll. I moved on down the sidewalk.

Dad said, "The families this place must ruin every day. The loss of livelihood, money that could be used to help their children thrive; better housing, better food, better education. The children should come first. It's really sad. Son, Bea's waving at me. I have to go. We'll be home as soon as she hits her goal. Love you. Bye."

"Wait, what's her goal?" But he'd clicked off. Why the hell did she *have* a goal? Or is that just something she'd told him to allow her to scratch that gambling itch a little harder? I texted him the address to the Summerset with the room number, told him I loved him, and then hit the redial for Helen.

"Bruno, are you really torching those houses?" She'd cut right to it as soon as she answered.

I stopped and put my back to the wall of a coin laundry, so I could watch the people moving by. Waldo sat next to my leg, his head moving with each person that came close, too close, and he let out a little growl. Closer yet and they'd get mauled.

"The houses belong to Johnny Ef. We're trying to motivate him to give up Sonny."

"Who's Sonny?"

I forgot that I hadn't filled her in on why I'd come up north. I started at the beginning and told her all of it. When I finished she said, "Burn 'em all down. I'll help you."

"Take it easy. It hasn't worked so far. I think we have to change tactics."

"You let me know if I can do anything more to help."

"I will, and thanks for the backup at the Coffee Hut."

"Three out of the four of those thugs are on parole. We violated their parole. Along with the additional charge for the guns, they won't see daylight for three to five."

"Excellent."

"The fourth one bailed out before we got the paperwork finished. What are you going to do about Sonny?"

"Do you really want to know?"

"I'm in it now, so yeah."

"We tried taking off his money flow and we tried burning down his assets."

"So, now you're going to go at him head-on? That's all you got left."

"Unless you have another idea I'm missing?"

"He's got a big organization and it's just you and Drago. Let me in."

"I'm not gonna do it. You think of anything though, something we missed, you give me a call. Oh, hey, did you run Langhari for her history?"

"We couldn't hold her. I plugged her prints into Interpol and I'm waiting on the return. I cited her out. I'm about to do a deep dive on her background. So far, the only thing I can find only goes back seven years. I'll get back to you. You call me if you need backup."

"I will. Thanks, Helen."

"Keep your head down."

It was something cops said to one another and caused a pang of yearning to be a cop again, the comradery, the brotherhood, something I sorely missed. The hunt and the satisfaction of coloring within the lines while putting away bad guys.

She clicked off.

On the Sonny thing, I'd gone too long without all the pieces to the puzzle. I needed a serious come-to-Jesus sit-down with Layla, get her to tell the truth about what was really going on.

CHAPTER FORTY-FIVE

I WAS STRETCHED out on the couch when the sun woke me as it sliced through the slit in the curtains—or it could've been Waldo licking my naked big toe. He needed to go out and do his business. I struggled into a sitting position and then up to my feet, old bones creaking and popping.

The bedroom door stood ajar.

I tried not to peek in as I passed and couldn't help myself.

Empty.

A walrus must've thrashed about in the bed, the blankets and sheets in twisted disarray, the mattress broken down at one corner. What kind of activity and weight did it take to break down the corner to a mattress and box springs?

Yikes.

The bathroom door off the bedroom opened and steam billowed out. I jumped from the doorway and moved to the kitchenette to put on some coffee, found a pot already made and half-empty. I slept too hard and hadn't heard a thing.

With the condition of that mattress, maybe that was a good thing.

I poured a cup and added six packets of sugar and six of powdered cream, a poor man's breakfast.

The light in the room dimmed. Drago appeared from the bedroom, his face flushed and beaded with sweat from a hot shower. "Hey, old hoss, you got a cup of joe for me?"

I poured him one. He took it, slurped some, and headed for the door, Waldo at his side. "I'm gonna take the little man here out to do his business, be right back."

"Drago?"

"Yeah, bro."

"I thought we talked about not doing any more houses?"

"I know. I didn't."

"Three more went down last night?"

He shrugged, sipped. "Those are part of the first group. I didn't do any more."

"They were on timers. That gonna be a problem?"

"No, I guess not."

I hadn't asked Drago direct enough questions when we talked about not burning any more houses. With Drago, if you didn't ask, he wouldn't volunteer information—something he practiced full-time in case he was ever arrested and questioned by law enforcement.

Or by bikers under duress, knives, fingernails pulled, electricity, waterboards, and acetylene torches. Though, I could never imagine Drago being captured by bikers—he would be like a giant dead man's switch on a bomb. You try and take him down, he'll just go nuclear and crater everyone around him.

Headed out of the hotel room, he stopped, reached on top of the refrigerator, took down a length of rebar, and stuck it up his sleeve. After he walked out the door, the room seemed to open up with more light and square footage.

The door opened again, and as if he'd read my thoughts, Drago said, "Dude, use the back door when you come and go from the hotel."

"Why?" I asked the direct question this time.

He'd started to close the door, stuck his head in a little. "'Cause, the Lusty Muff is owned by the CCS. It's their HQ."

He closed the door before I could protest. He'd rented a room two doors down from a Celtic Cross Syndicate property?

Was he crazy?

No, that was just Drago. He didn't experience fear like normal folks. And the idea of having your enemy close at hand somehow seemed logical to him.

I should've asked him where Layla was—he shouldn't let her go out on her own, more so now with the CCS so close.

I sat on the couch and drank my coffee.

Layla startled me.

She appeared out of nowhere clad in a white fluffy robe and sat on the couch a little too close, her long black hair wet, a towel in both her hands trying to wring out the water, her face flushed from wet heat. I continuedly reminded myself that she grew up in Costa Rica, a people who related easily to others in a friendly manner where personal space wasn't an issue like with Americans.

My mind all on its own flitted to the shower, how could they both fit?

I shook it off. I didn't need those kinds of images chasing me around all day.

She sat less than a foot away. Moist heat from her body prickled the skin on my arm. She stared at me with those dark eyes, her hands working at drying her hair.

I didn't have much time. Drago wouldn't be gone long. I didn't want him defending her if I had to push a little for the truth.

"I spoke with Aimee last night."

Layla stopped drying her hair. "Is that right? What did she say?"

She didn't ask how I'd found Aimee Langhari.

Hers a general question in reply, a good interrogator's primary weapon. I didn't want her working me for information when I had to be in control. "What exactly is your relationship with her?"

She broke eye contact and looked away. "I met her in my abnormal psych class. She's nice. We really hit it off. How did you come to meet her?"

"Look, Layla, you need to quit messing around. No more games. Aimee works for Johnny Ef. You know it and I know it. What does she have to do with Sonny?"

She got up and tried to walk away. I grabbed her arm and pulled her back down. Her hands went to the white robe to hold it together. She stared at me. She was trying to figure out what to say. Her answer regarding how she met Aimee was a little too pat, as if they'd both practiced it ahead of time to get the same lie just right.

Her tone turned a little terse. "What exactly are you asking? What are you implying?"

"Tell me about the money."

"The money?"

"The ransom."

"What are you talking about? My mother handed the money over to Johnny and Johnny let me go. That's how kidnappings work. He was holding me against my will. He wanted the money."

I squeezed her arm.

"Ouch, you're hurting me."

"A hundred thousand dollars is nothing to a man like Johnny Ef."

"His name's Johnny Fillmore—he doesn't like Johnny Ef."

I shook her arm. "Stop it. Tell me."

She looked to the hotel room door. "Where's Karl? He should be back."

"He's not going to help you with this. You've been lying to us."

Her head whipped around; her eyes alive with a dark fire. "No, you're right, that little bit of money is nothing to him but that's all my parents had that was liquid. He takes what he can get when he can get it. That's what he does. That's what he did with me." Her voice caught. She tightened her grip on the robe. "*He took me.*"

Tears filled her eyes. I almost fell for the act until I remembered how she'd been holding back the information about the Comstock. That should've been the first thing she told us when the whole thing started.

"You've been to the Comstock; you knew about the freeway being close to the fifth floor. You knew too many details."

"No, I haven't been there. Someone told me about it."

"You're lying. If you want Sonny back, you quit lying right now."

"Okay! Okay, I've been there. I've been there. Are you happy now?"

"Why did you lie about it?"

She looked away. Her voice came out in a whisper. "Because I . . . was ashamed."

"Tell me."

"I'm ashamed I knew about what goes on there and did nothing about it. All those poor people. I didn't grow up in that kind of world. I didn't know places like that existed."

Tears filled her eyes and rolled down her cheeks. I did feel sorry for her, couldn't help it.

The hotel room door opened. Waldo and Drago entered.

"Karl?" She jumped up and ran to him. "Oh, Karl?" She jumped into his arms.

"What's going on? What'd you do to Layla?"

The rebar slipped out of his sleeve and into his hand.

CHAPTER FORTY-SIX

I HELD UP both hands as I stood. "Now hold on, Drago. Just wait a minute and listen before you start swinging that iron."

Waldo gave a loud bark that came out more of a roar. He charged me. He stopped short, and if given the go-ahead, stood ready in easy striking range of my crotch.

Drago took two long steps toward me, vengeance in his eyes. He stopped. He held Layla up with one arm pinning her to the side of his chest.

I said, "She was just telling me about the Comstock and how she's been there before."

I threw her under the bus. A better tactic than getting a piece of iron upside the head. The physical pain wouldn't have been as bad as the violent blow coming from a good friend.

He froze and set her down. She stood looking up at him. Her size in comparison to his reminded me of a cartoon a deputy posted on the corkboard in the narco office that depicted a giant eagle swooping down on a tiny field mouse, the mouse standing tall giving the middle finger to the eagle. The caption read: "One last act of defiance."

Layla had that kind of steel in her backbone.

"That's true," she said. "I've been there. I'm not proud of it."

Drago's expression shifted from anger to confusion. "In what capacity? I mean, why did you go there?"

He was worried she'd been a victim, an occupant of one of the rooms on the upper floors, someone who entertained men. Damaged goods in dire need of psychological help.

She reached out and took hold of his big hand. She dropped her chin and moved a step closer, her eyes growing larger if that were possible.

"I told you about Johnny Ef, about what he did to me."

"No, you didn't. What did he do to you?"

"Hold on," I yelled. "Stop talking, Layla." She was about to light the fuse to an unstoppable laser-guided missile.

"Don't talk to her like that. Layla, tell me."

I said louder this time, "Johnny . . . you know slick-talking Johnny. He wormed his way into her heart and . . ."

Layla started to talk over me. I held up my hand. "Wait. If you care anything for Drago—"

Drago shoved me. I fell back flat onto the couch. Waldo moved in, his muzzle next to my face, a low rumble coming from deep in his chest.

Layla hesitated, looked at me then back at Drago. "It's nothing. It's just like I told you, Sonny is Johnny's son, that's why he won't let me have him. He won't let me anywhere near him. He won't tell me where he is."

In a half-whisper I desperately said to her, "You're doing it again."

She reached up on tiptoes.

Drago bent down.

She took hold of his ear and pulled him down the rest of the way to kiss him on the lips. A gentle, long kiss that even I could mistake as sincere.

The Beauty knew how to control the Beast.

She turned to face me with a smug little smile Drago couldn't see. Drago put his arm around her. She was using him as her own personal weapon. She'd been around Johnny Ef too long, and the street had corrupted her beyond repair.

All the biker gangs in Southern California couldn't take down Karl Drago, but a cute, hundred-pound Costa Rican girl with black hair down to her ass could.

I asked her, "Who has the hundred thousand dollars your mom paid to get you out of hock?"

"Johnny does. Why would you ask that? Karl, why would he ask me that?"

Drago looked me hard in the eyes, then looked down at her and said, "Because Johnny wouldn't touch any money like that; he'd have one of his cutouts handle it—this Aimee Langhari or Ennis Freemantle."

"No." Layla shook her head. "Not Aimee. She's not involved in this. She's my friend."

I had to step delicately and carefully word what I said next. Layla held her finger on the trigger and could fire Drago off on a violent mission of blood and bone.

"Last night when I came in and you were doctoring Karl, I'd just come from a meet with Langhari."

I waited a moment to let that sink in. "She set me up to be taken down by four CCS members."

Drago's jaw muscle bulged as he ground his molars.

"No. No," Layla said. "That's not true. She's my friend. She wouldn't do that, she's not involved. She has nothing to do with this. She's a student like me at University. Karl, she's my friend."

Drago ignored her and asked me, "What happened?"

"Helen swooped those four assholes, booked three for parole violations, and the fourth one bailed on a gun charge. She took Langhari in but couldn't hold her. She's out."

He gently pushed Layla away and shoved the rebar back up his sleeve. "I think it's time we gave Ms. Langhari a visit."

Layla took Drago's hand in both of hers and yanked. "No, I won't have it. She's a friend. I don't believe she did what Bruno said she did."

"Are you calling my friend a liar?"

They both stood still and took a moment to think it through.

"Karl, honey, can I talk to you in the bedroom, alone? Just for a minute that's all, just a quick sec?"

Now Drago looked torn, unsure what to do with a little Bruno on one shoulder whispering in his ear and Layla with her big brown eyes that worked on him like a tractor beam sitting on his other shoulder. She won out.

He said, "Okay, babe. Bruno, I'll be right back. Wait right there."

"Hey, ah, buddy, could you call Waldo off?"

Drago stopped at the bedroom door. "No, I don't think so. I think you need a few minutes to think about how you were talking to my girl."

He said one word in German. Waldo growled and moved a few inches closer to my face with his torturous halitosis.

The bedroom door eased closed. There wouldn't be a lot of talking going on in there. She was probably going to affix a ring in his nose to guide him around. I didn't have room to talk. When Marie said jump, I was already in the air.

"Hey, Waldo, how about we go out and get a couple of Whoppers with extra cheese, huh? Whattaya say?"

He growled.

"A strawberry shake?"

Another growl. He couldn't be bribed. Just my luck, a dog with integrity.

"Fine."

The bedroom door didn't open for forty minutes, until Drago finally trudged out headed for the hotel room door. "Come on."

I hadn't moved a muscle and had a kink in my neck. Waldo pulled off and headed over to catch up. I stood and hurried behind the dog, which shouldn't have been the pecking order.

Drago turned at the door and said, "You stay and keep an eye on her."

For one terrible second, I thought he was talking to me. Then he gave the same command in German to Waldo.

Waldo actually shuddered as if his body wanted to stay as ordered and his mind wanted to come along with us. Drago started to close the door. Waldo let out a little whine, the first I'd ever heard uttered by him. He didn't want to stay with the Ice Princess. Even after forty minutes of being stared down with fetid dog breath in my face, I still felt sorry for him.

In the hall, headed for the stairs that led down, I caught up to Drago's long stride. "Where are we going?"

His head jerked around. "To throw this Langhari broad on the grill, get her to tell us what the hell's going on."

"Huh, I did not see that comin'."

CHAPTER FORTY-SEVEN

DRAGO GUIDED US out the back door into the parking lot and over to a brand-new one-ton dually truck, black with red pinstripes and paper plates, a vehicle he must've leased with fake ID and credit. The new-car-interior smell hit me as soon as I opened the door, and when I closed it the air pressure worked on the ears.

Funny how a person became accustomed to soured strawberry shake mixed with dog smell. I buckled up, Drago didn't. He didn't believe in safety belts, said they were for those who didn't know when they were going to die.

He had not said a word on the walk to the truck. He started up, put it in drive, and maneuvered out onto the street, sweat still beaded on his bald pate. I was worried about him. I had never seen him conflicted, never seen him try to balance his world with a woman in the mix.

I finally said, "We going to talk about this, partner?"

He said nothing.

The crowded streets had thinned after all the eight-to-five folks made it to their place of toil; three or four hours of work, an hour lunch, four hours more, then the long traffic-filled trudge home, dinner, a glass of wine or four, bed, then start over the next day.

Drago pulled down the sun visor and drew out a fat marijuana cigarette from the inside flap. He lit it and took a long toke.

Drago never used drugs. He stuck his hand out to offer me the fattie. I took it, rolled my window down, and tossed it.

He sat back against the door, trying to get a better look at me as if I'd lost my mind.

"Pay attention to the road," I said. "What's the matter with you? You don't smoke weed."

He went back to driving.

More silence.

That girl had worked like some kind of galactic acid on my friend, eating away at him from the inside out.

"You know," I said, "I'm worried about you, big man. You're not yourself."

He nodded and said nothing.

I said, "I'd never talk against your girl, you know that, right? I think it's great that you've found someone. Just . . . Just be careful, okay?"

This time he didn't even nod.

Halfway to the Shimbuto, his eyes still on the street, he said, "You know I went to the grocery the other day, thought I'd cook me some turkey."

"That right?"

He still didn't look at me. "I get home and find that the turkey is boneless. Can you believe it, a boneless turkey?"

"What?"

"How do you think those turkeys hold up their little heads to eat if they don't have any bones? They strap them in a sling or something like that while they grow?"

He said it straight without cracking a smile and continued driving.

My big friend Drago was going to be okay.

He had a heart that could resist galactic acid.

My cell buzzed.

Marie.

The morning sky dimmed a little from guilt over going to the States without her direct knowledge. I should've been home with her and Tobias, or at the very least calling her every other hour to hear her voice.

I took out my wallet and from it the folded bindle with her lock of hair. I held it touching the hair between thumb and index finger. The softness, the color, conjured her smile, her beautiful eyes. What the hell was I doing up in the States chasing my tail?

"Hi, babe," I said, as cheerfully as I could.

The greeting was met with silence.

Then a sob leaked out. "I miss you, Bruno."

This wasn't the Marie I knew. The old Marie would've been holding back anger about me being in the States.

I closed my eyes tight and gripped the phone. She didn't deserve this. "I miss you too, more than you know."

I would've preferred the anger.

"I shouldn't call you like this. I know you wouldn't stay there any longer than you have to. You must be really busy. Please forgive me, it's the hormones, postpartum. You know, we talked about how it would change me for a while."

"No, it's okay. You call me anytime you need to. I'm sorry, *it has* been busy here."

Another sob and sniffle that tore my heart out.

"I called because of what's on the news . . . Is that you? I mean with those houses burning down? That apartment building, the Comstock?"

I fought back tears. I hated like hell to hurt her; her pain was my pain. I nodded and realized she couldn't see the nod and said, "Yes, we're trying to apply some pressure. So far it's not working."

"Ah, Bruno, really?" More tears. "Do the best you can. I won't bother you anymore."

"How's Tobias? I miss him something terrible."

"He's doing fine. Great really." Her tone shifted. "He misses his father."

"Hey, ah—" The words twisted on my tongue and wouldn't come out.

"What, Bruno? What's wrong?"

"No, wait, it's not like that, nothing's wrong."

"What then? Talk to me."

"There are three infants without a home. Maybe three, I don't know yet. Helen's working on finding their parents, but it's my guess the parents gave the kids up to . . . to satisfy their addic—" I couldn't finish the words that described something so vile.

Her tone shifted back to the strong Marie I knew so well. "You bring them home, Bruno. You don't even think about leaving them there. You hear me? You bring them home."

"I thought you might say that."

"We'll deal with the extra children just like we always have. Tobias can have some little brothers and sisters his own age to grow up with."

"Babe, you're a beautiful woman. I mean it. I won't be much longer, I promise. A couple of days at the most. That's only forty-eight hours. And I promise I'll call you more often."

"I can't wait to see you. You be safe and keep your head down. I love you."

"I love you too."

Drago pulled up and parked in the red zone in front of the Shimbuto. We couldn't stay there too long without being noticed.

"Babe, I have to go now. I'll call you. I promise."

I clicked off, sniffled, and swiped at my nose. I looked out the window at the Shimbuto.

"We need to finish this."

"I'm with you, bro. Let's get after it." He opened his door and rolled out into the street. I followed on my side. We would only have a few minutes to work on Langhari; security would call the cops on us. I was confident that just the sight of Drago would solicit the correct responses from her as to where Sonny was being kept. Then I could go home to Marie and Tobias.

I yanked open the door to the apartment building, and Drago entered with me behind him. The podium with the security guard stood empty. I went around to the back and found a heavyset black woman on the ground, half-propped against the wall. Blood from a head wound leaked down to her cheek, her neck, and to the light-blue uniform blouse. She opened her eyes, saw me, whimpered, and tried to inch away. I put my hand on her booted foot. "It's okay. We won't hurt you. What happened?"

Her eyes rolled up and closed. She was going into shock. "I'll call for paramedics, you hold on."

She didn't hear me.

Drago stood looking over my shoulder. He pointed at two buttons with labels on the counter's edge. One read "Elevators," the other, "Police."

The second one, marked "Police," was a panic button, a direct line to police dispatch. If the security woman, hurt and lying on the floor, had pushed that button the police would already be en route to the Shimbuto.

Drago said, "No time now, bro, we gotta roll outta here or deal with the blue bellies."

I wanted to get home to Marie. I didn't answer, pushed the button for the elevators, and headed over.

The elevator doors opened just as a black-and-white police cruiser skidded along the curb out front behind Drago's truck, trapping us inside the Shimbuto. Drago stepped in with me. The elevator bounced a little from the weight exchange. The doors took their sweet time closing. Drago said, "Looks like it's time to rock and roll."

He lowered his tone and sang—more to himself, humming and hitting every third or fourth word. "Through the desert . . . Demon . . . no rain . . . hat full of hate . . . the insane."

In violent, no-win situations, Drago tended toward the dramatic. When the odds crimped down on us, he'd start singing song quotes I never recognized.

I'd only heard his song quotes two other times in the past.

This was bad, really bad.

What the hell was I doing?

I should be at home with my wife and children.

Home with Tobias, my newborn son.

CHAPTER FORTY-EIGHT

THE ELEVATOR DOOR opened on the penthouse floor to a reek that permeated the air. I might not have recognized it had I not chased violence most of my life. When the body is threatened with imminent death, it naturally secretes hormones mixed with adrenaline and noradrenaline.

The metallic odor of blood.

This was the scent that belonged to the worst emotions: fear and regret and most of all a begrudged sorrow.

I started to step out of the elevator car. Drago grabbed my shoulder, pulled me back in, and went first, the iron already in his hand held down by his leg.

The door to Penthouse Three stood ajar, the dead quiet an insidious ugly thing warning all to run for their lives.

When death brushes by, it leaves something behind—something contagious.

Drago didn't hesitate. He bulled through the door, the rebar up and at the ready to bite into a skull. Eat those who didn't immediately yield.

The penthouse had windows across the entire front that looked across the wide boulevard to the Staples Arena. The interior was exactly how I imagined it: tall imitation Asian vases, Asian rugs, chrome, and black leather furniture, bamboo wall covering, and elegantly dressed geisha dolls trapped in glass cases.

To the left, a jutting wall had a mirror that reflected the view out the windows and gave the illusion of a more expansive space.

A tall-backed living room chair faced that wall of windows with a delicate human arm that hung down toward the floor. Fresh blood ran in rivulets to a widening puddle in the expensive carpet.

I didn't have to look to know the arm belonged to Aimee Langhari. Her long beautiful hair cascaded down and lay in the blood, dark black on bright red, black widow colors.

And still I looked closer without moving and caught her reflection in the window.

And wished I hadn't.

A sight that would remain forever in my memory.

Drago's head moved from side to side as he searched for the interloper who'd done the dirty deed. The same criminal who whacked the security person down on the bottom floor.

The apartment was empty.

We'd missed them by seconds. He walked over to the chair. My legs wouldn't cooperate and were happy to stay put.

Drago looked down at her then looked up at me. "Dude," he whispered.

More sirens out on the street below. Once the two cops down in the lobby discovered the brutalized security guard, they'd called for backup. We didn't have much time left before our freedom became an endangered species.

LAPD weren't fools; they would cut off our exit to the stairs and put a watch on the second elevator as they came up in force in the other one. We were trapped like rats just like we'd trapped the pervs in the Comstock.

What goes around comes around.

Drago moved to the window and looked down. "We've had it, bro."

I said, "I'm sorry I got you into this."

He smiled. "Best job I ever had."

I nodded.

He said, "You know I can't go back inside, and I know how you don't like to fight the cops. But I'm not going back to the joint. I can't do it. I'll try not to hurt them too bad. If we're going to go, we better get after it. They're just going to keep coming."

They were going to gun down my big friend.

He didn't have a chance. It's what LAPD did best, gun down wanton criminals.

This was all my fault.

And I would end up in prison for the rest of my life. A large knot rose in my throat, my eyes burned with tears at the enormous loss.

Until I saw it.

I moved closer to the puddle of blood under Langhari's hand and saw a small device. "Get the door," I yelled. "Close the door. Hurry."

Drago knew me well enough not to ask questions. He ran to the penthouse door and slammed it, then turned back, his expression neutral.

He waited.

I didn't look over the top of the chair to see Langhari and the terrible waste of life. I plucked the device from the blood and hoped the wetness had not shorted the electronics inside.

"What's that?" Drago asked.

"Shhh. Listen. Don't even breathe." I pushed the button on the device. The activation brought a barely audible click. I quickly looked around and realized I had missed where the noise originated. I missed the movement that would reveal our salvation.

I hurried over to the wall of books, all leather-bound classics, and pulled on the shelves. Nothing.

Drago came over to my side. "Hey, old hoss, you gone coo-coo for Cocoa Puffs?"

"No, this." I held up the device. "I've seen it once before, one like it, anyway. It's an electronic release for a safe room."

"No shit." He snatched the device from my hand and now we both had her blood on our hands.

He pushed the button.

The click came again but not as loud. I turned to the wall that jutted out, the one with the long mirror on the other side. The bookcase covered the short wall to the extended leg in the "L" configuration—the continuation of the bookcase. I pulled on this bookcase, and it swung open revealing a hidden room.

Outside the penthouse door, LAPD yelled their advisal that they demanded entry and were coming in. They'd have their guns drawn looking for a target. A black man with someone who looks like Drago, they didn't need any more probable cause to pull the trigger.

They'd pull the trigger, again and again and again.

Seconds. We only had seconds.

"Come on," I said to Drago in a hushed voice.

He didn't need to be told. He shoved me in ahead of him and swung the wall closed behind us.

Inside on that same wall was a long lever. He pulled it down. The door vacuum-pressed the room, shutting out all sound.

The mirror, two feet off the ground and running the length of the wall, was bulletproof glass, the kind used in banks as "bandit barriers." Attached to the exterior of that was a one-way mirror allowing a view of the entire room without anyone able to look in.

The secret room also allowed us to see the chair and the back of Langhari's head, her hand drooping down into her coagulating blood.

Aimee's blood from the secret door release device was smeared across my palm. I wiped it on my pants, leaving a crimson streak.

Four LAPD uniforms rushed the room, guns drawn.

I flinched and stepped back as if they could see us.

They cleared the room, holstered their guns, and met over at the chair to gawk at the cooling corpse of the once beautiful Aimee Langhari. They made jokes, smiled and laughed, gallows humor, a vent that allowed the cops to do their jobs, absorb the violence of the world Joe citizen rarely experienced.

I'd done it myself, but this day I didn't like the cops very much for it.

The supervisor, a sergeant, advised dispatch of what they found and asked for Homicide to respond along with a forensics team. He also asked that the elite Robbery/Homicide division be notified.

This murder might cause a blip on the media radar.

Drago stood close and elbowed me. He whispered, "This is too cool, bro, it's like reality TV but this is really reality as it happens. Hey, and the best part, there's no commercials."

He looked around, found a nice comfy chair, pulled it close to the window/mirrored glass, sat down, and put his feet up on the sill, ready to watch. "Now all we need are some cold brewskis and a big bowl of popcorn."

My friend Drago adjusted to violent death quicker than I could.

Her sudden death hit me hard. I'd looked into her eyes at the Coffee Hut. She'd been a living, breathing human not hours before. Now, never again. What a terrible waste.

I looked around and found a small refrigerator, the college dorm type, opened it, and found it stocked full of food and beverages. I took out a can of ice-cold Miller's Highlife and handed it to Drago.

"Are you kidding me?"

"Shhh."

"Oh, right. Right."

He went back to watching the cops exploring the apartment, violating policy. They needed to wait for the detectives before they searched. One cop came up and put his face close to the mirror as if trying to see in. Drago brought his feet down and picked up the rebar he'd let drop to the carpeted floor.

I put my hand on his shoulder and whispered, "Easy, big man, he can't see us. Just don't move or talk too loud."

He whispered, "We're a couple of animals in the zoo, aren't we? Or like on *National Geographic*, the one where the lions chase down the gaknews. Not that I'm a friggin' gaknew. I'm not, but you know what I mean."

Yeah, I knew what he meant. He meant gnu.

CHAPTER FORTY-NINE

I GUESS IF I were Aimee Langhari and worked with Ennis Freemantle on one side and Johnny Ef on the other, I too would have an escape hatch.

If I'd been smart enough to think about building one.

Langhari knew her day would come and had depended on security personnel at the front door to give her enough warning, something she probably paid extra for under the table.

Whoever killed her rushed the poor woman downstairs at the front desk and clubbed her senseless before she could give out the alarm to Langhari.

A fatal mistake.

Langhari had the activator in her hand when we found her. She must've kept it on her person once the McMansions started burning down. Someone's head had to roll for such a large error, such a large loss of laundered money.

If Johnny let the affront go without sending a message, he'd appear weak.

Freemantle had too many biker buddies backing him up for Johnny to touch him. That meant what happened to Langhari had been Freemantle's work at Johnny's behest. They jumped her too quick for her to use the safe room. Too bad. She could've waited them out forever, right under their noses.

If she'd just made it behind the fake wall in time.

The room was the size of a cabin on an ocean liner and had a single bed, a hot plate, a cupboard filled with edible dry goods— cans of soup, cups of noodles, protein bars, that kind of thing— running water with a sink, and an airplane-size bathroom with a shower, neither of which Drago would be able to fit into.

The safe room was constructed of ten-inch walls with sound-proofing and a one-way speaker that allowed her and us to hear the conversations in her apartment. She'd thought of every possible contingency except the most important one.

She should've barred her apartment door with reinforced steel.

That way the noise from an attempted breach would've given her ample warning. But then once the killers got in, they'd see the door had been barred from the inside and realized . . . well, the what-ifs could go on and on.

Now we'd be trapped for eight to ten hours while law enforcement worked the crime scene. Better than the alternative. The cops would get all they needed the first time and then walk away never to return. Movies and books had the cops put seals on doors with warnings, but in all of my career, I'd never seen one. If the police had to come back for whatever reason, they'd need another search warrant.

I stretched out on the single bed. Drago drank his beer and watched the apartment activity, enthralled with the procedure, ut-tering things like, "Hey, they don't do it that way on TV." Or, "Yeah, buddy, go ahead, that there violates the rules of evidence, I know that much from my trial."

He let go with a loud belch. "Hey, bro, toss me another, would you?" He crumpled the aluminum can into a perfect little ball and tossed it in the corner. I lay on the bed, ignored him, put my arm over my eyes, and fought off the anxiety over losing eight to ten hours when I could've been looking for Sonny. The minutes slid by, taking twice as long as they normally would. I lost count.

"Drago, what are we going to do next? I'm outta ideas."

He grunted, got up, and rummaged around in the small room, curious. He started in one corner and worked his way around checking everything out, the half-dresser with spare clothes, the makeup, the jewelry.

When he came to the single bed where I lay, he got down on both knees and peered underneath. "Hey, what's this?"

I got up on one elbow as he pulled out a simple brown paper bag from a local grocery store. He unrolled the top and said, "Well, now I don't feel so sorry for the broad getting her throat cut."

He held the open bag for me to look inside. Bundles of U.S. currency with paper bank wrappers from a Costa Rican bank.

"Son of a bitch."

Drago stood and went to the one-way glass, looking out at Aimee Langhari. "She did have the money. We were only guessing. This means she knew about the kid, Sonny. And now she can't tell us a damn thing."

"Just because she has the money doesn't mean she knew where Sonny was—it means she was involved up to her pretty little neck, just like we suspected."

Drago nodded. "Hey, your girlfriend just arrived."

I jumped up. "Who?"

Helen Hellinger had come in and stood talking to a homicide investigator from LAPD, one I didn't recognize.

Helen walked around the chair to view the corpse. I turned up the volume on the speaker. The fat homicide investigator dressed in a rumpled dark blue suit ogled Helen and said in a salacious manner,

"Baby, that there is called a South American necktie. They cut the throat of the rat and pull the tongue out through the slit. Someone's sending a message."

Helen didn't look at him and continued to look at Aimee Langhari. "Yes, I'm fully aware of the implications, thank you."

Drago stood next to me. "It's also the calling card for the CCS. I say when we get out of here, we pay the Celtic Cross Syndicate a visit, put a little iron in their blood."

"There are too many of them—there's just the two of us."

He looked at me strangely as if I still had my mojo tucked between my legs, when I didn't.

I said, "A hundred grand might not be a lot to Johnny Ef or Langhari, but it means a lot to Ennis and his cohorts."

I took out my phone and dialed Helen's cell. The buzzing from her pocket came over the speaker in the safe room.

CHAPTER FIFTY

OUTSIDE THE SAFE room's one-way glass Helen said to the homicide detective, "Excuse me, I have to take this." She stepped away from the homicide detective and over to the mirror with her back to the homicide dick to watch him in the mirror if he came over to listen in.

"Bruno, where are you?"

"Out and about, why?"

Drago smiled at the misdirection I'd fed her and said, "That's nice. Work it."

Helen said, "You're not going to believe this . . . well, maybe you will. Somebody just took Langhari off the board."

"Is that right? Where?"

"At her apartment—and before you ask—I can't get you in to see the scene. This is LAPD's baby and they are being assholes about it. I barely got in myself."

Drago slapped his leg and chuckled. "She said she can't get us in to see it. That's choice, ain't it? I mean grade-A hundred percent choice."

The detective called to her. She said into the phone, "Just a second." She put the phone to her chest and walked back to the detective. They spoke in murmurs too low to hear. She came back to the mirror where she'd been before.

She stood less than two feet away staring into the one-way mirror and caused a little fight or flight to jolt through my body, making me want to run and hide under the bed before she saw us and accidentally put out an alarm.

The scar on her face and her intense brown eyes gave her an exotic air. The light scar, more a line that started on her forehead and curved down the side to the bottom of her cheek, could only be seen when up close. It added to her character, enhancing a striking mystique.

She was a deputy made of case-hardened steel. A living, breathing legend. Her peers tagged her *Wonder Woman*. Cops had to categorize people: good guys and monsters. It made their world easier to understand.

It was how she earned the scar that propelled her into legendary status. She'd crashed her marked patrol car underneath a gas hauling truck that was leaking fuel. Pinned her in. She took her gun out and waited for the fire department knowing they wouldn't get there in time.

Back in the safe room, Drago said, "That's it. I'm putting one of these rooms in my pad, this is way too cool."

Helen said, "You sure you and Drago had nothing to do with this?"

"Damn right, I'm sure, why?"

Drago moved over and put his extra-large head down next to mine, so he could hear the conversation. I leaned away from him and put my hand over the phone. "You can hear what she says from the speaker on the wall."

"Oh, yeah, right, sorry."

He shrugged and returned to his usual blank expression.

Helen lowered her tone even more. "I've just been told the woman security guard at the front desk said the man that whacked her in the head was a black guy who looked like an older Richard Pryor."

I put my hand over the phone again. "I don't look like an older Richard Pryor."

Drago elbowed me and nodded his agreement with her, a sappy grin filling his face.

Helen continued, "And the big white guy looked like a fat Gene Wilder."

Drago tried to grab the phone from me.

I fought and waved him off and said into the phone, "You know full well those descriptions don't match us."

She'd heard our tussle. "You sure it wasn't you and Drago who did this?"

"Does it really matter?"

"Of course, it does."

"We didn't kill Langhari. We got there after the fact and barely got away before the cops pulled up. The security woman only remembers us—not the thugs from Celtic Cross Syndicate because they whacked her over the head and scrambled her memory. We came in after the fact when she came to. That's why she remembered it wrong."

She asked, "You sure it was CCS?"

"Yeah, as sure as I can be under the circumstances. That's where I'd take the investigation if it were me."

She nodded. "I'll tell LAPD." She paused. "I came up with a big zero on any infants missing with the exception of one, but I don't think it applies. Happened a couple of months ago."

"Okay, good."

Those poor kids without concerned parents out there looking for them, caring about what happened to them. The thought of three more children to take down to Casa Bruno had a dizzying effect.

Helen said, "Does one of the infants have a birthmark on his foot?"

All the air left our side of the glass, turning the safe room into a giant vacuum.

My voice came out in a croak. "Why?"

CHAPTER FIFTY-ONE

ON THE OTHER side of the one-way glass, Helen said, "Frankie Toliver, from Silver Lake, one month old—now three months old—was kidnapped. The FBI bungled the million-dollar ransom exchange, lost the money, and the kid was never recovered. He's got a birthmark on his foot."

I turned to look at Drago. All the color had drained from his face and his jaw muscle bulged as he ground his teeth at the implication. His girl Layla had been lying to us—not only lying but might even have some serious mental issues.

I had believed every word of her Sonny story and I'd been a cop for close to three decades and knew how to read people. She really believed Sonny was hers. *Having mental issues* was the only way she could have slipped by me.

What a colossal mess.

I watched Helen manipulate her phone buttons. "I'm sending you a photo of the birthmark and of the child. Check the children you have to make sure. Just in case, okay?

"Bruno, did you hear me?"

I didn't have to look. I'd already checked their feet and none of the three had birthmarks. "It's not Frankie. None of our children have a birthmark."

Sonny—Frankie Toliver—was still missing. I couldn't imagine what his parents were going through, especially not hearing anything for two months after the ransom had been delivered. How thin can hope stretch, before it diminishes and then disappears and turns into a chasm filled with permanent pain?

Helen nodded. "As you can imagine, the mother and father are frantic. They have some influence with a supervisor on the LA County Board of Supervisors. As soon as I made the inquiry on the computer, it set off all kinds of red flags. FBI jumped me wanting to know why I was asking. The FBI kept it out of the news to cover up their blunder. They want this screwup off their balance sheet."

"I told you—he's not one of the kids. You can check them yourself if you want."

"Take it easy. Why are you jumping down my throat? I trust you."

She didn't sound all that convincing with the trusting part. She understood that I sometimes championed the child's rights over the parents'. The line between a good parent and a bad one is more restrictive for me, more black and white than the court or Child Protective Services allow.

I shouldn't have been so terse with her. "I'm sorry, I just really want to get home."

"Call me later, Bruno." She clicked off.

"Shit," I said.

Drago stared out into Langhari's apartment with the forensic personnel in white paper suits, goggles, and paper booties doing their job, diagraming the room, shooting detailed photos, taking samples.

Drago understood what Helen had said about Sonny, how Sonny was really Frankie Toliver, what this meant for Layla, the impact it would have on their white-hot relationship.

He shook his head. "Sometimes you just want to lay the day down and shoot it in the head."

I put my hand on his shoulder. He didn't pull away this time. I didn't leave it there too long.

I wandered the few steps over to the bed and lay down again to wait out our temporary prison term. I curled up and put the pillow over my head and tried to think.

My phone buzzed. I pulled it out of my pocket and found two text messages from Eddie Crane, our child who wanted us to adopt him. For a second, seeing his name cheered me up.

The first text message said, *Missing you hope you come home soon.* It about ripped my heart out.

I lay on the bed trying to rest, knowing sleep wouldn't come if I coaxed it. I had to sneak up on it.

*   *   *

I woke with Drago tugging on my ankle. "Come on, old hoss, time to saddle up and get the hell outta here."

With the cops so close on the other side of the wall, I shouldn't have been able to sleep, but my body was still recovering from being shot point-blank in the chest ten weeks earlier. Plus, I was a horse's ass for sleeping when I should've been talking to Drago about Layla—how she'd lied to us—how she'd lied to him. He had to be angry and feeling like a fool. And most of all, hurt.

I'd slept for six and a half hours when I could've been searching the safe room for other clues besides the money. No time now.

I got up just as Drago pulled on the long handle.

The door let out air with a whoosh.

We hurried to the apartment door. He had the grocery bag with the hundred grand under his arm. I didn't look to the left to the aftermath, the remains of Aimee Langhari, now nothing more than an abandoned puddle of coagulated blood.

I stopped at the door. "Hold on, big man." I took the safe room door activator over to the bookshelf. I slid the activator on top of *A Tale of Two Cities*, a green leather copy with the page edges gilded in gold. Then I closed the safe room door until it clicked.

Back out in the hall while we waited for the elevator, Drago asked, "Why'd you do that?"

I shrugged. "Don't know, guess it's because a safe room's most important advantage is that it's a secret."

I think I did it out of some screwed-up respect for Langhari. I couldn't help her but I could help keep her secret.

He pushed the DOWN button. "Yeah, enough secrets have been aired out today."

Down on the street, LAPD had towed away Drago's new truck. I followed him two blocks north where an Uber ride stood waiting.

The night air never tasted so good.

It tasted like freedom.

CHAPTER FIFTY-TWO

WE TOOK TWO different Ubers back to the Summerset, watching to make sure we weren't followed. On the way up the stairs to our third-floor room, I said, "Hey, ah . . ."

"Just say it."

"It might be better if I ah . . . controlled the conversation when we talk with Layla."

Drago's anger radiated off him in an invisible aura. I worried for Layla, about the future of their relationship.

Drago took the steps up two and three at a time. "In your dreams," he said over his shoulder.

I hurried to keep up with him.

At the hotel door, Drago put the key in the lock. On the other side, Waldo barked and scratched at the wood.

Inside, Waldo smiled and jumped up on his master. Drago ignored him. "Layla?" His feet thumped the floor.

"I'm in here. I'm taking a bath." A warm humidity hung in the air generated from the open bathroom door.

Drago stomped into the bedroom and then on into the bathroom. He slammed the bathroom door.

I fought the urge to listen to the conversation.

I sat down and Waldo came over and let me pet him. I waited, my ears listening hard for yelling by either one of them.

And waited.

Nothing, not a peep. Suddenly, the shower came on.

Forty minutes passed. The bathroom door opened, and the bedroom door closed. Another thirty minutes passed.

Someone knocked at the hotel room door. Waldo growled and hurried to the door looking for a juicy calf on which to take out his canine anxiety after being snubbed by his master.

I pulled a gun, stood off to the side, leaned all the way over, and peeked in the peephole. I put the gun away and opened the door.

"Dad."

I took him in a tight hug and held on. "It's so good to see you. I'm glad you're back."

Bea bumped past in her wheelchair. "What am I, chopped liver?"

I pulled Dad back to get a look at him. He wore his regular clothes: khaki pants and a flannel shirt with a cardigan sweater.

I closed the door. "Well, how much did you win?"

Dad's smile tarnished, and he silently waved, pointed to Bea, and shook his head no.

I whispered, "How much?"

He whispered. "All of it. Gone."

I wanted to go over and gloat, throw a few verbal jabs at Mom, but Dad's sad expression held me back. I took his arm and escorted him over to the couch. We sat. I loved having him in the same room safe and sound.

He looked around. "Only one bedroom? I guess we better see if the room across the hall is available."

I handed him the key. I'd already rented it for him. He nodded, the smile gone, replaced with exhaustion.

I said, "Get some rest, we'll talk later."

He nodded again, took hold of the wheelchair, and rolled it toward the door.

"Hold it." Bea said, "I'm not ready to go yet. Let go of my chair. Unhand me."

"Be quiet, old woman."

I hurried around and opened the door. I waited until he got the hotel room door opened across the hall and closed behind them.

The bag with a hundred thousand sat on the counter. I stood there alone with Waldo. I wasn't used to being alone, not with so many children at home. I opened the bag, took out a bundle of ten thousand, and fanned the hundred-dollar bills. The entire predicament had been caused by man's greed and avarice.

The sight of Dad back safe, holding him in a hug, his familiar, comforting scent, brought on an overwhelming desire to be back home in Costa Rica. Done with this mess.

I put the bundle in my pocket, took out the two .357 pistols from my waistband, and laid them on the counter.

I didn't leave a note.

Drago would figure it out with the guns right there in plain sight. I opened the hotel door and started to close it, but Waldo had tried to get out to tag along. I said, "Not this time, pal."

Half in the door and half out, he looked up and growled. "Okay, okay, take it easy. You can go. But you better be on your best behavior."

We came out onto the street rife with night people: the dope slingers, the B girls, the con men on the prod, and all the victims driving slowly by looking for the vice they most desired—the vice they needed to ruin their lives.

Two outlaw motorcycle gang members dressed in their denim cuts, denim pants, and black boots worked the door at the Lusty

Muff, the topless bar run by the Celtic Cross Syndicate. Both had long greasy hair and tattoos visible on their necks and faces.

I tried the ploy of pretending like I owned the place and walked by them into the door. The shorter biker, with "Buck" embroidered on his cut, put his hand on my chest. "Sorry, no smokes allowed, *Caucasians* only."

Waldo growled. I waved a hand down by his face. He stopped. I said, "I have an appointment to see Ennis Freemantle."

The taller, dumber of the two had KNIGHT embroidered on his cut. He said, "Oh yeah, and I'm the king of England."

"Is that right? What's the king of England's name?"

Knight clenched his fists and took a step toward me. Buck got in front of him, holding him back.

I said, "You had better call Ennis and tell him I'm here or you two brain trusts are going to be demoted to cleaning toilets."

I didn't like bikers.

Buck hit a speed-dial number on his cell. "Yeah, there's a smoke out here who says he has a meeting with the boss. Yeah, I didn't think so."

I said, "Tell him it's Bruno Johnson."

Buck and Knight exchanged looks.

Knight said, "Can't be. Bruno Johnson's dead."

"Yeah, yeah, yeah." I pulled up my sleeve and showed them the BMF tattoo on my shoulder.

Buck said into the phone, "It's Bruno Johnson. No. I know that's what I said, but he's got the tattoo. Are you sure? All right." He hung up. "Let him through."

We started to go in. Buck stepped in the way and said, "Not the dog."

"If the dog doesn't go in, neither do I."

I took out the bundled ten thousand. "And then your boss won't get this money."

"Straight to the back then. Don't let that cur stop and sniff the cooze."

The entire motivation for the Lusty Muff was to exploit women. All of a sudden, I'd had enough. These two might've been the ones who'd brutally killed Aimee Langhari.

I let my right foot slide back going into a horse stance and said to Knight, "I'll give you this ten thousand if you can spell England."

In a snap he shifted to anger and pulled a fist back to hit me. I rabbit punched him in the nose as the distraction, stepped back, and leaned into a roundhouse to the jaw.

His jaw shattered. He dropped straight to the dirty sidewalk.

Pain shot up my arm, into my shoulder, and up to the top of my head. I'd hit him at the wrong angle and had broken my wrist.

Buck reached under his denim cut behind his back, going for a weapon. Waldo jumped forward, latching onto his crotch.

Buck screamed and grabbed hold of Waldo's head with both hands—screeching like a girl. "Get him off. Get him off."

Pain flashed bright stars in my vision and I cradled my arm. "Let the big dog eat," I said. "Go ahead, Waldo, take a big bite."

Waldo braced his feet and swung his head back and forth, his teeth still locked onto the man's genitals.

Buck screamed and fell to the ground.

I patted Waldo's head. "That's enough, boy." He let go and took a step back, still on alert, ready to go again if given the command.

Buck's natural instinct was to roll over on his belly to protect what was left of his mauled and bleeding manhood. When he did, his cut pulled up, exposing a Beretta model 92F tucked in his back waistband. I reached down with my good hand, relieved him of the weapon, and stuck it in my waistband.

Buck writhed and moaned.

I said to Waldo, "My hand's broke. You think we should call this thing off?"

He looked at me, turning his head from side to side, not understanding what I'd said.

"Yeah, I agree. Let's get this thing over with."

I pulled on the door to the Lusty Muff, and we entered into the smooth darkness.

CHAPTER FIFTY-THREE

THE CELTIC CROSS Syndicate, according to Drago, had five strip joints across LA County, which they used as crime hubs to gather and launder their ill-gotten gain. Money derived from tyranny, blood and bone, and drug sales. The five strip joints—the Moose Knuckle, the Bearded Clam, the Hot Muff, the Steamy Muff, and the Chick A Dee—acted as precincts similar to the police station concept—the Lusty Muff being the headquarters.

Each location had a rank and file just like law enforcement, with presidents who acted as captains, vice presidents as lieutenants, and sergeants at arms as group enforcers. For the time being, Ennis Freemantle reigned as king, lording over all of CCS.

Inside the Lusty Muff, Waldo sensed my pain from the shattered wrist, sensed my need to lean on him. He stayed at my side and with every step brushed against my leg to let me know he was there.

We walked on by a topless woman with smooth skin and eyes older than her age. She stood at a podium and took the cover charge from customers coming in off the street. She had to have heard the ruckus right outside the door. She saw my skin color—one not normally allowed in—and saw Waldo.

She said nothing as we passed.

We slipped through some black curtains into the poorly illuminated main room. The walls all painted black helped with the cave effect. The loud music would preclude any form of normal communication—a beat that banged against my face and hurt my ears. The place smelled of body odor and nicotine and a pungent chemical reek from smoking meth.

Three women danced on an elevated runway, their eyes glassy from drugs, their bodies marred with tattoos and augmented to meet the standards of the perverse who sat on all three sides of the runway, one hand on their drinks, the other out of view down in the dimness turning to dark.

The men didn't hoot and howl like in movies—they sat and stared and nursed the watered-down drinks and lusted. Cigarette and meth smoke hung from the ceiling, further diffusing the low light.

Five other women writhed on men's legs and laps at tables on the outer perimeter. More tables filled with men waiting their turn for their lap dance. Deviant behavior was alive and well in the Lusty Muff. How much better off would the county be if all five CCS joints were bombed at the same time? How many unsuspecting victims of future sex crimes would be saved?

But this was America, land of the free, home of the brave.

Yeah, right.

More than ever, I needed to get back to my family in Costa Rica.

I counted four more bouncers throughout the room. One large one sat on a stool at the bar lit with ground effect lighting. The lighting shadowed the faces of those who sat and drank and gave them a skull-like appearance. The fat bouncer wore black pants, a long-sleeve shirt, and a black vest that couldn't contain his obesity, the buttons screaming for relief.

My wrist throbbed with each step. I had to ignore the pain and concentrate on the task at hand.

As Buck had instructed, we moved on through to the back without stopping. The path veered left to what looked like four doors down a short hall: the bathrooms and the dressing rooms. I took the stairs to the right going up and came to a single door on a short landing.

I entered without knocking.

In the room to the left sat a desk and chair, both mottled with age and, if allowed, would tell many a tale of heartache and pain centered around vile human exploitation.

Straight ahead, a fully outfitted bar.

To the right sat a displaced red vinyl restaurant booth that faced a glass window and looked down upon Ennis Freemantle's domain.

He sat in the booth with two of the youngest women in the Lusty Muff, both topless. Behind the booth stood two thugs wearing the CCS colors, their hands crossed at their waists. The fools wore sunglasses in the near-dark room, preferring to look cool over good tactics.

One broke away and came toward us.

Waldo growled. "Easy, boy. I'll tell you when," I whispered.

The thug had "Blinky" embroidered on his cut. He said, "Raise your arms, I'm going to pat you down."

"You can kiss my black ass."

He turned and looked over his shoulder at Ennis, who nodded that it was okay and to let me through. He shooed away his two girls, who got up in a hurry, glad to be away from him.

"Boss, he's got a dog here, a real shit eater."

Ennis slapped the table. "That dumbass Buck, he knows better."

I said, "It's not Buck's fault. You might want to have one of your dumb shits down there take him to the hospital. Knight too."

A slow smile weaseled out onto Ennis' narrow lips across teeth yellowed from too many cigarettes and chasing the dragon with meth. "Is that right? You took down two of my boys?"

"I didn't say that. When me and Waldo walked up, your two thugs tripped and fell on the sidewalk. Clumsy, I guess."

Ennis looked at Blinky and waved his hand. Blinky pulled out his phone and made a call.

Down below, the fat bouncer sitting at the bar answered his phone. He got up, waddled over to another bouncer, and whispered in his ear. That bouncer nodded and headed for the door to scoop up the trash out front and take it to the hospital.

Ennis said, "Sit down and tell me what brings you to my fine establishment."

"Thank you, but I prefer to stand."

Blinky tried to move from standing behind the booth by his boss to a flanking position behind me.

Waldo quickly shifted from my right side to my left to counter the move and stopped him with a growl.

I said, "I wouldn't come any closer if I were you."

Blinky put his hand inside his denim cut.

Ennis kept his gray beard long and bushy like some kind of wizard. The wiry gray hair disappeared down below table level. It might even reach all the way down to his belt buckle.

The scars of his face gave the illusion of an ancient oak that had lived through too many hurricanes. On his fingers he wore three rings: one a skull, another a Nazi swastika, another a Nazi eagle. Next to his hand sat a large-framed chrome revolver with inlaid gold on the make and model: Colt Python.

His other hand constantly serviced his narrow lips with a long brown cigarette, his whole demeanor twitchy.

"You gonna tell me why Bruno Johnson thinks he can just walk into my place and jack two of my best men without getting his head handed to him?"

"I want you to answer one question," I said. "Just one and then I'll leave you be."

"Heh, heh."

He flicked ash onto the table, put the cigarette between his lips, and sucked hard for a lungful. He blew it out through his nose.

"You're a damn fool. You know someone put a bounty on your black ass, twenty-five thousand dollars dead. What's to stop me from collecting that easy money right here, right now?"

"Johnny Ef can do better than twenty-five, the way I hurt him, you'd think it would be more like two hundred and fifty. Maybe he's hurting for money. You might want to ask for the money up front. I pay in advance."

I took the ten grand from my pocket and tossed it on the table. "That's ten-grand against ninety more if you answer one question. You can't find easier money anywhere else."

He took a long pull on his cigarette and watched my eyes. "An answer to some questions can cause trouble worth more than a hundred large."

"That's ten-grand good-faith money and I guarantee the answer will be no skin off your nose."

"Okay, I'll bite. But I'm keeping the ten whether I know the answer or not. Ask it so you can get your black ass outta my establishment. I have a reputation to uphold."

"I'm looking for a child—"

He held up his hand to stop me. "I don't deal in children."

"Johnny Ef does—and you work for him."

"I work for no one. I might have an understanding with Fillmore but nothing else. And I would advise you not to call him that to his face. He doesn't take to it."

"You do deal in kidnap, rape, robbery, and murder. This kid was kidnapped two months ago. His name is Frankie Toliver."

He sucked on his cancer stick, held it in for a long couple of seconds, and let it out. "I'm not a fool. I wouldn't cop out to a kidnapping to you or to anyone else. You think I'm a chump? You take me for a chump?" He raised his voice.

"No. But you know a lot about what happens on the street. This happened on your turf so whoever did it had to pay you a piece of the two-million-dollar ransom."

He stopped mid-puff and eyed me. "Two million dollars, you say?"

"That's right." He knew all about Frankie Toliver. The ransom had been for a million, no reason why I couldn't sow a little deceit among those who'd killed for much less.

He said, "Let me get back to you. Keep that other ninety ready. I might be hitting you up for it."

"Just tell me, is Frankie still alive?"

"I said, I'll be talking to you. Leave your number where you can be reached."

I tossed a paper napkin with my cell number on it to the floor. "The deal's good for twenty-four hours."

"Get out before I forget my manners."

CHAPTER FIFTY-FOUR

DRAGO CAME OUT of the suite door into the hallway as Waldo and I approached. Drago's face flushed red and beaded with sweat that made the black-ink tattoos on his scalp stand out.

I asked, "Where're you going?"

He'd returned to the stoic man of few words. "Layla has a hankering for shrimp scampi."

He kept walking, his back to me. Waldo left my side and went with him. That was it, that was all he had to say?

I said, "Did you tell her?"

The part about Sonny really being Frankie Toliver?

He stopped, didn't turn around. His shoulders pulled back as if I'd stuck him in the back with a spear. After a moment, he shook his head, still without turning, unable to look me in the eye. "I couldn't. I . . . I guess I don't want to know if she lied to us . . . to me. It doesn't matter to me."

"You got it bad, big man."

Now he slowly turned, anger plain on his expression. "What are you talking about?"

"You're in love with her."

The anger faded and shifted to confusion. He turned and walked off down the hall.

He didn't understand love, how it could pull a man apart or mold him like a lump of Silly Putty. Love turned men into silly fools and sometimes into babbling dupes.

I watched him until he disappeared down the stairs with Waldo at his side. Drago had always had a crush on my Marie, but this wasn't just a schoolyard crush. What he had for Layla was different, it was the real thing, and he was in denial, driving straight for the cliff. Drago was Thelma driving the car and maybe I was Louise sitting next to him.

I entered the room and found Layla in her white fluffy robe with a towel wrapped around her head in a beehive configuration. The girl sure liked her showers. She stood in the kitchenette pouring sugar and creamer in her coffee. She smiled, smug and comfortable in her little world with Drago wrapped around her finger, an ICBM she only need point and push the red launch button.

"Can I talk to you?"

She kept the smile and said, "I don't like you, Bruno. I don't like the way you treat me. So, no, I would rather you leave me alone." She sipped her coffee holding the cup with both hands as if it might run from her.

I nodded. "Aimee is dead."

The coffee cup slipped from her grasp and shattered on the floor, spewing a tan liquid. Her hand shot out to grab the counter for support.

I hurried around into the kitchenette and picked her up with my good arm pinning her to my chest to keep her from cutting her bare feet, her body hot against mine. I carried her over to the couch and set her down.

Her hands flew to her face as she wept with grief.

After a time, she spoke through her hands. "Are you sure?"

"I'm very sorry, but yes, I saw her."

She brought her hands down. "What happened?"

"You don't want to know."

"Tell me."

"CCS is what happened to her."

Her chin trembled as she shook her head. The towel that wrapped her hair threatened to fall off.

She saw that I cradled my arm, her eyes full of tears.

"What's happened to your arm?"

"I broke my wrist."

"You poor man, and you're here helping me while you're sitting there in pain."

She jumped up and disappeared into the bedroom. Talking about my broken arm somehow made it hurt worse.

She hurried back with a pillowcase and two nightstand drawers, tears still streaming down her cheeks. She laid one of the drawers on the floor upside down and stomped on the flimsy construction, knocking the bottom out. She picked up the frame and slammed it on the floor until it shattered. She yanked off the metal rail that had guided the drawer in the dresser frame. She did the same thing to the second drawer.

She was a very capable girl.

The towel for her hair finally fell away.

My mouth, all on its own, dropped open. She now sported a pageboy haircut. She'd cut off all that luxurious black hair. All that beautiful hair.

She sniffled and put a hand up to her hair. "You like it?"

"Ah . . . of course I do. It just takes a little getting used to." It totally changed her appearance and, in some way, made her look even more exotic.

She nodded and started to tear the cheap pillowcase into strips. When she had enough for the job, she gently took hold of my arm and felt the bones.

I gritted my teeth from the pain.

She sniffled again. "Yes, I think your right, it's broken. I'm going to have to set it."

"I figured that was coming."

Without any warning, she pulled on my wrist. Pain blasted into my brain as broken bone grated against nerve endings. Bright stars lit up the inside of my eyelids. She held on tight, so I wouldn't misalign the bones. "There, it's over. All done. Now don't move." She put one of the metal rails on each side of my arm. "Here, hold this."

I did. She started wrapping my arm with the torn strips. I watched her eyes that continued to weep tears.

"Did she . . . did Aimee suffer?" She looked up.

I whispered the lie. "No, not at all."

She nodded, her chin quivered, and she went back to work fixing my arm.

"This is only temporary. You're going to need a cast."

I said nothing.

She started in on another strip of torn pillowcase, wrapping it tight. My arm already felt better.

"Thank you for this. You'd make a helluva doctor."

A little half-smile slipped out.

I didn't want to hurt her, but she had to move forward. "I know about Frankie Toliver."

She stopped wrapping the strip for a moment, then continued on. More tears.

"Layla," I said softly. "Why don't you tell me about it?"

She said nothing.

"Layla, please?"

She wouldn't look at me and continued splinting my arm.

She finally spoke. "What do you want me to say, that Johnny Ef is a real bastard. It's just as I told you before, the way we met. I didn't figure out until later that he had stalked me and planned to use me

all along. It was all just a game to him, a distraction. Then ... I guess
... No, I knew he figured out I wasn't going to get pregnant. That's
what he wanted all along. He wanted me pregnant. He would pat
my tummy and say, 'Babies are money in the bank.' As if my womb
was a piggy bank he could just crack open. When I wouldn't give
him what he wanted, he cast me aside. He sells babies, Bruno. That's
what he does along with all those other vile and disgusting deviant
moneymaking schemes. I hate him. I hate him. Now he's killed my
good friend Aimee."

I put my hand on hers. She stopped wrapping, buried her head in
my shoulder, and cried, my skin turning warm and wet through my
shirt. Johnny caused nothing but pain and grief and needed to be
taken off the board, permanently.

She spoke into my shoulder, her words muffled. "But I did get
pregnant. I didn't tell him. No way could I tell him."

She paused. Her body stiffened.

"I lost the baby, miscarried. God could see the life I was bringing
my baby into and said no, not this time. I didn't tell Johnny. The
doctor told me I could never get pregnant again. It only made me
want Frankie more. This was God telling me that Frankie was my
child—my last opportunity to be a mother—a good mother.

"I'm a good mother." She said it as if trying to convince herself.

With my good hand I gently pulled her away to see her eyes and
asked, "Johnny had Frankie Toliver kidnapped?"

She nodded. "He had me watch Frankie, take care of him for the
first couple of weeks. I didn't know he was a kidnap victim until
much later. I swear I didn't.

"I just thought he was ... like the others, bred for money. I fell in
love with the cute little guy and called him Sonny.

"I knew Johnny wouldn't give him to me. Money meant more to
him than I did."

"That's why you told your mother you were kidnapped to get the money to buy Frankie?"

She nodded. "I didn't know he was kidnapped until Aimee told me. I think she told Johnny about how I loved Frankie and that's why Johnny took him from me, so I wouldn't try and run off with him. Johnny wanted me to get the money, the hundred thousand from my parents to make up for the baby I couldn't have.

"He'll do anything to anyone for money. He's a demon, a fiend. Aimee, I loved her like a sister, but she was all about the money too. God rest her soul."

"Do you know where Sonny—Frankie—is right now?"

She shook her head. "Wouldn't matter anyway. Aimee has the money and now she's gone. If I had the hundred grand, I know Johnny would sell me Sonny. I just know he would."

She wasn't thinking straight. Even if she could buy Sonny—Frankie Toliver—he belonged to his parents, not to Layla. She desperately wanted an infant she couldn't have.

I said, "You know Johnny . . . I mean, now you know what Johnny is really like. Do you think that Johnny wouldn't just take the money from you and not give you the baby?"

She hesitated. "That's why I gave Aimee the money. She said she could make the exchange happen. I've been waiting. And waiting. She didn't do anything with the money." Her voice lowered, "I think Aimee kept the money for herself. Now it's too late. She's—"

My cell phone rang.

I looked at the number.

It was Ennis Freemantle calling.

I said to Layla, "It's not too late."

I got up, stepped away, and answered the phone.

CHAPTER FIFTY-FIVE

ENNIS WANTED ME to come back; he wanted to make a deal. I clicked off the cell phone and said to Layla, "I have to go."

"Here, you need a couple more strips to secure the arm, and you should have a sling. I'll make you one."

I waited while she finished. I thought I should take Drago with me back to the Lusty Muff, but that would be too much like pouring gasoline on smoldering embers. He hated bikers, CCS in particular. And they hated him. I couldn't risk it.

When she finished, I kissed her forehead. "Thank you. I have to go out for a few minutes."

"Are you going to get Sonny back?"

"If I can, but if we do, he has to go back to his parents."

She nodded. "I know, I just don't want him with those people anymore. He's not safe. It's unhealthy. He's at risk every second he's with them." She got up, went to the kitchenette, and stooped down to clean up the mess, the broken cup.

If we did get Sonny back, we'd have to pry him from her hands.

I stopped at the counter and took the brown paper grocery bag with the hundred thousand from her parents. "After we return Sonny to his parents, are you going back to Costa Rica?"

She looked up from kneeling on the floor, her hands full of cup shards. "No, Drago's asked me to stay with him. I haven't told him yes, but I think I'm going to say yes. He's the only person in this city who's been straight with me. Nice to me."

I nodded and left through the door and headed down the hall. She did love Drago. I was wrong again. I'd been misreading her. She was a good person. She no doubt would change Drago, maybe even settle him down, get him to step away from his vendetta.

Hopefully.

In front of the Lusty Muff, two different thugs had replaced Buck and Knight guarding the front door. They had been given the word and stepped aside to let me pass. This time the topless girl taking the cover charge smiled and whispered, "Thank you, that Buck is a real asshole and you fixed him good. He'll never bother me again."

Buck was now minus his rape equipment.

I winked and continued on through. Word had gone out. Everyone in the place stopped, turned, and looked as I entered. I forced myself not to hurry, not to look up at the window where Freemantle sat watching.

I made it to the stairs and to the landing. I stopped, took a deep breath, and opened the door.

Three hard-core biker thugs, all black leather and denim, stood by the desk to the left. One held a sawed-off double-barreled shotgun, enough firepower to literally cut me in half.

Ennis sat at the table in the red vinyl booth, alone, smoking, his movements twitchy from too much meth. He waved me over.

I missed having Waldo at my side and was decidedly more vulnerable with my arm trussed up minus my fur-covered partner.

I pulled open my shirt to expose the Beretta I'd taken off Buck, establishing the rules early.

"Don't be an ass, you pull that pea shooter, and Simian back there will cut you down with the gauge. Sit. What do you want to drink?"

I sat. "I don't drink." The back of my head prickled, having those three behind me.

I was a damn fool.

I might as well have been wearing sunglasses in the darkened room.

"Anyone who sits with me and makes a deal has got to seal that deal with a drink. That's what gentlemen do. What's it going to be?"

The irony, him using the word *gentleman*.

I said, "Tequila, top-shelf or nothing."

Ennis wanted to do a verbal dance, play the bullshit drinking game for a while before getting down to business.

He chuckled, raised his hand. One of the thugs at the bar brought a bottle and two glasses.

Ennis pointed. "That there is twenty-six hundred dollars a bottle. Is that top-shelf enough for you?"

I ignored his question and poured a glass. "I'm guessing you didn't pay for this tequila and it fell off someone's truck."

He smiled at the jab. "You were favoring your arm when you came in the first time. Now you got it all bound up. My guys do that to you?"

I said nothing.

He stared at me and took yet another deep pull off his cigarette and smiled.

That's when I saw it, something crawling about halfway down in his long shaggy unkempt beard. It disappeared down into the gloom below the table edge. I tried not to stare. I only saw it for a second and waited for whatever it was to show itself again.

Ennis reached, took the bottle, and poured himself a slug. He held up his glass toward me. The last thing I wanted was to drink a toast with this piece of shit.

I clinked his glass with mine while snatching glimpses of his beard. I slugged down the liquor.

Back home I worked at a cabana bar, and even though I wasn't a drinker, this tequila was the best I had ever tasted. It went down smooth and warm and made me crave another.

A dangerous proposition.

He set his glass down on the table. "I gotta tell ya, this is the first time I've ever in my life had a drink with a smoke."

"You call me that one more time and it'll be your last."

He sat back as if slapped. "You got a set a gorilla balls on you, don't you, boy?" He looked over his shoulder at his three thugs and laughed. "That's more than we can say for ol' Buck, your dog done gone and gelded him."

They all got a chuckle out of that.

I poured another drink and held up the glass. "Let's chalk one up for thinning the gene pool."

Ennis laughed and slapped the table. The critter in his beard made another showing, and this time I got a good look. It was a fat black widow spider with a waxy body and a red hourglass on its underside. Ennis had a poisonous spider living in his beard and didn't know it. That's what happened to people who let meth rule all their decisions while ignoring common hygiene.

The thought of a spider running free range over my body caused me to shiver. I slugged down the second shot of tequila. He immediately poured another.

The liquor started to work, the pain in my arm diminishing. Ennis raised his hand and waved. Another thug came over and placed stacks of U.S. currency bound in rubber bands on the table in front of me. He waved again. The three thugs filed out of the room and closed the door behind them.

I drank and poured another tequila, promising myself it would be the last. I held up the paper bag. "For this deal *I'm* supposed to bring *you* the money. What's going on?"

He leaned over a little. This time I watched two smaller black widows duck deeper into the gray hair of the beard. He had a whole family living in there.

I moved back some. No way could he know they were there. Any day—any minute now—they would bite the shit out of him, put him in the hospital, maybe even kill him.

He said, "I don't know where no kid is being held."

"Ah, shit." I started to slide out to leave.

"No, wait. I got another deal, a better one."

I waited. "I'm listening."

He checked over his shoulder to make sure his men had not returned. "Right there on the table is your ten that you dropped off plus another hundred thousand."

I shook my head. "No, I won't do it. For that kind of money, you could only want one thing. You want me to kill Johnny Ef. You want the top-dog position and you want me to do the dirty work for you."

"You're one smart smo—"

"Don't you say it!"

"Take it easy, it comes natural to me. No offense intended. Not this time, anyway, heh."

I eyed him and took another shot of tequila. The clear liquid went down too smooth and sanded off the sharp edges, made the world easier to understand. I poured another. This time a little version of Dad on my shoulder kicked me in the head. *Son, alcohol steals your brain, it befuddles and makes bad choices you can never take back.* His favorite quote, but for the life of me, I couldn't remember if it was his own or if he was quoting someone.

The liquor had already stolen that part of my brain.

Ennis leaned over even more. I slid away from him.

"What the hell's the matter with you? Don't you like white folks?"

I ignored his stupid comment and said, "We've been coming at Johnny Ef hard. He's going to be untouchable, sleeping in a different place every night, taking different cars and different routes, changing up his routine, no way can we get a line on him now. And if we do, he'll have tough men all around him. We'd never get close enough, not now."

"That's what I'm tellin' ya. You agree to do the deal, I'll tell you when and where he's most vulnerable."

I needed Ennis' information to get to Johnny and force him to tell us where he had Frankie/Sonny stashed so I could go home.

"I have twenty-four hours left, then I'm out of here. That's my clock and I'm sticking to it."

"That's okay—that'll work. Tomorrow night there's a poker game, one he never misses. He always cleans out the chumps he invites, and the dumbasses keep comin' back because he gives them something else that they want more than money. Ol' Johnny's low on cash right now, thanks to you. He really needs this."

I said nothing as his offer swirled round and round looking for a place to land.

"And," Ennis said, "the best part is that it's a hundred-thousand-dollar buy-in. Eight players including Johnny, that's nine hundred thousand to you."

"You somehow got the wrong impression of me. I'm not about the money. I just want the kid back and to be on my way."

"Sure, sure." He winked. "I understand. In this poker game I'm talkin' about, he'll only have four of his most trusted men covering him. Just four. Any more and his marks get nervous and think they're going to get ripped off. Two at the door and two inside the room."

"Those men covering him are not going to be CCS?"

He sat back. "Naw, that's parta why we're having this conversation." He reached out to put his hand on mine and suddenly remembered who I was—what I was—and jerked his hand back.

"You take this poker game down; you get to talk to Effin Johnny up close and personal. He'll tell you whatever you want to know if you put his feet to the fire. And you get nine hundred large, ta boot. I'm givin' ya another hundred grand on top of all of that to make it a cool million dollars. You can't pass up a deal like this. It's too sweet."

Yeah, if it was so sweet why was *he* passing on it? I downed another shot and slid out of the booth, my head swimming from the alcohol. I took ten grand off the top of the pile his men had left on the table and put it in the grocery bag. "I don't want your blood money. Keep it."

"You going to do the deal? You gonna take out Johnny?"

"Once you get the time and location of the game, you text me, and I'll think about it."

"That's not the way we do things around here, boy. It's either yes or no." He pounded the table with a pointed index finger. "Right here, right now, I gotta know. You in or out?"

I stopped on my way to the door. "Okay, I'll hit the poker game. And I'll have a talk with Johnny. That's all I can promise. If it goes down bad or he doesn't want to tell me where the kid is, you might get what you want."

Ennis smiled. "I guess I can live with that."

The poker game gave me access to Johnny Ef and Johnny Ef knew where I could find Sonny.

CHAPTER FIFTY-SIX

THE BEDROOM DOOR to the suite was closed when I got back, Drago and Layla in conference or congress or both for the rest of the night. I set the grocery bag of money back on the counter to the kitchenette, the day catching up to me all at once.

I stretched out on the couch. Waldo followed me over, sat next to me, and rested his big head on my shoulder, his halitosis easier to take with all the tequila on board numbing my senses. He was sad that his best friend had found a mate.

The tequila had really taken hold and made the room shimmy every now and again. How many shots had I taken? Something that good should be outlawed.

I closed my eyes to make the shimmy go away and made it worse; it turned the world into the pitching deck of a ship at sea. I rested my good hand on Waldo's head. I should've called Marie, but she'd instantly know I'd been drinking. I was ashamed enough already that I'd let the entire day slip through my fingers—all those hours lost asleep in the safe room waiting for the police to finish with the forensics deconstructing what happened to Aimee Langhari.

My cell buzzed. I checked it. A text from Eddie:

Is it wrong that the game Monopoly is only made by one company?

I chuckled and closed my eyes. That kid really knew how to cheer me up.

*   *   *

Later, I woke with a start, frantically brushing black widow spiders from my nose and face and spitting them from my mouth—a tequila-fueled bad dream—and my limbs felt abnormally heavy.

I held my arm up for a better look. Layla had put a plaster cast on it, and I never woke. Note to self: good tequila acts as anesthesia.

Then I noticed Bea sitting in her wheelchair with Dad in the hotel chair right next to her—both staring at me.

Mom took a slug from a highball glass with orange and red liquid, probably a tequila sunrise. The thought of tequila, ugh.

Bea said, "That's not a healthy way to wake up. Come on, get your ass up. You going to sleep all day?"

I tried to sit and lie back down, my head an anvil with someone using a hammer on it. The ping-ping-ping throbbed behind my eyes. Tequila was not my friend. I let a groan slip out.

"Son, is it your arm that's hurting you? How did you do it? Maybe we should take you to a doctor."

I swung my legs around and put my head in my hands. "Oooh."

Bea said, "He's groaning from a hangover. I can see the signs."

"Bruno doesn't drink. You didn't drink, did you, Son?"

More shame piled on top to smother me. "Never, except when I have to."

Mom held her glass high. "Spoken like a true drunk. Hear, hear."

"Why don't you go—"

"Bruno!" Dad cut me off before I said something I'd regret.

I looked at Mom. "Back so soon? Did you reach your goal?"

That took the air out of her sails. She set her glass down on the table, spun in her wheelchair, and left. Dad opened the doors for her and then came back.

He gave me the dreaded "I'm disappointed in you" look. I much preferred yelling and screaming. But he never yelled and screamed, at least not in my lifetime. He apparently had an entire other life before I came along, one filled with intrigue and adventure he'd never told me about and only hinted at with inadvertent verbal clues. He might tell me one day as advanced age threatened to snuff out his legacy. He was a lone candle with high winds in the forecast and it hurt just to think about him not being around.

He sat on the couch next to me and put his hand on my leg. Sunlight had not been kind to him and the evening dimness aged him ten years. "I'm sorry, Dad, it's just that . . . well, she lost your entire life savings and then has the gall to spout off at me."

"It was *my* life savings."

"I know, I know."

"And it's none of your business."

"I might fight you on that one. I love and care about you, and that gives me the right to say something when I think you're being taken for a ride, cheated."

He squeezed my leg with his hand. "You don't know what you're talking about."

"Then tell me."

"Bea asked me not to."

"Did you promise?"

"Well, no, but—"

"Then tell me. If our roles were reversed, you'd do the same for me."

He looked away as he thought about that one. He finally moved and sat with his back against the cushion. "It's more complicated than you think."

I said nothing, letting the silence do my bidding.

He waited a minute then said, "You know your mother had a . . . ah, jaded life in the past. I call it 'the before' and 'the now.' She's different in 'the now' and she's having a hard go of it. And, Bruno, you're not making things any easier on her."

He waited for a comment from me.

I said nothing.

"It's guilt," he said. "It's crushing the life out of her. The old Bea could care less about guilt but the new one—"

"So, she burns through all your money to assuage her guilt."

He pointed a finger at me. "Bruno! I won't tell you again. What's the matter with you, Son, have you lost all compassion?"

"I'm sorry, go on."

"As I was saying, this newfound guilt is crushing her. She even went to see a psychiatrist and he told her to make amends, that it might help."

I started to say something.

He held up his hands. "Wait. Before you say anything more, let me finish."

"Go ahead."

"Back in the day when she was . . . who she was before, she hurt people."

I said in a lowered tone, "You more than anyone."

He scowled. I crawled back into myself.

He continued. "She consistently fell in with the wrong people looking for the fastest path to easy street. She was arrested many times. Each time the consequences grew more severe, her criminal record compiling until finally she was going away for a long time. Friends came to visit her in jail while her case crawled along through the justice system. She talked those friends into bailing her out. She never told them she wasn't guilty, she just wanted out of jail. She wanted her freedom.

"Once out, she absconded, jumped bail."

He shook his head in despair and disgust. "Those nice people, two families, lost their houses they put up as collateral. Houses that had been in their families for generations."

"Oh, my God."

I had been a fool. Mom was trying her best to be noble, to make amends, and I'd only seen her bad side, the pessimist's point of view. I owed her a huge apology. How had I missed it? Of course, Dad would help her in that sort of endeavor. If I didn't trust her, I should've trusted Dad. All of a sudden, the love for my mom returned in a rush.

"That's right. She can't live with it. The guilt is killing her."

"I'm sorry, Dad. I feel about two feet tall. I wish you'd told me. What can I do to help?"

He beamed.

His integrity and her shame had kept them from telling me. I'm not sure I'd ever heard of a more magnanimous gesture. I'd have to get down on my knees and beg her forgiveness.

I said, "Cards might not be the best way to go."

"I know, but how else can she raise six hundred and fifty thousand dollars—legally?"

"Six hundred and fifty thousand dollars? Dad, my God!"

"It's a lot, I know. But you should've seen her in Vegas. While she was winning, all the guilt melted away and she was the old Bea, the beautiful Bea with that sparkle in her eyes, with that lust for life. She wasn't bitter and angry, she was alive just like in the old days.

"Son, I'd gladly spend that money all over again to give her that same twenty minutes. She was truly happy."

I struggled up to my feet and stood. Dad said, "What are you going to do?"

"Eat crow, a big double serving. I've been a horse's ass for too long."

"I'm not going to argue with you on that one, Son." He smiled.

I picked up the glass of tequila sunrise Mom had left behind and walked across the hall. I knocked on the door before sliding the card key and entering without permission.

Bea sat in her wheelchair looking out the back window at the massive wood pallet yard behind the hotel. She didn't turn to see me come in.

I sat on the couch and put the drink on the coffee table where she could reach it. She said nothing and kept staring.

"I came to tell you I'm sorry and to ask you to forgive me."

"Forgive you for what?"

"For the way I've been acting. I'm protective of Dad and sometimes it keeps me from seeing the big picture."

She turned and looked at me, my mother who I'd only known for little more than a couple of months.

She said, "This isn't on you, Son. I am a bad person. I deserve everything you can dish out. I went to prison when you were very young, and when I got out, I never came back. I hurt a lot of people in my life and I'm trying to atone."

Tears filled her eyes and flowed down her cheeks, leaving glistening tracks on wrinkled brown skin.

I stood, a lump growing in my throat. I knelt at the wheelchair and held her hand. "I know you are. You should've told me what you were doing. I am so sorry I treated you the way I did. Can you ever forgive me?"

She pulled me into a hug and held on tight. All those missed years without a mother vibrated and leapt up between us in a flourish of long-forgotten love. All of a sudden, she became a part of my world as if she'd never left.

That's the power of a sincere hug.

We hugged until my legs started to cramp and hurt from being on my knees too long. Finally, I tried to pull away. She held on a second longer and whispered, "I love you, Bruno."

"I love you, Mom." I said it without reservation. I pulled away and we both wiped our wet faces.

She stared me in the eyes. "Your dad obviously told you about my debt, and you have to know I can't leave here until I get the money to pay those people back. I don't care what I have to do to get it. I'd appreciate it if you took your father with you to Costa Rica while I do what I have to do."

"I understand. And that won't be necessary. I'm here for you now. I'll get the money you need. I'll get it tonight. That is if everything goes according to plan."

"*What? How?*"

"I don't want Dad to know but all this mess should be over tonight, and I'll have your money. We can all go back to Costa Rica together."

"You already said that. How are you going to do it? I want in, whatever it is that's going down, I want in. I can't let you do this without me. I caused all my problems. I don't want charity. Let me help earn it. I have to help earn it or it won't mean anything."

I shook my head. "It's going to get ugly."

"You think I haven't seen ugly? Bruno, I want in."

I stood and walked toward the door. "Me and Drago will handle this. I couldn't live with myself if you got hurt."

I stopped and turned. "I just got you back, Mom. I'm not going to let anything happen to you now. End of discussion."

She followed along in the wheelchair. "You've seen how I can handle myself. Let me in, please, I have to earn my way out of this ... mess, or this God-awful guilt will be the end of me."

CHAPTER FIFTY-SEVEN

MOM FOLLOWED ME across the hall back into our suite where Drago now sat at the kitchenette table with Layla eating shrimp scampi mixed in dirty rice. In front of Drago sat a pile of three steaks cooked but still raw. The food came from a high-dollar restaurant as evidenced by the empty bags on the floor: *Mastroianni's of Beverly Hills.*

That was a long drive for takeout.

Had Layla asked him to make that trek? Drago talked around a mouthful of food and pointed with his serrated knife to several other bags on the counter with the restaurant logo. "Got a bunch of stuff off the menu, didn't know what you wanted. Help yourself."

Had to be two thousand dollars in highbrow cuisine, the scent wonderous even with my hangover.

"Xander." Mom wheeled over to Dad. "Would you please tell Bruno that I'm in on whatever he has going tonight?"

"Bruno?" Dad said

Drago looked at me. I said to Drago, "We're going to finish it tonight. We're going to have a little talk with Johnny Ef and whisper in his ear." Drago nodded and kept eating.

Layla said, "I'm going, too."

Drago stopped chewing. "No, you're not."

His tone carried such finality, her eyes opened wide and she sat back in her chair as if slapped. He apparently had never used that tone with her.

Mom said, "Bruno, I—"

"No, you're not going, and that's the end of the conversation. Drago and I will handle it. Be packed and ready to fly home tomorrow."

Drago nodded his approval about it just being the two of us tonight and went back to devouring the meat in front of him, the caveman element overpowering the civilized man.

My cell vibrated in my pocket.

I checked the screen. Spiderman—Ennis Freemantle.

I stepped over to the front door, turned my back to my friends and loved ones, and answered it. I said nothing, waiting for him to talk.

"You there?"

"I'm here. Talk to me. Have you made the call to find out where he's going to be?"

"I've been thinking on it. I can't get the information from our . . . ah friend by just asking. He'll know something's up. He's gonna ask me why I wanna know. You're gonna have to give me a name and description of someone who will play in the game tonight. And it can't be you or your big friend—he knows you two on sight. It has to be someone who knows cards at least well enough to make a good showing."

I turned and looked back to the room. Everyone watched me. I looked into Mom's eyes and nodded. Even though she couldn't hear the conversation, she nodded and knew I was letting her in.

I came back toward the living area and said into the phone, "Tell him Ms. Beatrice Wentworth. She's visiting from Vegas where she owns two small hotels on the old strip. Wentworth is an alias, so he can't background check her."

Mom smiled hugely.

Because Mom smiled, Dad did too.

Freemantle said into the phone, "Good, that's real good; he'll eat that up with a spoon. Does this Beatrice bitch know how to play poker?" I gripped the phone tight and fought back the rebuttal on the tip of my tongue, remembering he was about to get his with multiple poisonous spider bites. "Yes, she does, and she will bring a bag full of money."

"Gimme her description."

"She's a black female about seventy, wheelchair-bound, and you can tell him she'll be an easy mark at cards."

"Excellent. Excellent. I'll make the call now and get right back to you." He clicked off.

Mom wheeled over to me and reached out her hand. I took it, reveling in the touch. She said, "Thank you." And meant it.

Drago, his eyes on the meat being shoveled into his maw, said, "What's the setup?"

"Johnny Ef has his weekly poker game tonight—"

Drago looked up from his plate. "Are you kiddin' me? That's perfect."

"He's going to have four pros guarding, watching his back."

Drago shrugged and went back to eating. "Pros go down under the iron just like everyone else."

I wished I had his confidence. These four guys would be armed and watching for a rip.

Dad came closer and stood next to me and Bea. "You're going to rob a poker game? That's not good, Son. People are going to get hurt. Bea . . . don't want Bea to be put in jeopardy." He turned to Mom. "No, honey, you can't do this."

"It's okay, Xander. Bruno's a smart boy, he'll have every detail planned out. You wait and see if he doesn't." She looked at me, her eyes alive just like Dad had said, alive with joie de vivre that I had never seen before. "What are the stakes?" she asked.

"Hundred thousand buy-in, you're the tenth person."

She let out a little squeak of excitement and clapped her hands. "I gotta pee." She jumped up from the wheelchair and hurried to the bathroom. Drago quit chewing mid-bite and stared at the retreating Bea, then back at me.

I could only shrug.

Layla's mouth dropped open in shock. "Oh, my God."

"Yeah," I said. "I know."

Layla pointed with her fork in the direction Mom had fled. "You mean she's not—"

My phone buzzed in my pocket. "Dad, Bea's *your* wife, explain it to Layla. Lord knows I can't."

I answered the phone. "Yeah."

"It's all set. I texted you the location and the time. Do the best you can regarding our deal, huh?"

He sounded content with what was going to happen to Johnny Ef.

He clicked off.

I checked the text message Ennis sent regarding the location and time.

I couldn't believe our luck.

I looked up to the ceiling. "Thank you."

Then over to Drago. "We finally caught a break. After all the problems with this mess, we finally caught a break."

CHAPTER FIFTY-EIGHT

SEVEN P.M., TWO hours before the poker game was to start, Drago put a duct tape strip across the semi-naked deskman sitting on his butt in the utility closet just off the lobby at the Shimbuto. His feet and hands zip-tied and taped.

Dad stood outside the utility closet door donning the man's uniform. The too-large hat needed rolled-up paper inside before it would sit on his head properly. The shoulders to the uniform blouse hung too far down, but he'd pass muster. Few people paid attention to the hired help, especially an elderly black man.

Across the street, the Staples Center hosted some grand event, with several thousand well-heeled twenty-somethings in a long line waiting to be let in and more coming every minute. They talked and laughed and vaped.

LAPD was there in force, monitoring the activity on foot and in frequent patrol cars passing by.

Not the best scenario for our caper.

Though, if the poker game rip went down wrong, the chaos on the street might act as good cover to escape.

Or not.

Drago and I had to get into the penthouse before the poker players started to arrive. This meant the front-desk man had to be taken out. Our team was short on players, so dad came in from the bench to pinch-hit. I had to admit he looked good sitting up on that podium with his huge smile, the blue-gray security guard uniform, and the hat at a jaunty cant.

"You sure you got this, Dad?"

"Son, I wore a postman's uniform for forty-one years and I am smart enough to know how to push a button to activate the elevators. I'll be fine, don't worry about me. You just be careful."

I nodded, scared to death the same as a dad would be for his son in a weird role reversal.

Drago closed the utility room door, and we headed to the elevators with Waldo tagging along. The elevator doors opened because Dad had pressed the button back at the desk. We got in; the doors closed. I said to Drago, "What if the guy in the closet starts to kick and make noise?"

"I already whispered in his ear and told him how the cow ate the cabbage."

I had to smile at the old adage he'd taken from me and I had borrowed from Dad, the passing on of Dad's legacy.

The elevator door opened on the top floor. My anxiety continued to rise. The plan had too many moving parts. Something was going to go wrong. When it did, people were going to get hurt.

I put my hand on the knob to Penthouse Three, tried to turn it, and at the same time bumped my shoulder when the door didn't open.

Locked.

Shit.

We hadn't planned on it being locked.

Of course, it would be locked.

Why wouldn't it be?

Waldo raised his paw and scraped the door—he wanted in. Drago put one of his hands on each of my shoulders and moved me aside.

From his pocket he withdrew a tool, an automatic lock pick that resembled a small gun.

He'd continued to be submerged in *the life* while *I* worked in a cabana bar on the beach where the most important thing to worry about was enough rum for making pina coladas.

Inside the apartment, Aimee Langhari's blood had been cleaned up and the carpet removed, leaving only a gleaming dark hardwood floor.

Waldo, his nose in the air sniffing, his paws clicking on the hardwood, moved right to the spot where the blood had been coagulating on the now missing carpet and sniffed the floor.

Two round tables had been added with green felt and ashtrays. Off to the side sat a portable bar on rollers and a short table covered by a white tablecloth with cold cuts and different types of bread and condiments on plates with Saran Wrap.

We had less than an hour and a half. The anxiety over the need for us to be out of view sent me to the copy of *A Tale of Two Cities* on the shelf, looking for the electronic controller that activated the safe room latch.

I found it and pushed the button. The wall of books moved almost imperceptibly as the latch let go.

I looked back. Drago stood at the short table making himself a huge hero sandwich while he dropped roast beef to his sidekick Waldo who snapped it out of the air.

"Drago," I hissed. "Get your ass over here."

He munched on his hero as he came over. "You need to chill. This here caper is all about nothin'. Easy pickins."

With one hand Drago swung open the partial wall. Waldo entered like he owned the place, went right over, jumped up on the bed, and lay down claiming the most comfortable spot for himself.

We entered. Drago pulled down the handle that vacuum-locked the room.

Now we just had to wait for the fun and games to begin.

I paced back and forth. Drago sat in his chair next to the one-way glass, his feet up on the sill, finishing his sandwich.

In combat, the Army tells the infantryman to sleep whenever you get the chance. For Drago it was eat whenever you get the chance. And he did. Took a ton of calories to keep a machine that large on the road.

I stopped at the bed and waved a hand at Waldo to get off, that I wanted to lie down. He growled.

I said, "Tell your dog, the people get the furniture."

Drago didn't look over. "He *is* people."

I glared at Waldo, who gave me a smug smile over the win.

I pulled a chair around and sat beside my big friend. "I'm worried my mom's going to get shot when we bust outta this room."

Drago's big head came around slowly to look at me. "I won't be the one to shoot her." He held up the rebar. Sometimes his comments came off a little rude and insensitive.

"Yeah, I gottcha, I'm the one with the guns."

I couldn't hold a gun in my dominant hand, the cast wrapped around my thumb and across the palm. I'd only be able to shoot with my left.

Drago said, "If you're worried, just stay outta my way and I'll deal with it."

A canned answer he'd given me on several of our other capers. He didn't mean it to hurt, but it did.

"You be careful with that iron. We need Johnny talking so he can tell us how to find Sonny."

He grunted.

I sat next to him, nervous, fidgety. Drago eventually reached over, put a large paw on me, and pressed down to get me to stop.

"Yeah, I know," I said. "I can't help it."

This time he watched the empty room on the other side of the glass without looking at me. "Just think about going home tomorrow, how you're going to be getting on that plane and—"

"Boat. We have to take the slow boat. No way can I explain three infants to American Customs or Costa Rican Customs for that matter. They'd pull us out of line and my fake ID won't hold up under close scrutiny."

Drago nodded.

I said, "Hey, you know I just realized I've never seen you sleep. Do you ever sleep or are you really some kind of android from the future, a Cyberdyne Systems Model 101 Terminator with living tissue over a metal endoskeleton?"

I only knew the description because the kids back home loved the movie and watched it over and over, yelling out the lines along with Arnold.

Drago grunted again. This time it was one of those "quit-being-an-idiot" kind of grunts.

I checked the digital clock on the small desk for the umpteenth time since we came in; only two minutes had passed since the last time I looked.

Drago said, "Make yourself useful and get me a beer outta the fridge."

"Sure." Anything to have something to do.

My arm itched under the cast. I handed him the beer and sat next to him in the chair. "So, Layla said she's staying here with you?"

He spun in his seat, grabbed a handful of my shirt, and yanked me up to his face.

Waldo barked and came off the bed like a bullet. He took my cast in his jaws, my arm feeling the pressure as he pulled me in the opposite direction.

Drago—up in my face. "She say that? She told you that?"

"Take it easy, big man. Sure, she said it. I wouldn't make up something like that."

A huge smile slowly crept across his face that had flushed red. "She really said that?"

"Yes. Yes. She said she was staying here with you. She didn't tell you?"

He let go and turned away staring out the glass, still smiling, and muttered. "She's staying here."

I yanked my arm out of Waldo's mouth, glared at him, and straightened my shirt. "Yeah, she is, and I think she's got a thing for you."

He whipped back again. "You think so? You're not just saying that, are you?"

"No, I'm not. I can tell she's got a thing, it's for sure. You two need to communicate better."

"Daaamn." Drago drew out the word, dimming it at the end. He slugged down the beer in one long glug.

"Hey," I said. "If she doesn't know how you feel about her, you'd better tell her."

He lost his smile, his eyes turned wild, something I'd never seen before. "I can't. The thought of sayin' those kinda words scares the hell outta me. The L word." He shivered.

I tried not to chuckle. He wasn't afraid of the devil himself, but a little hundred-pound girl put him back on his heels with a couple of simple words.

I looked askance at the empty bed. I made for it taking three giant steps. Waldo saw the play, knocked me out of way, and jumped up on the bed.

He growled.

Damn dog.

The nerves rose up inside me, and I had to move around. I wandered into the bathroom and checked out the medicine cabinet and looked under the sink. What I found suddenly made everything clear. Instead of sleeping the last time we'd been in the safe room, I should've been tossing the place.

I'd been a fool from the very start.

I came out to tell Drago.

On the other side of the glass, the door to the penthouse opened.

In walked Johnny Ef with four of his cohorts dressed in tuxedos.

Four lethal penguins.

Game on.

CHAPTER FIFTY-NINE

THE FOUR MEN could easily be ex-special forces, square-shouldered, square jaws, hair cut short, their movements agile and economical. They looked like highly capable James Bond clones.

Four against two, five if we counted Johnny Ef.

Not good odds.

The cast on my arm suddenly became more prominent. I looked around the room for something to saw it off, at least the plaster strap across my palm so I could hold a gun.

No tool came to mind.

While we watched and listened, Johnny issued his orders not to interfere in the game and to only monitor if a verbal disturbance broke out. If someone got "froggy," Johnny would give the two men inside the nod and they would quietly as possible eighty-six the offender. He offered to let the men eat if they wanted. The game was going to go twenty-four hours or more.

They declined.

Hunger made predators more dangerous and unpredictable.

I could only hope Johnny didn't see the dent Drago and Waldo put in the cold cuts.

Johnny assigned one of the men to be in charge of the bank. He'd take the hundred thousand cash buy-in and issue the chips. He'd also be the one to cash them out at the end of the game. The two designated outside men left the room to stand watch in the hall in front of the penthouse door.

Johnny moved around the room checking out the décor in an up-close examination. He'd obviously been in the room before and acted as if he owned it. He had probably been making the lease payments for Aimee and now laid claim to the spoils of war.

A trophy.

What a perfect venue for an impromptu poker game.

He made his way over to the mirrored one-way glass, and for a brief second, I worried he might know about the safe room but then realized that would defeat the purpose for having one—the secrecy.

He opened his coat, took out a Sig Sauer 9mm pistol from a shoulder holster, pulled the magazine to check the loads, and put the gun back. He moved away, over to the window to watch the craziness down below and across the street at the Staples Center.

Drago said, "I get the first whack on that guy."

I started to tell him that wouldn't be a good idea, that we needed Johnny talking, when my cell phone buzzed. Eddie from back home had sent another text message:

I was going to wear my camouflage shirt today, but I couldn't find it.

I chuckled as I always did with his text messages and showed it to Drago.

He grunted.

I don't remember ever seeing Drago laugh. He'd give a chuckle now and again, but never a full-on belly laugh. What a life he lived, one without mirth.

Twenty minutes passed. Johnny started to move around the room, the same as an animal in a cage. I wanted a piece of him for what he'd done to Aimee Langhari. The unmitigated gall to use her condo after he'd had her killed. The act matched his demented mentality.

The penthouse door opened from the outside by one of the penguins and in came a man I recognized from the Comstock. The guy in the Porsche crossover, the bronze Cayenne that drove away when we first arrived on scene.

Waldo sensed some invisible response from me or from Drago to the man entering the penthouse. He put his paws up on the sill to the window to see out into the room.

He growled.

I said, "Tell him not to bark."

Drago said something in German. Waldo looked at him, dropped down, and went back to the bed to lie down.

The man handed a Nike gym bag to the security guy inside, who took it over to the counter and started counting the money inside. The machine made a quiet whirring noise.

The new arrival smiled hugely and shook Johnny Ef's hand. Johnny had taken the chair at the first table with his back to the outside window to keep an eye on everyone in the room and the entrance to the penthouse.

Johnny called the man Edward.

Edward was elegantly dressed in an expensive dark-blue suit and yellow tie, his fingernails manicured and buffed. This guy lived at the top of the financial food chain and frequented Johnny's houses of ill repute, where he ruined young lives to satisfy a vile and perverted craving.

The next man in wore a burgundy velour gym suit with a white stripe and swung from two crutches, one leg in a cast all the way up to the hip and one arm in a cast from his wrist up to his shoulder. He maneuvered the crutches with great difficulty.

He was a Drago rebar recipient from the Comstock. He too handed off his money in a plastic CVS bag and hobbled over to sit beside Edward. Johnny had a big smile for him as well and called him Franklin.

Within twenty minutes the two tables filled with the broken and the maimed from the Comstock incident, all of them out on bail. All of them, first thing, came over to shake Johnny's hand to pay tribute before taking a seat.

They made sandwiches and cocktails and talked among themselves—all to the man—reliving the horror that befell them at the Comstock. They described Drago as an inhuman beast with eyes that glowed red hot—a Conan the Barbarian wielding his long sword.

In their conversation, none of them admitted any criminality and thought themselves victims of an unjust violent encounter and worried the world had degenerated and had been taken over by the lawless.

Their bodies were broken and plastered, heads bandaged, their emotions scrambled and destined to be massaged and manipulated by head shrinkers for the next ten to twenty years over the massacre they would revisit every night they laid their heads on their pillows and closed their eyes. Still, that wasn't a large enough penalty for what they had done. Tonight, if all went well, we would penalize them with another fine of a hundred thousand dollars each and a few more broken limbs.

Franklin finally said, "Well, are we going to get this show on the road?"

Johnny checked his watch. "We have one more player before we can get started."

Mom—she was late. She probably wanted to make a grand entrance. Tonight wasn't the time for theatrics.

The penthouse door opened and in wheeled Mom.

I slowly stood from the chair, my mouth agape.

She looked like some kind of genie escaped from a bottle, dressed in purple satin with gold trim and some kind of turban made from the same material. From around her neck hung a violet glass bauble on a gold-colored chain. From her ears fake diamonds winked when they caught the light. She looked regal and rich, if not a tad eccentric.

She handed the penguin a brushed-aluminum Halliburton briefcase that contained the hundred thousand that belonged to Layla's parents.

Pure class.

She knew how to handle herself in a short con. That's why she was late; she had been preparing.

Once she was inside, one of the penguins pushed her wheelchair over to the tables.

I chuckled and whispered to no one, *"A turban? Really, Mom?"*

Johnny's table had filled up and only one spot remained at the second table. Mom wheeled over and introduced herself to Johnny. Johnny stood like a gentleman and kissed her hand.

I wanted to break his face for touching her.

He introduced her to the rest of the players as "Ms. Bea." Everyone said hello, anxious to get to the cards and a chance to win stacks of chips. Johnny held out his hand like a maitre d', indicating the empty seat at the second table.

Mom smiled and said, "This place right here would be best for me." Indicating the spot where Edward sat, the first to arrive to get the prime seat next to Johnny.

She fluttered her eyelids at Johnny.

He chuckled. "That'll be fine. Ed, why don't you move to the other table?"

Ed's expression showed his silent anger. When he didn't move right away, one of the penguin James Bonds came over, scooped up his chips, and moved him along.

Edward sat in the empty chair at the other table and shot Mom the stink eye.

She coyly cocked her head to the side, smiled, and shrugged as if she didn't mean to cause such a problem.

Yeah, right.

She wanted to put the men off their game before it even started.

Great job, Mom.

CHAPTER SIXTY

I TRIED TO do the math in my head: two of the inside penguins had guns and Johnny Ef had a gun, which equaled three. Then once the operation went loud, the two guards outside would rush in, guns out. That was five against two, odds nowhere near what they should be for the op to fall in our favor.

People were going to get hurt.

We *did* have the element of surprise.

We were going to pop out of a wall. That would give us about a second-and-a-half distraction.

Drago sat calm and quiet watching out the one-way glass, the same as if at a tennis match sipping a mint julep.

Waldo got off the bed and came over and sat next to my chair. I looked over at the bed. He saw me and looked to the bed then back at me as if daring me to go for it.

I said to Drago, "It's five against two and that's not counting if one or more of the pervs are heeled."

Drago took some sunflower seeds from the navy pea coat he wore, put them in his mouth, cracked one, and spit the shells onto the floor not caring about DNA. "I don't expect any trouble from any of them turds."

I said, "How are we going to play this?"

He shrugged, spit some more shells. "This is your gig, I'm just following your lead."

"Oh, terrific."

Out in the room, Johnny Ef rose from his chair and held up his cocktail glass. "I'd like to make a toast to the late great Aimee Langhari, who in her absence, generously donated the use of her condo."

The mentally deranged around both tables slapped the wood and made noise: "Hear. Hear. RIP. Hope it's not too hot for her where she's going." Things of that nature.

I'd briefed Mom on the setup, the orientation of the room, and the safe room. She looked over to the mirror we sat behind and shot me a knowing glance.

Johnny sat down.

Mom next to him said, "I'm not sure I understand the link to this Aimee Langhari person?"

Johnny gave her his best womanizing smile. "She was a woman who overstepped and is no longer with us."

Then I caught on, pulled out my phone, and started recording.

Mom opened a pack of cards sitting in front of her and with great alacrity began to shuffle them. "You used the past tense with her. Is there something I need to worry about?"

Franklin guffawed. "Just don't get on Johnny's bad side, am I right, Johnny?"

Mom gave Johnny a coy smile. "By overstepping, I hope you don't mean playing cards, because tonight I intend on cleaning out all you boys."

A few of the walking wounded sitting around their table let go with unsure laughs.

The other table had already started playing and only paid heed to their cards and the chips in the pot.

Mom dealt the cards after calling the game: Texas Hold 'Em. Johnny picked up his cards as they came to him and said, "You have nothing to fear from me. I only gave Aimee what she had coming to her."

Franklin said, "Yeah, a South American necktie from what I hear."

Johnny shot him the stink eye. Franklin crawled back into himself.

Mom smiled. "This is a pretty rough crowd. Maybe I should've brought my dog Fifi for protection."

The men at the table laughed at that. "Yeah, Fifi sounds like just the kind of dog to keep you safe."

Johnny's mood shifted. "Play cards."

They played a few hands before one of the guys with a bandaged head said, "Johnny, that Comstock Hotel was one sweet operation, you going to get some other place like it started? I got an itch that needs scratching."

A guy with red hair and a cast from his shoulder down to his wrist said, "Yeah, we'd really appreciate it if you got another one up and running. And soon."

Johnny said, "Yeah, it's already in the works, but I have to pass on some of the expense so be ready to pay a little extra." He let a creepy smile wiggle out. "Now are we going to jibber-jabber or play cards?"

I queued up the video and sent it to Helen Hellinger. Seconds later, Helen texted back and asked, "Where are you?"

I ignored her. The recording gave her more than enough to prosecute Johnny Ef. Mom had been on the ball and got me thinking in that direction. Helen would recognize the location in the video and come running. We didn't have much time. I'd made a mistake sending it so soon.

Drago stood and stretched. "You going to call this thing? It's getting late and I need to get back to Layla."

He acted like this was an everyday eight-to-five job and he needed to clock out.

I didn't know when to say go. Nothing was going to change the odds. Mom was still right out there in the field of fire and could get hit once the rounds started popping off.

And they would pop off, there was no two ways around it.

Call it now or wait. I didn't know what to do.

Mom suddenly tossed her cards in. "I need to get a Courvoisier. I'm bone dry and spittin' sand."

Johnny raised his hand to one of the James Bond penguins. "Don?"

"No one waits on me. I'm my own woman." She wheeled over to the cocktail bar, hesitated, then wheeled behind it.

Drago stepped over to the long handle to the door of the safe room. "I guess she's calling it for you."

He pulled down the handle and shoved with his shoulder.

Waldo barked and barked.

The secret door swung open.

CHAPTER SIXTY-ONE

WITH ALL DEVASTATING events, there is a pause, a deep gasp by those caught by surprise.

That one second of widened eyes and mouths, their breath trapped in lungs failing to obey.

In that one second Drago charged the two tux-clad guards, issuing the guttural bellow of a water buffalo, the rebar pulled back to slay the enemy, reap them like stalks of wheat.

Waldo roared and made it to the first man who reached inside his tux for a gun.

Waldo leapt, his jaws closing on the wrist as it started to withdraw.

Crunch.

Scream.

The iron in Drago's hand came down and chunked the guard in the head. He wilted to the floor.

The group of poker players shook off their stunned silence and screeched, jumping to their feet knocking back chairs, wild-eyed, looking for someplace to hide. A couple of them got down on hands and knees and crawled under the table. One man stood in the same place and pissed his pants.

Waldo had his man down on the floor, his gun hand in his jaws wiggling, tearing, chomping. The man kicking at the dog as he whimpered for someone to help.

Maybe he wasn't ex-military.

All of that happened as I rushed toward Johnny Ef not twenty feet across the room and at the same time miles away.

My legs and feet moved in air that had thickened, slowing normal speed.

Mom popped up from behind the bar, her turban gone, her makeup—the red lipstick and kohl around her eyes—made her a naked clown, a vulnerable clown.

She pointed a small gun at Johnny Ef and yelled, "Don't move! Don't you move!"

Johnny, angry, continued to draw his gun from under his suitcoat

I raised my .357, pointed at Johnny. "Don't do it. Stop. Stop."

Johnny's gun made it out and swung toward Mom.

Behind me, the penthouse door forced open.

Gunshots rang out, tamping down the frightened screaming around the tables.

I didn't have time to look back.

Drago would have to deal with it.

Mom's small gun popped and jumped in her hand.

Smoke rose in the air.

Johnny flinched as the round hit him.

My mind gave my finger permission to pull the trigger, but in that new slowed time zone, nothing happened right away.

Johnny's gun fired.

"Noooo!" I yelled.

The .357 in my hand finally fired, kicked with heavy recoil.

Mom flew back against the wall, hit by Johnny's bullet.

My first round missed Johnny and shattered the window behind him, changing it to a million-piece puzzle held together by nothing.

My second bullet caught Johnny under the chin. He flew backward through the shattered window, disappearing into the night.

Eight of the poker players made for the door in a herd. I sensed it more than saw it as I moved toward the bar. "Mom? Mom?"

Drago went to work chopping the losers with his rebar, breaking legs and arms he'd missed the first time at the Comstock, giving the men matching sets.

Waldo chomped and barked and mauled, the humanity piling up in blood and bone.

I finally made it around the bar.

Mom lay on the floor laughing. "Did you see that asshole get flung out the window when you shot him? That was really something else, wasn't it? I was right there to see it, not ten feet away. It was really something."

"Are you hit?"

"Help me up."

I took hold.

My hand touched damp and slick purple silk. "Mom, you're shot."

"It's just a nick. Get the money. Get a bag and get the money."

My hands moved over her body looking for the GSW and found it, high right shoulder.

"Bruno, snap out of it. Get the money. Can't you hear that outside, the screaming? Johnny made a big splash down there. The cops are coming on the run. We gotta move. Get the money."

"Forget the money. I'm helping you out of here."

She stopped and took hold of my arm with her good one, her eyes right up in my face. "Son, I won't tell you again, get the damn money."

"Right. All right."

"Wait," she said, turned, and took a Louis Vuitton bag, a knock-off that had been folded and collapsed on the seat of her wheelchair. She handed it to me and eased down in the wheelchair. She un-wrapped her turban and draped it over her shoulders like a shawl to cover the wound and the blood. I wheeled her over to the counter with the stacks of cash. She held the bag open while I loaded it.

She giggled like a little schoolgirl.

I yelled at Drago to clear a path for the wheelchair. He took hold of the downed poker players by their ankles two at a time and dragged them to the center of the room and left them in a broken pile.

The Louis Vuitton was loaded to the top. Mom covered the bounty with part of her purple shawl. We made it to the elevator, the three of us and Waldo.

I pushed the lobby button.

I took in a huge breath for the first time in the last two minutes. That had been all the time that had passed since the secret door burst open.

"Drago," I said, and pointed at the rebar still in his hand.

He pushed it up the sleeve to his navy pea coat while I tore off a piece of my tee-shirt, folded it, and pressed it against Mom's shoulder wound.

Drago moved me out of the way when he saw she was injured. He got down on one knee, took a woman's sanitary napkin from his pea coat pocket, and gently placed it against the wound.

"She's going to be okay. The bullet just caught the top part of the muscle." He'd been wounded enough times in the past and knew what to carry.

The elevator door opened to the lobby.

Dad stood by waiting. "Hurry, we have to hurry. There are people all over out there on the street and police. What the heck happened—did someone go out a window? I think someone went out a window."

He took the handles to his wife's wheelchair and off we went, no one answering his inquires, all of us too caught up in the moment.

The traffic on the wide boulevard was stopped. All the twenty-somethings had migrated into it to see the man who took a header into the concrete. Four blue uniforms ran into the Shimbuto.

I quickly texted Helen Hellinger telling her to get down to the Shimbuto code three if she wasn't already en route.

We walked slow to the first corner, turned, and found Drago's new truck parked where we'd left it.

CHAPTER SIXTY-TWO

TWENTY MINUTES LATER, Drago pulled into the hotel parking lot. The adrenaline had just started to diminish and no longer pulsed behind my eyes. My hands shook with a palsy.

I helped Mom get out of the truck with her wheelchair and the bag of money. She wouldn't turn loose of the Louis Vuitton bag and held it tight against her chest, a cool million dollars.

I had not known my mother long, but her smile was the largest I had ever seen—she lit up the night with it. Dad smiled because she smiled. He caught my eye and winked. That one wink made everything worthwhile and warmed my heart.

Mom kept saying, "We have to divide up this money and get it to those two families tonight." She said it again and again.

Not the words of a woman on the con. "Bruno, you sure it's okay to have all this money?"

"Yes, I'm sure. But a hundred grand of it goes back to Layla's family in Costa Rica."

"Of course," she said. "That leaves four hundred and fifty thousand for each of the families. Come on, Xander, push faster."

I said, "You guys get upstairs. I have something I have to do."

Dad lost his good cheer. "Son, it's over. We can go home now. Let's go home."

I put my hand on his shoulder. "I won't be long, I promise. I'll be right back."

He nodded and pushed Mom toward the elevator. I waited until the elevator closed.

Drago stood by with Waldo waiting. He said, "You want me to go with you?"

"No, I got this, but let me borrow your truck."

He tossed me the keys and said, "I'll catch ya on the flip."

He and Waldo shambled off to the stairs going back to the room and to Layla.

I headed for the hotel office. I paid the clerk fifty dollars and he gave me the room key. I walked to the room on the ground floor. I swiped the card key and opened the door.

Inside, Layla jumped off the bed, her eyes wild as she shielded Frankie Toliver . . . Sonny.

"You! What are you doing here? How did you get here?"

Behind her cowered a younger-looking Hispanic girl, a babysitter for when Layla was away. Layla never left the child unattended.

I held up my hands flat. "Take it easy. I'm just here to talk."

The room had everything a child needed, a basinet, a changing table, a refrigerator for the formula, a couple of boxes of diapers, and a ton of baby clothes folded neatly on the dresser.

Layla really loved that child.

Frankie cooed and sounded happy.

"I'm not giving him up, if that's why you came here. He's mine, and you can't have him. I paid for him fair and square. A hundred thousand dollars."

I closed the door and eased down onto my butt, my back to the wall, the least aggressive position in the room. I waited for her rapid breathing to calm. Her short pageboy haircut took five years off her age, too young to be in a dive hotel holding a kidnapped child demanding ownership. She should be out living her young life before settling down with a kid.

Why had she cut that beautiful long hair, hair she'd had all her life? Why was she acting so irrational, saying things like she bought him fair and square? Why did a girl like her find Drago attractive, as sad as that sounded?

I was placing my values based on my life's experiences on her. She came from a different childhood and growing environment.

Then I realized, she was emotionally damaged.

She didn't have any physical scars from her time with Johnny Ef, but he'd broken her just the same. She now lived in a different world, one where keeping a kidnapped child somehow made sense. Johnny had introduced her to his world, forced her into it, and this was the result. Johnny got exactly what he deserved, a one-and-a-half gainer right into the asphalt.

She slowly eased down to sit on the bed. "How did you know?"

I didn't answer right away, letting time stretch and calm her even more. "I followed you to the Shimbuto the night you came down from Aimee's apartment and went to the coffeehouse. I saw you with Aimee together at the high-top table talking in the coffeehouse.

"I met Aimee. She seemed like a very nice woman."

Layla shook her head; she didn't understand.

"I was in her apartment tonight in the safe room where you and Aimee kept Frankie safe, away from Johnny. I found the diapers and all the other baby stuff under the sink in the bathroom. Then I remembered how you sent Drago off on a snipe hunt to get takeout in Beverly Hills and realized how often you weren't with us since we'd been here."

She nodded and gently stroked Franklin's head, his soft downy hair, tears brimming her eyes and rolling down her cheeks. "It's not right that babies can be sold like chattel."

"No, it's not."

"I can't have a baby, because of Johnny—not one of my own. I want this one. He needs me."

I didn't argue with her. I wanted her to come to the right decision on her own.

"Did you take care of Johnny? He's pure evil. He needs to be taken care of."

In a whisper I said, "Johnny's never going to hurt you or anyone ever again."

More tears. Her chin quivered as she nodded her approval.

I eased to my feet and walked toward her.

I sat on the bed next to her, put my arm around her. She buried her face in my shoulder and let the emotions take her. She let them all out in a flood of woe.

I took out a wad of cash, several hundred in twenties, and offered it to the Hispanic girl and waved goodbye. She smiled, took it, and left.

After Layla's body stopped shuddering, I whispered in her ear, "You've only loved Sonny a short time. His parents knew him the first time they went in for an ultrasound, heard his heartbeat, saw the photo, the first time he kicked in his mother's tummy. They went through the upset stomach, the sleepless nights, all the horrible pain of childbirth. A pain that's given as a gift to the parents, so they'll love and cherish the life they brought into the world." I spoke from the heart. It was easy. I'd just been through it with Marie.

And now Dad's words took on new meaning. He'd been right, of course.

She looked up at me, her face wet and childlike, seemingly too young to have a child of her own, but there was no doubt she loved this baby with all her heart and wanted him to be hers.

She should be in college enjoying her youth. Johnny Ef had interrupted her life's path. Johnny had been like a tall rock in a river disrupting all he came in contact with, breaking and smashing all that he touched.

"Bruno, I know what you're saying and a part of me, an old part of me, knows giving the baby back is the right thing to do, but I can't. I just can't. When I first met Sonny, I didn't know he'd been kidnapped. I thought he came from one of those other people who sold their children."

I'd never in all my years come across a problem like this. I didn't know what to say. "Listen, I know it's hard. I have a son back home who has been sending me text messages. Here, look." I showed her my phone and all the short quips Eddie had sent. She let one little laugh escape around her heated emotions, a sign the real Layla was still there, only buried deep below the pain.

I said, "I wouldn't give Eddie up for anything in the world and Sonny's parents feel the same way. Layla, it's the right thing to do."

She put her face back into my wet shoulder and shook her head no.

I said, "Drago and I rescued three other infants that need a home. You can have one of those."

She pulled back to look me in the eyes for the truth of the statement. I nodded to reaffirm I meant it.

"I couldn't. I love Sonny."

"I know you do."

I worked on her some more using kind, gentle words.

Thirty-five minutes later we sat out front of Sonny's home in Silver Lake. Layla started weeping all over again, her face wet with tears as she held Sonny—Frankie Toliver. "I can't do it, Bruno. I can't hand him over. Will you do it? Please?" She looked up at me, her eyes tearing my heart out of my chest.

I reached and took Sonny from her arms.

She didn't resist.

"Wait. Wait." She pulled him back and kissed the top of his head. "Bye, Sonny."

I got out and before I closed the truck door I said, "Call Drago. He'll be going crazy not knowing where you are."

She nodded.

I walked up to the front door, the house quiet with only one light on at eleven in the evening. Frankie Toliver, warm and wiggly in my arm, smelled of baby products. I yearned to be home holding Tobias, my son.

I used the large knocker on the center of the door and waited.

I pulled out my old flat badge from when I was still a detective with the Los Angeles County Sheriff's Department and held it up to the peephole in the door. A black man with a white baby standing on the porch of a house where a child had been kidnapped had a good chance of being misinterpreted.

The porch light came on and the door opened. A woman stood in slippers and a robe, holding the edges together. Her face looked skeletal with dark half-circles under her eyes. She had not eaten or slept in years and years. And it had only been two months.

The mother of a lost child. A gone forever child.

She'd accepted the loss so entirely, her mind had not put together the purpose of my visit.

"Yes?"

"Sheriff's department, ma'am." I showed her the badge. I handed her Frankie. "I think he's yours."

Then she realized it was for real.

She let out a yelp. Several yelps. Hugged Frankie and cried and walked in a circle. "Oh my God. Oh my God. Jim? Jim, come down here. It's—" She choked on the name. "It's Frankie. Frankie's back."

I stepped out and faded into the night.

I'd almost made it back to Drago's truck when Jim Toliver caught up to me running in his robe and slippers. "Wait. Wait. Who are you?"

I was glad he came out and tracked me down so Layla had a chance to witness the pure joy on Sonny's father's face.

I showed him my old badge again, flipping it open and closed. "LA County Sheriff."

He took hold of my hand, the one with the cast, took it with both of his, and shook. "Thank you. Thank you. I cannot thank you enough."

His wife appeared across the street in front of the mansion, holding Frankie.

Jim said, "Come back inside. I want to do something for you. I want to give you money—anything you want, it's yours."

"Jim," his wife said. "Have him come in for a drink. Have him tell us all about it."

"Thank you, but I have to be getting back. The investigation came to a head tonight, and Detective Helen Hellinger thought you should get Frankie back as soon as possible. This was Helen's investigation. If you go in and watch the news, you'll see what happened. It's across the street from the Staples Center."

"What's your name?" Jim still had not let go of my hand.

"My name's not important. Helen Hellinger is responsible for getting your child back. Call and talk to her." I broke away from him, got in the truck.

And drove away.

CHAPTER SIXTY-THREE

THE STREETLIGHTS FLASHED past as I drove the big black dually headed back toward the motel.

Layla had not stopped crying.

I wanted to help her. I needed to help her.

"You're in your second year of college. Don't you want to finish your degree before you start a family?"

She stopped mid-sob and looked at me. "You don't understand. I told you I can't have any kids, none of my own. Johnny saw to that."

Johnny wanted her to have a kid so he could sell the baby for profit. She'd chosen, on her own, once pregnant with his child, to take a different path and that path had scarred her physically. Something she had to believe was her just deserts.

At the same time, I did understand the "why." She didn't want to bring into this world a child sired by Johnny Ef. I wasn't a psychologist, but I understood how her choosing that other path could affect her with an all-encompassing guilt and how she wouldn't be able to think logically about her future until she made amends for making the choice not to have Johnny's child.

The idea of keeping a kidnapped kid just didn't make sense. She knew that now, but I'd seen how she handled Sonny, how deeply she cared for him, how devastated she was to lose him. She'd proven herself a good mother; she was mature enough to take care of an infant. She had so much to offer a baby—and a baby may be the only intervention that could help her now.

I couldn't blame her. I loved being a father.

Halfway back to the motel, Drago called Layla who sat next to me in the front seat of the big dually truck, weeping over the loss of Frankie Toliver.

Forever.

She answered. "Karl? Oh, Karl?"

His loud voice came over the phone. "Where are you? I'm coming. Just tell me where you are?"

"We're almost back to the motel." She looked over at me for confirmation.

"Less than ten."

"Ten minutes. Karl, I . . . I gave up Sonny." She sobbed.

Silence on the other end. Drago had little experience with women and even less with emotional issues. I felt bad for him.

Drago was pacing in the parking lot when we pulled in and hurried over to the passenger side. He scooped up his true love and hugged her. I wanted to warn him to be careful not to crush her.

He held her off the ground carrying her to the stairs, both talking quietly.

My cell phone buzzed.

Helen Hellinger.

"Bruno?"

"Yeah, kid?"

"Bruno . . . You shouldn't have told the Tolivers it was me who recovered their child. Sweet Jesus. I mean . . . thank you, but . . ."

"You're working this case. You deserve the credit."

Silence.

"The sheriff himself is coming to the scene to congratulate me. Sweet baby Jesus, Bruno."

More silence.

I said, "You should make sergeant out of this."

"Hell, they'll probably make me a lieutenant."

Silence.

She said, "Johnny Ef got what he deserved."

She didn't ask over the phone if I had anything to do with it.

"The babies—you get anything back on the three babies?"

"I was going to call you. With everything happening so fast . . . I didn't have time."

I held my breath. I wanted the kids to have their rightful parents but worried about Layla's state of mind.

Helen said, "I think we have a solid hit on two of the children. Good families, parents of the women who had the children and gave them up for cash. These are good people who want to raise them."

"Can you vet them for me? I know you're busy, but I really have to get back."

"You got it."

"I'll leave the two here with a good caretaker until you say it's okay to release them. If the families for some reason don't look good, I'll come back and take them south."

That kind of conversation should never have been happening, not in a civilized world.

"You going to take the third one?"

"I am."

I'd have time to make sure Layla was a good mother on the boat trip down to Central America. But I didn't have any doubts. Marie and I would look in on them in Tamarindo.

Helen gave me the description of the two babies staying.

I went upstairs, found Layla, asked her if she wanted to go pick up her child.

She looked at Karl.

Karl said, "It's up to you, babe, but I say hell yeah."

I drove over to Fruit Town in Compton and introduced them to Layla's new baby.

Karl said, "I'll take it from here—get Layla and the baby on the boat and down to Costa Rica."

Thank God for Karl Drago.

I collected Dad and Mom and we caught the next flight out. Karl and Layla would take the boat to avoid customs and passport screening.

AUTHOR'S NOTE

About the Dedication to Mike Fasari

During the writing of this novel, I lost a good friend whom I worked alongside for a number of years. We had a lot of great laughs—what a sense of humor. There is no stronger bond than one forged while risking your life.

Mike and I were in two violent confrontations together. One remains vivid in my mind. It started as a landlord-tenant dispute that quickly devolved into a gunfight. The suspect had us pinned down with blistering rifle fire. He reloaded several times. Mike had been caught short with little cover—between six and ten feet away. He held his ground and continued to return fire with a shotgun so the suspect couldn't advance on us. Another brave deputy risked his life to flank the suspect and ended the gun battle.

I'll miss Mike. I think about him all the time. His laugh, his smile, the way his eyes lit up while telling a story.

Why Bruno? Why the Kids?

Growing up, I had five brothers and sisters—six of us who required school clothes and three hot meals a day. Our stepfather worked as a pipe fitter; the jobs were sporadic and made the family money fluctuate. Until my mother figured out how to make it all work, we would periodically go on welfare. But this was back when the government gave out food instead of money or food stamps. She'd take me to stand in a long line outside a defunct movie theater with all the other unfortunates.

When our turn came, Mom handled the paperwork; then we shuttled the food boxes to the green Belvedere station wagon. Boxes loaded with inexpensive food: rice and pasta, large cans of mystery meat, powdered milk, powdered eggs, big blocks of American cheese, and butter. The labels on the food came with recipes that helped make the bland food half-palatable. Rice pudding was my favorite. Mom made big vats of it to keep in the refrigerator for her always-hungry kids to nosh when their stomachs growled. And that was all the time.

She also made big vats of macaroni and cheese with chunks of mystery meat. We didn't talk about it, so I naturally thought all of our friends' families were doing the same thing. Mom worked at cake decorating, sewing, and selling toys to put clothes on our backs and food on the table.

Before there were any regulations, she also took in extra children. She babysat while their parents both worked. At one time there were twelve plus our six: eighteen children in one house. I was tasked with making lunch. I'd take a loaf of day-old Wonder Bread Mom got at the day-old bakery. I'd lay out the entire loaf on the breadboard and start an assembly line, slathering each piece first with peanut butter then with jelly. Not the other way around—it didn't work that way. I became accustomed to all the extra kids. Mom was too busy with her other moneymaking duties to supervise the children. I became the sheepherder and the sheepdog, both. Maybe this is why I can relate so well with Bruno and his mob of children down in Costa Rica.

BOOK CLUB DISCUSSION GUIDE

1. The two plotlines start with two very different requests for Bruno to accompany a vulnerable individual from Costa Rica to Los Angeles. Do you feel that these plotlines were two separate stories or were they intertwined? If so, was there an overarching theme?

2. Did you think that Bruno would leave Marie and their infant son to travel to Los Angeles? Do you think he was justified in doing so?

3. How did you react to Layla's parents' rejection of their daughter . . . virtually "scorning" her? Do you predict they will reunite?

4. Did your opinion of Bea, Bruno's mother, change as the story progressed? What do think happened to her after the card game? Did she stay in the U.S. or did she go back to Costa Rica?

5. Do you predict that Bruno and Marie will ever legally adopt the eleven children that they have rescued and taken to Costa Rica for safe haven?

6. What do you think of the blatant illegal tactics used by Bruno and Drago? And even LA County Sheriff Detective Helen Hellinger? Are they justified?

7. Bruno Johnson: Do you accept the premise that a man with his background can be both so ultra-tough and so ultra-tender?

8. What do you think Waldo adds to the story?

9. What do you predict for the future for Drago, Layla, and the baby?

NOTE FROM THE PUBLISHER

We hope you enjoyed reading *THE SCORNED,* the tenth novel in the Bruno Johnson Crime Series.

While the other nine novels stand on their own and can be read in any order, the publication sequence is as follows:

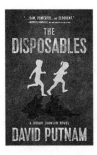

The Disposables (Book 1)

Bruno Johnson, ex-cop, ex-con, turns vigilante— nothing will stop him and Marie as they rescue battered children from abusive homes.

"I really loved *The Disposables.* It's raw, powerful, and eloquent. It's a gritty street poem recited by a voice unalterably committed to redemption and doing the right thing in a wrong world." —Michael Connelly, *New York Times* best-selling author

The Replacements (Book 2)

Bruno and Marie, hiding out in Costa Rica with their rescued kids, are pulled back to L.A. to hunt a heinous child predator.

"While laying low in Costa Rica, former LAPD detective Bruno Johnson must return to California—and risk everything to stop a ruthless kidnapper. The action won't slow down"   *—Booklist*

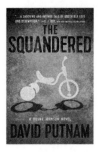

The Squandered (Book 3)

Book 3—Again, Bruno and Marie leave the kids in Costa Rica with Bruno's dad to intervene in the L.A. County prison system—and face a murderous psychopath.

"Putnam puts his years of law enforcement experience to good use in *The Squandered*, a shocking and intense tale of brotherly love and redemption realized in the midst of moral decay. It's a raw and gritty story I couldn't put down."   —C. J. Box,
New York Times best-selling author

The Vanquished (Book 4)

A woman from Bruno's past lures him and Marie back to L.A.—the result is an unspeakable tragedy that will haunt Bruno for the rest of his life.

"Bad Boy Bruno Johnson comes out of hiding to battle a vicious biker gang that threatens his family. Bring an oxygen tank with you when you read *The Vanquished* because you'll be holding your breath the whole time."   —Matt Coyle,
Anthony, Lefty, and Shamus Award–winning author

The Innocents (Book 5)

The first of the young Bruno prequels—Bruno is a new cop when he's handed a baby girl, becoming a single dad. Meanwhile, he's working a police corruption case—infiltrating a sheriff's narcotics team involved in murder-for-hire. Family and professional life for Bruno collide violently.

"*The Innocents* is a terrific read, reminiscent of the best of Joseph Wambaugh. David Putnam provides an insider's knowledge of the Los Angeles Sheriff's Department. His characters and settings are rich and authentic, and his dialogue is spot on accurate." —Robert Dugoni, *New York Times* best-selling author

The Reckless (Book 6)

The second of the young Bruno prequels—Bruno tackles the roles of the single dad of a two-year-old daughter and an L.A. County Deputy Sheriff in the Violent Crimes Unit. He is assigned a law enforcement public relations nightmare—apprehend a gang of teenager bank robbers without killing them or getting killed.

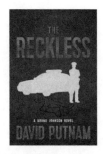

"Reading a novel by David Putnam is almost as good as riding shotgun in a patrol car. He writes what he knows and what he knows is that justice on the mean streets isn't always black and white." —Robin Burcell, *New York Times* best-selling author

The Heartless (Book 7)

The third of the young Bruno prequels—Bruno has stepped down from his beloved position in the Violent Crimes Unit to be able to spend more time with his teen daughter, Olivia. Now a bailiff in the courts, he gets a frantic call to extricate Olivia from a gunpoint situation in a L.A. gang-infested neighborhood—thrusting him back into violent crime mode.

"David Putnam's *The Heartless* is terrific—a smart, well-written, relentless account of a battle against evil, fought by a protagonist who has a real man's flaws, but also shows us the kind of heroism that's real."

—Thomas Perry, *New York Times* best-selling author

The Ruthless (Book 8)

The fourth and last of the young Bruno prequels—Bruno is plunged back into the Violent Crimes Unit when his friends, a judge and his wife, are murdered. Bruno's daughter is now the mother of twins; and the father of the babies is a drug-addicted criminal—abusive, and brutal. This is the setup for Bruno's time in prison as he takes justice into his own hands.

"Dark, disturbing, and all too believable, this is the tale of one man's quest for atonement in a world where innocence is a liability."

—T. Jefferson Parker, *New York Times* best-selling author

The Sinister (Book 9)

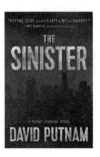

Bruno Johnson and his wife, Marie, hide in plain sight from the law in an upscale L.A. hotel as Bruno heals from a run-in with a brutal outlaw motorcycle gang—and the loss of his son—a son he didn't know he had until it was too late. Bruno is shaken to the core, but still a formidable force when it comes to saving a child.

"*The Sinister* Riveting, scary, but with plenty of wit and humanity, author David Putnam brings ex-cop Bruno Johnson's world alive in a way that only another ex-cop could. In Putnam's capable hands, the characters jump off the page—even the dog." —Janet Evanovich, #1 *New York Times* best-selling author

We hope that you will read the entire Bruno Johnson Crime Series and will look forward to more to come, specifically *THE DIABOLICAL*, coming in 2024.

If you liked *THE SCORNED*, we would be very appreciative if you would consider leaving a review. As you probably already know, book reviews are important to authors and they are very grateful when a reader makes the special effort to write a review, however brief.

For more information, please visit the author's website: www.DavidPutnamBooks.com

Happy reading,
Oceanview Publishing
Your Home for Mystery, Thriller, and Suspense